PROOF OF POISONED LIVES

PROOF OF POISONED LIVES

A Novel

Ian McLeod

ARCHWAY
PUBLISHING

Archway Publishing books may be ordered through booksellers or by contacting:

Archway Publishing
1663 Liberty Drive
Bloomington, IN 47403
www.archwaypublishing.com
1-(888)-242-5904

ISBN: 978-1-4808-1097-6 (sc)
ISBN: 978-1-4808-1098-3 (e)

Library of Congress Control Number: 2014916005

Printed in the United States of America.

Archway Publishing rev. date: 9/23/2014

CHAPTER 1

VIETNAM

March 1968

Near noon, Sergeant John Gooding paused at a plaza in the center of a jumble of streets crossing each other. His Colt 45 semiautomatic rested in its holster.

He thought, Saigon City smells of spoiling fish and shit. The sun is bright enough to boil my eyeballs like a poached egg. Heat waves radiate from the pavement, jumbling my vision. At night, Vietcong in black uniforms scuttle along in the shadows like overgrown black rats. Not safe for soldiers on the streets then. This is no place for an almost lawyer with a degree in chemistry from the University of Michigan. Fortunately I am near the end of my tour of duty.

Turning to walk down one of the streets, he adjusted his mirrored sunglasses, the lower rims resting on his cheeks, puffy from the sunburn. He sweated and his skin itched as he walked down the street. American soldiers and Vietnamese looked away from him after recognizing the military police identification on his helmet and armband. He was known as a hardnosed soldier who followed the rules and expected others to do so as well.

Well suited for the work, John was tall at well over six feet and muscular, towering over most Vietnamese. Few of the US soldiers on leave in the city from fighting in the jungles and plains of Vietnam, were prone to argue with him when ordered to return to the base. To reinforce his command, John carried a nightstick which supported his superiority in any given disturbance. Well-known for his ability to fight hand-to-hand, his reputation was enough. The soldiers kept in line for fear of going into the lockup on base, known to be a very unpleasant place. He thought, I am thankful that Officers are not my problem.

He thought, High noon has arrived and the American soldiers in the bars are already drunk. Some of the most belligerent will be hauled back to base in a stake rack truck and put into the brig to dry out. The most violent of them are sent back to front line units or court marshaled. I arrest them only in the most extreme circumstances.

John pulled a crumpled and soiled letter, dated June 25, 1966, from his wallet and reread it, which took him back to remembering days with his wife, Ann, just before he came to Vietnam almost two years ago.

"Dear John-I think of you constantly, wanting you in my arms again. Your picture is beside our bed. I hold it every night and morning and remember our making love. I know you will think of me for a few minutes each day. I love you. Happy 23rd birthday next week."

The rest of the letter was about their friends in Ann Arbor, where he finished his second year in law school before he was drafted. The letter was signed, "All my love Ann". This was the first of many love letters from her which he kept in his foot locker.

He pictured Ann at five feet six inches tall, a fulsome twenty three year old blond-haired woman. He thought, She has the body and face of Monroe and attracts men as if she also appeared naked on the cover of that first issue of PLAYBOY magazine like Marilyn. He thought, I trust her, even though I have been away so long.

Carefully refolding the letter, he put it back in his wallet and stroked a picture of Ann in a plastic insert. This ritual made his day feel better and less lonesome for a few minutes.

Suddenly, John's attention turned to an old, white haired Vietnamese man standing in the center of the plaza. He doused himself with gasoline from a US Army can. Quickly flipping open the top of a Zippo lighter and lighting it, he exploded in flame like a burning tree. Nobody moved to douse the flames as they came and watched by the hundreds. A crowd of Vietnamese around him cheered with approval.

John could do nothing. He thought, I'll never understand these people. It seems that they would rather die than have us here. I don't want to be here either. I feel that something bad is going to happen.

He was on alert. Walking down a side street, he came to the Lucky Lady bar, which, as usual, was lit up like a Christmas tree with many colored bulbs on the front of the two story building. The bar was a favorite of US soldiers, easily seduced by the beautiful mixed French and Vietnamese whores and cheap booze.

He thought, A lot of these men are going to North Nam after their leave is ended to die or be horribly wounded. I don't blame them for wanting the relief.

John walked through the entrance and stepped up to the bar tended by a strikingly beautiful French and Vietnamese woman. "So, Dragon Lady, are our soldiers behaving themselves?" The bar was beside a wall of the building and loaded with many liquor bottles.

Smiling, she said, "They go upstairs with my girls and when they come down, all of the meanness is drained out of them. Maybe you would feel better too. It's on the house, your pick sergeant John. You could pick me because I am attracted to you. I never go upstairs with men. I'm not a whore."

John said, "I am tempted, but don't want sex today, but I appreciate your offer. My tour ends in two weeks. All I have to do is stay alive so I can go home to my wife. By the way, your Japanese kimono is beautiful. I would like to buy one for my wife."

Dragon Lady nodded and said, "It's silk, I will find one for you to take to your wife, my gift to you. I hope you Americans stay a long time. It's good for business. If the Viet Cong win this war, I'll be shot as a collaborator."

John said, "Be careful today. A man just burned himself to

death today with gasoline on the plaza. I think there may be an attack close by."

Turning away from the bar, John walked out the entrance and stopped a few feet in front. He scanned the scene in front of him slowly and carefully.

Alarmed, he focused on a North Vietnamese dressed in black clothing, pointing a shoulder fired Rocket Propelled Grenade launcher at the entrance to the Lucky lady. He fired the RPG.

John yelled "Hit the deck" and fired seven shots from his Colt at the shooter, emptying the clip. His bullets ripped through the assassin. The shooter dropped the empty rocket launcher into a baby carriage. Men grabbed the body of the Vietcong soldier and ran, leaving only the baby carriage.

The grenade exploded, bellowing out the wall next to the bar and Dragon Lady, sending fragments of steel inside and outside the building in an expanding ball. John's left forearm was cut deeply near the bone, up to the elbow, by the shrapnel. He bled, as if a vein or artery was cut.

Blood dripping from his arm, John walked into what was left of the Lucky Lady bar. American soldiers and girls had been killed or badly wounded, shredded by the blast. Fortunately many of the soldiers survived the blast by dropping to the floor, as commanded by John. Dragon Lady was lying on the floor behind the bar bleeding from a chest wound.

She said, "I'll see you in the afterlife, Sgt John."

Bending down, John said, " Our medics will be here in a few minutes and will treat you. Hold on."

She gasped with a gurgling sound, blood bubbling out of her mouth and died. John gently closed her eyelids. His eyes filled with tears at the carnage in the bar.

Tearing off off a piece of the kimono she was wearing, he twisted it around his upper arm to stem the bleeding. Feeling faint, he sat down on a wooden remnant of the bar.

In a few minutes, Dragon Lady's relatives arrived and loaded her body, face down, onto a hand pulled cart used for food and liquor deliveries to the bar. Her kimono and arms skidded on the pavement of the street as they dragged her away.

Ambulances arrived. The medics put a tourniquet his arm to stem the bleeding and dropped the bloody strip of kimono on the street. Inside the bar, medics helped the living and examined the bodies, sorting out the parts which were American and those which were Vietnamese. The latter were taken by family members. The former were taken to the American hospital or the morgue on the base.

The military ambulance finally took John to the base hospital, where stitches were sown in his arm. An officer told him that he would receive a Purple Heart for being wounded and possibly the Silver Star for saving some of the men in the bar by his actions. He was informed by the doctors that he would be sent home which, was the best news.

He thought, Skip the metals, I just want to go home. I'll be glad to leave this place. We have no reason to be here and we are going to lose this war in the end. The report on the attack I filed out goes on top of hundreds of other similar reports of bombings in Saigon. The flaming suicide was possibly a diversion to position the RPG launcher, but I didn't put that into the report. I never could not have seen the RPG from the Plaza. Later he was told that there were no metals since he was not in a war zone.

CHAPTER 2

GOING HOME

Capt. Max ordered John to meet with the base minister and psychologist, who worked in a makeshift tent, which also was as a church. John walked over and stepped into the makeshift sanctuary with chairs and an alter. A tall, fit black man in his early forties stood up and greeted him.

"Good day Sergeant Gooding. I'm Casey McTavish."

John said, "I'm pleased to meet you sir. I was ordered here."

Casey said, "I know. There is no need to be formal with me. My first name, Casey, will do just fine. Your captain said that you are a first-rate soldier. I understand from Capt. Max that in the last two months you've done a lot to stop the soldiers from hurting themselves or the Vietnamese while on leave. You saved many lives in the bar."

John said, "Thank you Sir-Casey, but I don't know why I'm here."

"Your captain felt that you might be feeling guilty about the attack on the Lucky Lady. The explosion might be a problem for you." Casey paused to let that thought sink in.

A vision of body parts, soldiers and girls being torn to shreds, flashed into his memory. "I'll remember that for the rest of my life. I have headaches from the blast. But, I have seen a lot of death in battles up north, before I became a MP here."

"John, I believe everyone goes to a place which is safe when they die. Most religions preach this conviction in various forms. Can you accept that this as possible?"

"John said "Maybe. I can only believe there is a place after death which is better than here. I don't believe I am one of those who will go there because of what I have done here."

"John, I will say a prayer for you. "Dear God please hold John in your hands so that he can forgive what he has done and be seen and be blessed and with the spirit of your counsel and grace."

John said, "Thank you Casey. I'm going back home in a few days and will re-enter law school for my final year to graduate. If you are in Ann Arbor Michigan, please look me up."

John left the tent and walked to MP headquarters to arrange his passage home. His captain said, "Casey is the best minister we've ever had on this base. Unfortunately, he is going home too. I hope he helped you. Thank you for your service." They saluted and John returned to his barrack on base.

The next day, John was transferred to a new barrack adjacent the airfield for transport home. He reread Ann's first letter and put her picture in his top pocket next to his heart. He felt the joy of being alive for the first time in two years.

He thought, I wonder how I can relate to the other law students and what it will be like in classes. The other law students have never been in Vietnam. This war will not be something that I can talk about with them. I read in the newspapers that the war is very unpopular at home, lots of protests.

On the airfield John saw soldiers loading Agent Orange onto helicopters and airplanes for dispersal on foliage. He thought, The US is going to regret spraying Vietnam with that shit. Our soldiers, and the Vietnamese, are going to have heath problems from exposure to the herbicide, particularly the compound dioxin. Our government makes serious mistakes

———

IN JULY OF 1968, JOHN arrived at the airport near Detroit in uniform. Ann picked him up in their old dark blue 1960 Chevrolet which coughed and sputtered as if it was ready for the junk yard. He jumped into the passenger seat.

They petted, hugged and kissed for several minutes, ready to make love right there, except an airport police officer told them to move on. In doing so, he thanked John for his military service. All of the rest of people in the arrival terminal did not say anything to him.

At home, naked in bed together, John drew her close. Ann said, "You have a wound on your arm." She touched it tenderly with her finger.

John said, "It's a cut from a piece of shrapnel." She did not ask any more questions.

They made love, her long blonde hair splayed out on a pillow. John was poised over above her body inside her. Ann said "I'm ready." John moved rapidly until he came.

Afterwards Ann said, "I'll bet you can do that again. She climbed on top of his erection and moved faster and faster. She came with a cry of joy. Panting for breath, they lay together hugging each other for a while without talking.

Ann said, "I missed you so much. I dreaded every day that you might have been killed."

John said, "I was lucky. We are losing the war. The Vietnamese people hate us. We should pull out. The attacks on our soldiers by the Vietcong in the field are deadly."

Ann said, "You're home now. You did your duty for your country and should forget that. It's time to be a husband and lawyer again."

John thought, She doesn't want to hear about my experience at all. It's as if it never happened.

The kissed and slept for a while in each other's arms and later Ann wanted to make love again. He thought, This a great time for me. I'm lucky to be alive.

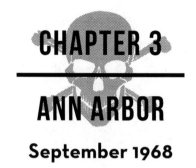

CHAPTER 3
ANN ARBOR

September 1968

John enrolled again in the University of Michigan law school as a senior. Most of the clerical people during registration were helpful and acknowledged his service in Vietnam.

On the first day of his Trusts and Estates class, Professor Allen Potts arrived a few minutes late. He had taught John Property Law as a freshman.

Potts said, "I'm glad you have returned safely from your tour of duty in Vietnam, but should have never been there in the first place."

John said, "Most of us were drafted and didn't have a choice. There are a lot of very brave men there who would rather be home. They die there for our country."

Potts said, "That is so. We are there because of the stupidity of our politicians."

John said," You need to at least acknowledge our service."

Potts said, "Yes, I do. Now we need to start class."

That was the beginning of the most boring class he had ever had. There was little said about the war or his service in any of his other classes.

———

ON TELEVISION, STEEL COFFINS AT Dulles Airport, wounded soldiers coming home, napalmed villages and night flashes of rifle and cannon fire in Vietnam appeared daily. He reacted with a cold sweat, nightmares and headaches, almost like he was back in Vietnam. John believed more than ever that this was a pointless war.

Other Vietnam vets at the local VFW had similar experiences and stayed away from the television news. He decided not to watch these programs. Ann did not to watch them, since they were of no interest to her, and so it was not a problem.

John knew that the war correspondents on the front lines were prevented by the military from sending home gruesome images of battles. Somehow President Johnson thought he could make the war more acceptable by limiting reporting about it. It was not the first time in history that horrible images of mangled bodies were withheld from the public. Reporters and war correspondents simply "went along to get along". John thought, The Presidential order, choking freedom of reporting by correspondents, is taking away Constitutional rights and hiding the real facts about the war. If the public knew what I know, Congress would end the war.

————

THAT FALL, THERE WAS A large and vocal minority of people who wanted the war to end, right now. Students were protesting at schools all over the country, even to the point of taking over buildings. School administrations and police were nervous.

John walked to the center of the Campus in front of the University of Michigan library, which was crowded with protesting students. A few professors were participating as well, risking their jobs. Some of the students were dressed in ragged clothing looking like it had been recycled from the Salvation Army. One of the protestors chanted into a megaphone, "HEY, HEY LBJ HOW MANY KIDS DID YOU KILL TODAY?" "END THE WAR" and "IMPEACH LBJ."

The Ann Arbor police were doing their best to keep a smaller group of uniformed students from the Reserve Officers Training Candidate School from bashing in the heads of the people they referred to as hippies. John felt sorry for what they would face in Vietnam.

Standing next to him was a girl, almost as tall as he was, with a white T-shirt and athletic shorts, barely covering a very physically fit body. She screamed "Desert to Canada" at the ROTC students.

John wasn't so involved in watching the protest that he couldn't appreciate the fullness of her breasts and her shapely, slim hips. She wore no lipstick and her hair was so blond in the sunlight that it almost appeared white, swinging wild just below her shoulders.

Her attention turned to him, hands on her hips. There was an aura of sexiness about her. As she came up to him, he saw her eyes were green and she had the straight nose of a British aristocrat.

John said, "You should feel sorry for them. They are bound by duty to our Country and training to fight in this war. They will be in Vietnam in a few months. Most of them will die there since they have no idea how to fight a guerrilla war in the jungles. The average time in there before they die or are wounded is less than a day. You're looking at terrific men who are brave enough to face almost certain death. I was there."

The girl walked close to John and smiled. Raising her eyebrows, and said, "I hope you're not right about the dying part. My brother Carl is there now." She paused to examine John as if she was making a decision. She quietly said, "Do you want to go over to the Women's Union and have a cup of coffee when this is over?"

John said, "I can't, I'm married," pointing to his ring.

The students at the University were not riotous by tradition and stopped protesting without incident when ordered by the police.

A black man and white woman embraced and kissed near John. Surprised, John recognized Casey McTavish, the minister from the base near Saigon in Vietnam.

Suddenly, a police officer used a night stick on Casey producing blood streaming down his head and over his face. The woman attacked the officer in defense of Casey. Both were thrown to the ground by the policemen and handcuffed with their arms behind their back, using metal cuffs. Infuriated, John started towards the cop, fists ready to strike.

Incensed by what they had seen, the crowd started to reassemble in front of the policemen as if to attack as well. The officer had his hand on the grip of his pistol.

Casey turned and sat up and in a booming base voice said, "John! Stop, I don't want anyone hurt here. You are not in Vietnam. This is a peaceful demonstration.

Casey continued, "I want everybody to sit down where you stand and link your arms with the person next to you. The politicians who started this miserable war are in Washington, DC and not here."

As if by some unseen force, everyone, including John, sank to the ground, linked arms and crossed their legs and watched quietly as other officers carefully lifted Casey and his wife from the ground and removed the cuffs. One of the other officers gently wiped the blood from Casey's face with a white handkerchief, staining it with blood. John's thoughts flashed back to the Dragon Lady and there were tears in his eyes.

Then the officers escorted the McTavishes from the campus to a van waiting to take them to the Ann Arbor jail, far away from the campus and the students. Casey smiled and waved at John as they left.

The young woman John talked to came over and stood close beside John. Her face was flushed from the excitement.

"Boy! I've never seen anything like that. It's almost enough to make you want to do the same thing to that cop, but I could never do that. She handed John a slip of paper with her telephone number on it. She said, "Just in case you change your mind."

John put it in his pocket, smiled and said, "I won't. It's time for me to go home to my wife."

CHAPTER 4

ANN

That Evening

John arrived home, sweating and exhausted. When he walked through the door, Ann, face contorted with tears in her eyes, came after him with her hands raised. She came within an inch of slapping him until he grabbed her wrists.

"What were you thinking? Channel 6 reported that a couple of people were arrested. I saw you standing in the background. If you were arrested, you might not become a lawyer. At the very least, you could not get a job in a corporate legal department or an important law firm." Ann was screaming, her mouth was drawn in a hard thin line.

"Reverend Casey McTavish, who is the man arrested along with his wife, is a minister and friend from Vietnam," John replied in a reasonable tone, trying to explain. Ann ignored what he said.

"How do you expect to support me? You're just going to waste all these years in law school, like you did in Vietnam," Ann said, turning around and stomping into the kitchen. She slammed pots and pans on the stove until she was finally exhausted. John said nothing to console her and he slammed the door as he left their duplex.

Returning home later, he said, "I'm not sorry Ann. Casey McTavish, helped me after I was wounded in Saigon City." I owe him my support and am going to give it to him."

Ann said, "Hopefully this incident will not ruin your career as a lawyer and our marriage."

John thought, It is pretty bruised right now.

CHAPTER 5

JAIL

The next day, Casey and his wife were charged with misdemeanor assault on a police officer in the Washtenaw Circuit Court in front of Judge Pierce. The *Ann Arbor Press* said Reverend Casey McTavish, a Methodist minister formerly from Alabama, was visiting the University to lecture on civil rights for the NAACP. He moved to Michigan from Alabama a few months before to live in Detroit. His wife, Claire, was originally from Charlotte, North Carolina. It was illegal for a black man to marry a white woman in Alabama where he was formerly ministering.

The county prosecutor was quoted in the *Ann Arbor Press* as saying they wanted to make an example of the McTavishes, and refused to dismiss the charges, even after the University President demanded that they do so.

In reality, John thought, The clubbing and arrest is because the police are afraid of the student protesters and this is a way to frighten them into disbanding. In fact, the arrests had exactly the opposite effect and now hundreds of students protested daily, both on campus and in front of the jail. The police avoided another confrontation with the students.

John volunteered to help their lawyer, Dick Rawlings, as a law clerk for a dollar a day. In Rawling's office, John told him he was a Law Review student at the U of M law school and very near the top of his class and would graduate this coming June. He said he had also met Casey in Vietnam.

Rawlings said, "I'm glad to have the help. Thank you for your service."

Rawlings and John visited the McTavishes in the jail that afternoon. On the way over Rawlings said, "The Judge set bond at ten thousand dollars each when they were arraigned yesterday. They present no flight risk and should have been released without bond. By the way, don't volunteer any legal opinions during the meeting." John nodded, yes.

————

THE NEXT DAY THE MCTAVISHES were shown into an attorneys' meeting room.

Rawlings said. "This is my clerk, a last year law student near the top of his class. He is going to help me with the leg work on your case."

Casey McTavish smiled so that lines furrowed his smooth dark face, and said, "Thank you John. Your involvement in a case for a black civil rights activist might ruin your reputation when you become a lawyer."

John said, "You helped me when I needed it the most. It's my turn to help you." He thought, There is no way that I would back out of this case. Ann will have to accept that.

Claire McTavish turned her head towards John, smiled and said, "It is a pleasure to know you John." Claire was slightly heavy, but her round face with her brown hair had a radiance which came only from love.

Rawlings said, "You know, Dr. McTavish, this case is quickly becoming national news. I want the two of you out of jail so you can talk to the reporters. As far as I know, Mrs. McTavish was not involved at all except to try protecting you from being clubbed."

"That's right. I want to get her out of jail as soon as possible. The white women prisoners are harassing her for being married to a black man. As for me, I've been in Southern jails many times for protesting against segregation, so I'm easily capable of staying here. I can minister to the inmates and maybe, if I am fortunate, find some converts to Christ."

Rawlings told them they were looking for still or moving

pictures of the attack and arrest. "John is going to be in charge of that." They both nodded their agreement.

Rawlings asked, "What caused the policeman to club you in the first place?"

"I hugged my wife and kissed her on the mouth in the excitement of the protest. I didn't see the policeman who was behind me. He said, "You fucking black bastard, let go of her," and clubbed me hard on the back of my head and then on my forehead as I turned towards him. My forehead bled and the blood ran into my eyes and my head hurt, so I had difficulty seeing him. Clair was facing him and says she can identify him."

Mrs. McTavish said, "The cop's hazel eyes closed to slits as he beat my husband. He looked like a KKK member in the south, only he was wearing a helmet and dressed in a police uniform. There was a large pistol in his holster and his right hand was resting on it while he used the club with his left hand. I sensed that if Casey had made any sort of aggressive move, he would have been shot. I can identify him from a photograph."

"Mrs. McTavish, can you tell us about your background?" Rawlings asked.

"I grew up in Charlotte, North Carolina. My family owns a number of companies in the food business. I have a Master's degree in business from Harvard, where I met Casey when he was lecturing. We were married a month ago in Detroit and we live there now. As you might suspect, none of my family and friends attended our wedding or even acknowledged the invitation.

"My family was so violently against the marriage that they disinherited me. They might bail me out of jail if I asked, to avoid any embarrassment to themselves, which I am not going to do," Claire said. She reached for Casey's hand and turned her head towards him with a radiant smile.

Dr. McTavish said. "I'm truly blessed."

John thought, This is certainly true.

The interview ended and the McTavishes were returned to their separate cells. Afterwards, Rawlings talked to Captain Bush in charge of the jail, while John waited outside the policeman's office. Loud voices filtered through the walls.

As they walked out of the jail, Rawlings said, "I've arranged for the McTavishes to be together in a separate room of the jail to keep them safe from the other prisoners. The police department does not want anything to happen to them. Negative publicity is Captain Bush's grave concern, as is the possibility of a lawsuit against the police department and the officer involved. The Captain said that the officer involved was suspended with pay."

CHAPTER 6

RAMIFICATIONS

Two Days Later

The arrest and arraignment of the McTavishes quickly became national news and Rawlings and John were mentioned as lawyer and associate in an article in the *Washington Post*. The Vietnam War protest on campus became a civil rights case for the Civil Liberties Union. Scores of police from all over Michigan tried unsuccessfully to make the protestors disband without violence.

The best signs in the protest at the jail, were FUCK THE COPS and BLOW ME MR. POLICEMAN, but they did not interfere. John thought, This is truly freedom of speech, He did not participate, since he was now acting like a lawyer.

After a week the Washtenaw County Prosecutor, in a hearing, asked Judge Pierce to release the McTavishes without bail, which he did with an audible sigh of relief from the bench. John thought, The Judge received a lot of the bad publicity for setting bail at ten thousand dollars and keeping them in jail.

Casey returned to his lectures on the civil rights movement in Hill Auditorium, the largest venue on campus. There weren't enough seats inside. Speakers were erected outside so that people could sit on the steps of the Auditorium and hear the lectures. He got standing ovations throughout his lecture on the goals of civil rights.

John thought, Public opinion is changing as is the law of civil rights. I am fortunate to be a small part of it.

The criminal charges against the McTavishes were dismissed by Judge Pierce after viewing the film in open court during a preliminary examination hearing. He ruled that the policeman attacked without any provocation.

Afterwards, Casey said, "I forgive the policeman who hit me," to the Chief of Police.

———

THE MCTAVISHES INVITED JOHN AND Ann to eat dinner in an Italian restaurant in town. Ann refused to go with him.

Over spaghetti, they talked about Casey's ministry.

"I was invited as pastor at the Methodist church in Charleston, West Virginia. It's in the heart of coal country. There is a large congregation of people who attend the church and receive a black man as their preacher. I accepted."

John congratulated him and wished him good luck. He said, "I hope I can visit there sometime." John did not offer any explanation why Ann was not there. He bitterly resented her attitude.

CHAPTER 7

GRADUATION

May 1969

In the final week of classes prior to graduation, John was courted to be a new associate by some of the best law firms in the country. They were interested in having help, based on his chemistry degree, to defend polluters for fat legal fees.

Ann was thrilled that prestigious firms arrived at the Law School from New York City and San Francisco. Each of these firms represented large companies accused of polluting. The recruiters said they wanted the best and brightest students with a chemistry degree. John was one of only a very few in demand, but he did not want to represent the polluters.

Ann talked gleefully about the prospect of living in a big city, particularly New York City. She insisted that he take one of the offers.

There were few chances for a job with firms who represented those injured by the pollution. They wanted only experienced lawyers, paid based on contingent fees.

John thought, Representing polluters, there are bonuses and a guarantee of a job for at least two years, possibly becoming a junior partner in five years."

John decided he had to go for the money for now. He thought, At least I don't have to listen to Ann bitch about the salary and I can become an experienced lawyer.

In one interview at the law school, Robert Taylor from New

York City sat across from John in an office in the Law Quadrangle, which was modeled after an English Tudor manor house. Taylor was self confident and arrogant.

A Harvard Law graduate, first in his graduating class, he was dressed in an expensive looking tailored black suit, which seemed to John to make him look a little like an undertaker. John thought, He is a little puffy in the face, probably from drinking too much booze. I don't like him at all.

Somewhat distracted, while Taylor talked about the wonderful benefits of joining his firm, John admired the grass and flowers of the inner courtyard through the leaded glass windows. He thought, I love living in Michigan.

Taylor said, "We're situated in the heart of the world. Everything which is really important happens in the City. All the major businesses have offices in Manhattan. There is unmatched culture."

"What kind of work would I be doing?"

"We're handling a pollution case in Delaware for one of the world's largest automobile firms. You will start immediately researching the law and studying underlying documents with one of the partners. If the case goes to trial, you will be part of a team of lawyers appearing in court each day and to help translate what the experts say into language the jury and the trial lawyers can understand. You will learn to be a trial lawyer from some of the best."

"What chemicals are involved?" John asked, feeling certain the answer would not be good.

"As far as I understand the matter, the lawsuit involves overspray from painting cars, which is being flushed into the municipal sewers. Our client has been doing this for at least fifty years."

"There are organic solvents in the overspray?" John asked, already knowing the answer.

"Well, possibly, I don't know. Residents of Wilmington are claiming that the overspray is causing illnesses, which is ridiculous."

"Sounds like the case could be settled if the company stops dumping the chemicals," John suggested.

"Our client indicated they will never settle," Taylor said with a smug smile. "This means large lawyer's fees."

Taylor offered John twenty-five thousand dollars a year, five thousand dollars more than the offer from the San Francisco firm handling a similar pollution case involving chemical-reaction byproducts dumped into the Pacific Ocean. The recruiter for that firm said, "Environmentalists are claiming that our client is killing dolphins." John wanted nothing to do with that firm.

John said, "I will think about your very generous offer, Mr. Taylor." John thanked him with a firm handshake and left having no intention of accepting the offer. He was disgusted with the idea of making money defending pollution without any hope of stopping it.

John walked outside the building. May on the Law Quadrangle was beautiful that year. The bushes were in bloom, and the grass was restored to green from winter brown. The wind was blowing patterns in the as yet un-mowed grass. John sat on one of the stone benches and basked in the noonday sun, trying to figure out how to cope with Ann, who wanted him to take the job in New York City.

John sat there for several hours, feeling very good, reading advance sheets with recent United States Supreme Court constitutional law decisions. His final exam was in a month, and he thought that one of the decisions might be on the final exam.

When he arrived home, he told Ann that he was going to decline job offers in New York and San Francisco because he didn't want to represent polluters. She threw a heavy law book of his at him, which bounced off his shoulder. He thought, Ann is very physical in expressing her displeasure with me. I worry about what she might do to me in the future.

"You selfish bastard! I suffered through all those long nights alone in bed while you're studying or away in Vietnam. For what? So you can take a job as an underpaid flunky at a second rate law firm?"

John said, "It's my career, not yours." This statement did not help matters at all. Ann stopped talking to him.

John spent the next two nights on the sofa in the living room.

John decided that he was going to have to try to placate Ann for the time being, but he formally declined the jobs in New York City or San Francisco.

His next interview was with an eighty-member firm, in Lansing, Michigan, which represented a large chemical company with a bad pollution problem he had read about. John met Albert Quinn in the Men's Union on campus for lunch. He brought Ann along.

Quinn had a laid-back likeable, mid-eastern manner, was about forty years old, and was handsome in a sort of movie star way. He was dressed in pants and a sports coat. John and Ann were greeted with a firm handshake and a friendly, "Nice to meet you. Call me Al."

Quinn said his firm represented companies in Michigan that needed to make sure injured employees obtained proper settlements from their Workmen's Compensation insurance and that their medical needs were being met. He offered John twenty thousand dollars a year.

"We have a very happy firm and everybody likes each other. Being from Michigan, you are going to fit in very well." Quinn said.

The work sounded boring to John, but he agreed to take the job. Ann said she was satisfied with his decision and that Al was a likeable guy.

————

LATER JOHN SAID TO ANN, "I'll only stay a couple years to learn about becoming a practicing lawyer with a good firm. After that, I want to join a firm representing injured parties as a plaintiff's trial lawyer."

Ann said, "John, you are taking a lousy job, but you need to be the best lawyer you can at the firm. Al Quinn sounds like a nice guy and I don't want you to disappoint him. Maybe you will decide differently leaving in a few years."John thought, maybe she will like Quinn.

CHAPTER 8

PRETZEL BELL

June 1969

After the final exams, John went to the Pretzel Bell with some of his classmates and ordered pitchers of beer. The Bell was crowded and noisy with young men and women who were drinking heavily.

John proposed a toast to all of the friends they used to know at the University, particularly those who had left school.

"A toast to absent friends!" John said. Beer mugs clinked together. He was thinking of Shirley.

John dressed in a dark blue sports coat with tan pants and black shoes so as to look lawyerly, now that he had graduated.

A number of young women smiled at him. His wedding ring stopped most of them from approaching his table. A well endowed young woman came over and asked to sit next to John, grabbing a chair from a nearby table, and said her name was Cindy. John smiled, shaking his head. "I'm married," pointing to his ring. She thanked him, took a sip out of his glass of beer, leaving a little lipstick on the rim, smiled at him, and excused herself.

John's friends kidded him about attracting women. "You're just jealous," he said. John drank far too much beer that evening and his friends took him to his apartment complex at about nine in the evening. Residents were sitting out on their porches, trying to find a breeze in the stifling heat. Four of them carried him into the apartment, one man on each arm and leg.

In disgust Ann, said, "Put him in the bathtub in case he has to throw up."

In the morning John apologized to Ann. He said, "Just letting off some steam. I had a nightmare about Vietnam." Ann did not ask what it was about. John thought, The nightmare was about the Dragon Lady as she was dying.

CHAPTER 9

LANSING FIRM

June 1969

When he hired John, Quinn was certain that once he was entrenched in the job, he would stay for years. Eventually, he was going to have John work on the defense of a lawsuit against Bromine Corporation of America lawsuit. It was filed against the company before John joined the firm.

BCA sold a flame retardant called TBIS, used in flame proofing clothing, particularly for children. TRIS was allegedly making them sick and producing a skin rash that wouldn't heal. The defendant's President, Dan Bigger, maintained publicly that TBIS in the clothing was not the cause.

In fact, Quinn and the management knew TBIS was a health problem, but by the time of the lawsuit, all of the evidence was destroyed. This was as a result of a routine document destruction program at BCA, which Quinn established.

Management of BCA, particularly Bigger, was very grateful to Quinn and paid his firm a five hundred thousand dollar annual retainer for their services, since Quinn was so flexible about the ethics of the matter.

The company continued to sell one hundred million dollars worth of TBIS as clothing fire retardant despite the lawsuit. The gross profit was seventy percent.

Quinn thought, John will never about the destruction of evidence of sickness caused by TBIS.

CHAPTER 10

SEPTEMBER 1969

That fall, John learned that he passed the bar examination. He was now a licensed lawyer.

The firm hosted a dinner dance, which included John and Ann along with two other new associates, with their spouses, who worked on trust and estate law. John rarely saw them. It was boring work and they had nothing in common with him.

Quinn sat at their table. He was divorced for a few years and did not bring a date. Ann danced with him several times during the evening. She said he was a very interesting man. He told several funny stories about his clients.

In the Workmen's Compensation unit John dealt with injuries to workers in BCA plants. Quinn concentrated on the BCA pollution litigation for a majority of his time. He did not discuss this case with John.

IN NOVEMBER OF 1969, JOHN met with an injured BCA employee. In a routine conference, Joe Hamilton, a supervisor in the production of TBIS for BCA, disclosed he was sick with a severe skin rash. BCA was opposing payment of compensation because, they maintained, there was no proof that TBIS caused Hamilton's illness.

John was shocked. Hamilton showed him copies of reports, supposedly destroyed, which clearly demonstrated that BCA knew, at least five years before Quinn's lawsuit, that TBIS produced skin rashes, when workers came in contact with it. The rashes would not heal. Included in the reports, there was a discussion of safety measures needed in making TBIS.

John made two copies of the reports, and gave the originals back to Hamilton. He thought, I should have refused to take the copies from Hamilton, because they are BCA property. If it is found that I withheld evidence in the BCA litigation, I could be disbarred.

Afterwards, John went to Quinn to discuss the matter. When John gave Quinn a set of the reports, he did not seem surprised. He told John not to disclose the existence of the reports to anyone, at the risk of being fired and possibly disbarred. Quinn destroyed the papers in John's presence.

Hamilton's case was then quickly processed as merely a skin disease of unknown origin. The Workman's Compensation payments were forthcoming and he retired from the company. Afterwards, Hamilton surrendered his papers to Quinn as part of the settlement of the Workmen's Compensation case, with a written agreement, signed in Quinn's and John's presence, that he would never disclose any company information of any kind.

Finally, John had the only set of the Hamilton papers left in existence. This presented a very serious problem for him.

Quinn called John into his office and ordered him to work fulltime on the BCA litigation. Quinn said, "You don't have a choice. All of the information about the reports has to be secret. The reports that Hamilton brought to you and everything else about this case is included in attorney client privilege. You cannot disclose them or discuss them with anybody. If anything comes out about them from you, you will be disbarred. Do I make myself clear?"

"Yes. Am I to understand that reports will never be produced by BCA in the litigation?" John said.

"We are not going to disclose them, because they were destroyed as part of the document destruction program before the lawsuit was filed. Hamilton was not supposed to have them at all. They do not exist. By the way, do you have any remaining copies?" asked Quinn. "Hamilton said you made two copies."

"I did have a copy, but I shredded it after the Hamilton case was settled," John lied. "I did not want to have them in my possession after Hamilton agreed to never disclose them to anyone else as part of his settlement."

"Now you're thinking like a trial lawyer. Without that evidence in the reports, the plaintiff has no case. You're will go far in this firm," Quinn said, beaming a full smile at John.

Quinn accepted John's story, but he felt sick to his stomach. He thought about the Hamilton reports he had tucked away in his old Constitutional law book at home.

That evening, John and Ann sat at the dinner table, eating by candle light the steak dinner she had prepared in celebration of his promotion to the BCA litigation. He had called her from the office and told her about being on the trial team.

"I'm proud of you John. You are moving up in the firm," she said as she reached over and stroked his hand.

"Well, this is a step up the ladder. This firm never had a second-year associate in a line position in a major case. I am uncomfortable about working with BCA."

"I think we should go to bed and celebrate. I'm excited," Ann took his hand and led him up the short flight of stairs to the bedroom.

The Constitutional Law book was resting in his bookcase, and he was distracted. Ann was insatiable and John held back from coming for a long time after Ann.

Thinking about the matter afterwards John was disgusted with himself. He thought, I should have quit the firm, but he didn't because of Ann.

CHAPTER 11

ANN

December 1969

Ann thought, Lansing is the most boring city on earth. The population is Oldsmobile factory workers and wives, blue collar to the core, with lots of screaming children. Apparently they haven't heard of the birth control pills, which I take every day to prevent pregnancy. The stores are full of cheap clothing lacking any style. John is working twelve hour days and is not interested in sex.

Ann worried now about her relationship with Quinn, which had started during the dinner party in September. She thought, He is my ideal man, given the setting. He is smart, decisive and without any qualms about having sex with the wife of an associate. I don't doubt that he has done this in the past with other associates' wives, looking to help their husband's position at work or bored, like me.

It's just a fling. Quinn came right out and asked me to sleep with him as we danced together at party. I give Quinn the full body press as we danced.

Since that evening, we have spent many hours together wrapped in each other's arms after making love. I enjoy the sex, but he is getting too serious. At forty years old, he is over fifteen years my senior. Besides, John has achieved as much as he could in the firm by being picked for the BCA litigation team. I am afraid he might find out about us.

———

I DECIDE TO END THE affair. Sex with Quinn is becoming routine, as if we were married. We meet in the evening on Michigan State University campus in East Lansing, parking their cars several spaces apart as usual. I walked over to Quinn's car and wave as I opened the door. Once inside, Quinn ran his hands over my breasts as he kisses me. I put a stop to that.

"Wait Al, not tonight. We need to talk. I want to stop meeting you. I'm afraid that John is going to find out." I move his hand firmly from inside my blouse.

He pauses and with a surprised look and says, "Hey, we are having a great time and I want to you."

"The sex has been great but our relationship isn't going any further, and I know when to stop." I reach for the door handle.

"What if I offer you more,---like marriage?"

"You are too old for me," I say in a quiet voice as I push the handle down and open the door.

Quinn looks stunned, and says, "Good-by Ann, I take back the part about marriage. I didn't think you would fall for my proposal."

I knew then that he was serious about me and ending it now was critical.

"No, Quinn, I wouldn't," I close the door firmly. This puts a punctuation mark on the end of our affair. I walk back to my car.

I like variety in sex and can get the mundane type at home. Besides, there is a whole world of men who are attracted to me.

Some of the lawyers I flirted with at the recent annual State Bar conference in Detroit are interested. Lots of opportunity there to meet rich lawyers, but they work too hard and long at the office, like Quinn. There has to be someone richer.

She sang, "I'm just a girl who can't say no------" on the way home," forgetting the rest of the words.

CHAPTER 12

BCA LITIGATION

December 1969–August 1970

Shortly after joining the litigation team, John participated in depositions of the plaintiff who claimed to have been injured by the flame retardant and of the defendant's executives and employees. Hamilton, who lied in his deposition, said that there had never been a problem with TBIS as far as he knew. Quinn threatened plaintiff's attorney, Wendy Hold, with a motion for a summary judgment to end the case, based upon lack of any evidence.

Wendy Hold stated she did not believe any of the defendant's witnesses, thus far, including the experts Quinn hired. So far, all of them claimed in their depositions that TBIS was harmless and that the flame retardant was necessary to keep the wearer, particularly children, safe from burning clothing.

In the Quinn firm's library, Harold Warsh, a medical doctor hired as an expert, was the current deponent. Quinn wanted his testimony preserved, providing the possibility of a very cheap settlement with the plaintiff.

After Warsh was sworn in and identified for the record, Quinn began his questions.

"Dr. Warsh, where are you employed?"

"I'm a doctor of medicine with Boards in dermatology and reconstructive surgery, licensed in Michigan. I practice in Ann Arbor at the University Of Michigan Hospital where I have been on the staff for ten years. I am currently chief of staff for both areas of medicine." Warsh's assured resonant base voice and smile said volumes about his self-confidence and importance.

"Where were you trained in medical school and as an intern and a resident?"

"I was at Harvard University as an undergraduate and in medical school, where I graduated with honors. I interned and trained as a resident at Johns Hopkins University Hospital. I had a near perfect score on my Michigan Boards to practice in this state."

"Dr. Warsh, in your capacity as a reconstructive surgeon, have you encountered patients who have been burned while wearing knitted clothing?"

"Many times. Their clothing catches fire. Certain clothing, particularly sweaters made of synthetic fibers, melt and stick to their skin, causing second- and third- degree burns."

"What does the skin look like after it is burned?"

"Generally the skin is totally destroyed down to the muscle. It takes a lot of time to remove the remnants of the skin and fiber from the burn, referred to as debriding by surgeons."

"What is the treatment after the debriding?"

"The patients undergo skin grafts, which are a long and painful treatment, and they are usually permanently disfigured to some degree in spite of our efforts."

"Dr. Warsh, in your experience, have you ever encountered patients wearing clothing containing the defendant's flame retardant, TBIS?"

'Yes, we did a five year study of burns from clothing where the patients were exposed to fire and were burned. We found that sweaters without the TBIS caused extensive burns of the face and hands. In patients wearing sweaters with the flame retardant, the retardant prevented burns in the covered areas."

"Dr. Warsh, was any of this work published?"

"It was published in the *Journal of Medicine* about two years ago. The recommendation was to ban clothing without TBIS. The plaintiff's product was the only one we found to be very effective."

"Turning to your dermatology practice, Doctor, have you ever treated a patient where you determined that TBIS in clothing was responsible for a dermatological condition?"

"Not that I can remember."

"Thank you Doctor. If plaintiff's counsel is agreeable, we will take a short break."

Wendy Hold voiced her assent for the record.

————

IN HIS OFFICE, QUINN REVIEWED the testimony. Dr. Warsh sat in a chair sipping a cola, still very calm and self assured.

"Great job, Doctor, very convincing." Are you foreseeing any problems?" Quinn said.

"No, you are doing an excellent job with my testimony. I don't expect to have any difficulty with attorney Hold."

For the next few minutes they talked about the beautiful fall day and how the Doctor was eager to get back and walk around the Michigan campus. He said, "Insufficient time for the simple pleasures."

Back in the library, Dr. Warsh resumed his position next to the court reporter. He asked her in his sonorous deep voice, if he was speaking loud enough so that she could capture his words and she nodded with a smile.

Hold said, "Thank you Doctor for testifying today. It must be difficult for you to take time away from your patients, so I won't keep you long."

"Yes, and thank you."

"Doctor, are you being paid for your services today?

Quinn objected merely for the record and told Warsh he could answer.

"I am, but haven't received any money to date and I understand the judge has to approve payment. I would rather be treating my patients, but this litigation needed my services."

"Thank you doctor. Have you ever performed a dermatological study on the defendant's flame retardant TBIS?"

"No, Up until now, there didn't seem any need."

Doctor Warsh, "If you had seen a need, what would you have done by way of tests?"

Quinn said, "Objection, speculative, but the Doctor can answer the question if he can."

"The best available dermatological starting test is to shave the skin of live rabbits and place pieces of clothing against the skin to gauge the reaction of the skin. It is a standard type of test."

"Has the defendant engaged you or anyone else at U of M to perform these tests?"

"Not that I am aware of."

"Do you have an opinion as an expert as to whether such tests should be performed?"

Quinn said, "Objection that is outside of his direct testimony."

"He testified that he didn't see any reason for the tests. He can answer the question or we can call the judge for a ruling and suspend the deposition in the meantime, your choice."

Quinn paused and then said, "Doctor Warsh can answer the question, subject to being stricken from the record by the judge, based upon my objection." Quinn was sweating now.

Warsh said, "In view of the allegations in this litigation, it could be important to run the tests."

Hold asked, "In this study, is it important to run blood tests to see if the flame retardant is in the bloodstream?"

Quinn said, "Continuing objection to this line of questioning."

Wash said, "Yes, I would want to know the basis for any skin rash, whether it was topical or internal."

"Continuing objection as speculative," Quinn said.

"If I presented you with the results of such a test, would you be able to evaluate it?"

"Yes, if the study was done properly."

"Thank you, Doctor. Mr. Quinn, any follow up questions?"

"No, I think we're done here for now, but I reserve the right to depose Dr. Warsh further in view of his unexpected testimony.

Quinn said, "The judge will decide the matter. We can go off the record."

The court reporter gathered her tapes and said the transcript would be ready in a week.

After the court reporter left the room, Quinn asked Hold, "Why don't we sit down and talk about the case? I'm interested in the tests you are having conducted."John knew where this was headed.

"Well, I can't talk about that," Hold said, but the preliminary results are very interesting. You will find out as soon as they're completed." Hold was smiling and Quinn was still sweating.

"We might be able to offer your client a settlement. Would you be interested?" Quinn said.

"Well I'm open to listening."

"We are prepared to enter into a confidential settlement open only by order of the court. Do you have any problems with that?" Quinn said.

"No."

"Your client has developed a skin disease that we agree is not presently life threatening. We do not admit the disease was caused by my client's flame retardant."

"It could become malignant, resulting in a huge verdict." Hold said.

"Our client is prepared to offer one hundred thousand dollars to get rid of this nuisance litigation," Quinn said.

John sensed that Hold was weighing a large fee from the settlement against a long and difficult trial.

"If you double that amount, my client might settle," Hold responded, taking out a cigarette from a pack which then twitched between two fingers. She lit it.

John saw this as a sign that she was nervous.

"I believe my client might accept that," Quinn said as he took out a large Havana cigar and carefully clipped the tip before lighting it, not to be outdone by Hold.

Hold and Quinn talked about other cases of local interest for a few minutes.

Hold said the smell of the cigar was making her sick and she left.

John remembered that cigar smell several times on Ann's clothes, when he returned home after working at the office.

———

QUINN AND JOHN MET WITH Bigger at his office in the plant to discuss the settlement. They both lit up cigars, causing John to start coughing. They opened a window and laughed at John. Bigger said, "You need take up smoking cigars like a proper lawyer."

Bigger said, "There is every reason for us to settle this lawsuit. We sell over one hundred million dollars of TBIS annually. We net about fifty million dollars after taxes, since there are no advertising expenses and it's simple and inexpensive to make. I need your assurance, Quinn, that this will be the end of this matter."

"I can't promise that there won't be another independent lawsuit with a different plaintiff. I can promise that this litigation will not be used against us. Since it will be a confidential settlement, any test results Hold has in her possession will be suppressed. We specifically state that BCA doesn't admit any responsibility."

Bigger said, "OK let's settle it."

––––––––

QUINN AND JOHN LEFT THE BCA plant. On the drive back to the office, Quinn said, "The Plaintiffs are going to destroy all documents which were not of public record, including the results of any testing." He gave John a lecture on how to stop a settled case from being used by another plaintiff again against their client.

Again, John was unsettled by the smell of cigar smoke on Quinn's clothing.

––––––––

TWO WEEKS LATER, THE CASE was settled in the manner that Quinn said it would be. The case, involving a young woman, named Short, was dismissed with prejudice to it ever being brought again.

John stayed out of work for several days trying to come to grips with the chicanery on Quinn's and BCA's part. He thought, I can't say with the firm. Also there is that cigar smell. I can't accuse Ann directly of being with Quinn.

––––––––

MUCH LATER, IN JUNE 1970, John saw Hold at a State Bar meeting in Detroit and invited her to have coffee. Hold was dressed in an expensive looking skirt and blouse. She looked like she just came out of the beauty shop.

After they sat down at a table in a cafeteria, John asked, "So, what kind of results did you get with the animal tests on the fire retardant?"

Hold laughed. "What results? They were never started."

John smiled and said, "Very clever."

"I went right out and bought a new Oldsmobile convertible with all of the options with part of my contingent fee." She smiled happily.

Wendy had a serious look come over her face and the smile disappeared.

Wendy said, "There were a lot of gossip about Quinn and the wife of a lawyer in his firm. I don't know who the woman was. The source was an unreliable one, a woman who had a relationship with Quinn that she hadn't gotten over."

John didn't comment, but felt downcast.

Recovering, he said, "Who are you companioned with?"

"I have a woman partner and we live together as a couple."

John said, "I would like to meet her. She must be terrific to deserve your love." John thought, I don't care if Wendy is a lesbian.

They parted company and John drove home. On the way he thought, I am leaving the Quinn firm, even if I don't have a job. I am starting out as plaintiff's lawyer. That's where the money and excitement takes place. Ann will be furious because of the loss of income and may leave me. I know how much she hates living in Lansing, but I am stuck here for now. She will have to go along with me.

CHAPTER 13

PLAINTIFFS' LAWYER

August 1970

John went to the 1890's Mason County Courthouse to listen to Zach Shamus, a famous Michigan plaintiff's lawyer, plead a case. There are trial lawyers who are so well known to other lawyers that they become legends, like Clarence Darrow. Shamus was such a lawyer. The gallery section of the courtroom was full of lawyers watching him work.

Shamus' client was sitting at the Plaintiff's table in a wheel chair looking sad, but trying to put on a brave face.

The jury box had six jurors listening. The judge's bench was raised above everybody and he was clearly in command. John watched a trial about a dangerously constructed mower which injured the Plaintiff.

Shamus mesmerized the jury with his melodic baritone voice, like a great radio reporter, explaining that a defectively designed riding lawnmower toppled over sideways down a hill and permanently paralyzed the legs of his client. He was summing up his case before the jury retired to reach a verdict walking back and forth between the plaintiff and the jury box. This kept the focus on his client.

"Ladies and gentlemen, you have heard my client, the witnesses who saw the accident and our experts. There is no question that the defendant's lawn mower permanently and tragically paralyzed the legs of my client, Ron Welt, for life. Just imagine if you could never walk again and were confined to a wheelchair," extending his right arm towards the plaintiff. The jury looked at his client and shuffled their feet and twisted in their seats, uneasy with the thought. Shamus paused for several seconds.

"Your duty is to decide who was at fault, my client or the defendant, Riding Mowers, which made and sold the mower, which rolled over and paralyzed my client's legs. The defendant's expert witnesses have testified differently. They suggest that Mr. Welt should not have been mowing along the side of a hill and thus was at fault. They have been paid by the defendant for their time here in this trial, which the law allows even though they did not witness the accident.

I ask you to consider whether a reasonable person driving the defendant's lawn mower would expect it to slide downhill and roll onto him on where there is a gentle grade of about seven degrees. Even a young child could walk along the side of this hill and not fall." Shamus took several steps towards the jury box.

"The defendant that lawn mowers tend to slide sideways on grass," he said, pointing to a cartoon in evidence resting on an easel in front of the jury. "This mower was top heavy causing it to roll over on a gentler grade.

This mower even slid on the grass when it turned to start another row as you have seen from the films in evidence, showing the X-100 mower slide.

These still pictures are from the film in evidence. I will ask Judge Harmon to allow you to have them in the jury room." The jury turned their heads to look at the picture on the easel. The judge said, "Agreed."

Shamus' voice softened as he moved back to the rail of the jury box. There was complete silence in the courtroom, except for the whosh-whosh of the ceiling fan and the click-click of the court reporter's machine.

"My client will never walk again because of the defendant's mower. You need to send a message to the defendant and other mower manufacturers that you will not tolerate selling a dangerous mower.

"Ron Welt is trying to recover his life before the accident. His wife Rosa has to help him in and out of bed every day for the rest of his life. He cannot continue to work as a door to door salesman. He has no cash to take care of himself. The Welts' are destitute if he does not receive a substantial award from you, enough to sustain them for the rest of their lives. There is a loss of consortium with his wife.

"You need to send a clear message to Riding Mower Company that they cannot terribly injure the Welts without suffering the consequences," Shamus said, pausing as if to gather his thoughts. There were tears in his eyes and in some of the jurors.

"We have demonstrated that the mower will roll over when the wheels slide on wet grass are wet and hits a drainage ditch. Certainly any manufacturer of riding mowers is expected to know that this will happen. Just imagine five hundred pounds of riding mower rolling over you or your loved one. We need to send a clear message that selling this shoddy mower is not tolerated by us." Shamus pointed at the defendant's president. Then he spread his arms wide like a cross at the jury box.

The jury was now looking at the defendant's president sitting at the defendant's table in a blue pinstriped suit and white shirt with a matching tie, a picture of wealth and importance.

"I ask you to award damages to the Welts in the amount of lost wages for life. In addition, I ask you to award punitive damages for willful negligence in selling a lawn mower which cripples. The defendant willfully manufactured and sold the unsafe mower.

Thank you."

Shamus walked back to his client who hugged him and smiled with tears dripping down his cheeks.

John was very impressed with the closing argument, inferring that the defendant's experts were money grubbing liars. He thought, If I was on the jury, he would have given the Welts everything he asked for and more.

John listened to the uninspired closing argument of the defendant's lawyer. It seemed to him that the jury was unconvinced, since they were looking everywhere except at the lawyer.

———

WHEN THE JURY CAME IN with a verdict two days later, they awarded three million dollars in damages and seven million in punitive damages, with a specific finding that the defendant was grossly negligent, bordering on intentionally marketing an unsafe mower. John thought, This is the lawyer I want to work with.

————

JOHN CALLED SHAMUS' LAW FIRM a week later and asked his secretary to set up an appointment with Shamus to discuss a position as an associate. He mentioned admiring Shamus' closing argument to the jury in the Welt case. She said, "Send him your resume." An appointment was arranged after he sent it to Shamus.

In the appointment in his office, Shamus said, "I see from your resumé that you have worked for the Quinn firm for about two years. Why do you want to leave a firm which represents clients with lots of money? I understand that you were made a member of the litigation team. That's very unusual in that firm."

"I want to learn how to be a skilled plaintiffs' trial lawyer like you. I don't like defense work for clients who injure people or to work for lawyers who want to win at any cost. It's a practice that is all about money. I would rather work for the injured party."

"Quinn is a very good lawyer who represents clients he may not personally like," Shamus said as he reached for and lit a pipe filled with an aromatic tobacco.

John said, "Quinn loves his work as a litigator. I just feel that I am on the wrong side."

"Well, I think I can find room for you here. The catch is that I can only pay you sixty percent of your salary at the Quinn firm. You certainly have a fine academic record from law school. I will consider paying you a small part of contingency fees.

"Your chemistry training will be useful in a product liability case I have just taken on. E. *coli* in a hamburger made my client deathly ill. It was ground by American Meat Packers and their machine was infected with the bacterium. It is likely he will die, leaving a wife and five children. Would you like to work on this case?"

"Yes! I had a course in biochemistry as an undergraduate. I know that the toxin from this bacterium can make people very sick. It generally enters the meat when it is ground by contaminated equipment."

————

JOHN LEFT THE QUINN FIRM in November of 1970 and became an associate lawyer in the Shamus law firm. Ann stopped talking to him except to say, "Pass the salt."

John helped Shamus prepare and try the ground meat case for trial for three months. The plaintiff testified from his hospital bed by a video deposition, looking like he was dying. In fact, he died a week later.

————

THE DEFENDANT, AMERICAN MEAT PACKERS, offered five million dollars to settle before the jury reached a verdict, which the family accepted. Shamus gave John a bonus of sixty five thousand dollars from his million dollar fee.

When interviewed by John at Shamus' request, the jurors said they were prepared to award a very large judgment. John finally felt he was in the right type of law practice.

————

AFTERWARDS AT HOME, ANN POINTED out that he got only a token amount from the case. "Shamus is a lot richer."

John said, "That one fee resulted in more money than I would have earned at the Quinn firm in three years. Obviously very large contingent fees result, between twenty five percent before trial or thirty three and one third percent if the trial begins."

Ann did not say anything more, she was at a loss for a response for a change.

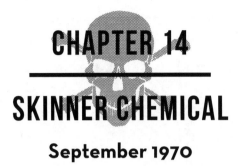

CHAPTER 14

SKINNER CHEMICAL

September 1970

Gooding and Shamus met with the Calders as possible new clients in their office. Wendy Calder and her daughter Paula were substantially overweight, dark-haired women with faces so pudgy you could hardly see their eyes. They claimed they had been poisoned by waste chemicals from manufacturing Agent Orange dumped into the Corn River by Skinner Chemical up river near Greenberg.

Wendy said, "Waste chemicals from the Skinner Chemical plant are dumped into the Corn River almost every day. The Corn River runs right by our farm."

Paula said, "Relatives of ours, Carl Brandt and Richard Stretcher, are high school graduates working on maintenance at the Skinner plant. They both said at a family picnic that they heard chemists at the plant suggest that dioxins in waste chemicals being dumped in the River could cause cancers. Their drinking water was from a well near the River.

After the conference with the Calders, Shamus warned John about the difficulties of the case. He said, "It is difficult to prove that their illness was caused by the waste dumping."

Gooding insisted that he wanted to try to get something for the Calders. He said, "Agent Orange is a poison. It's making a lot of Vietnamese and Americans very sick."

JOHN VISITED GREENBURG TO FIND out more about Skinner Chemical. The town was surrounded by thousands of acres of corn, wheat, beans and pickles.

John learned from the Calders that after work Brandt and Stretcher frequented the Hamburger Palace, a small fast food and watering hole in the center of town by the Corn River. Wendy had told Brandt and Stretcher that they needed meet John there today.

As he walked into the bar, he turned on a small tape recorder in his pocket. This was a useful tool that many lawyers used, rather than taking notes. The recording could not be used in court in any event.

John sat at the bar after five in the afternoon drinking beer and talking to the two Skinner Chemical employees. They introduced themselves as Buddy and Runner and were sitting on the barstools next to John. They started drinking about four o'clock. There were several empty bottles on the table, apparently left there to keep count. John suggested that they move to a corner table so as to not be overheard.

John thought, These guys are 'real beer drinkers' and must pack away a case each of Miller's beer a day. They chain-smoked and drank beers without the slightest hint of drunkenness, flirting with Bess a pretty waitress with fulsome breasts and a low cut blouse. After a while John did not try to match them beer for beer, but they did not seem to care. By seven o'clock they were really talkative.

"We work at Skinner Chemical on the Corn River. We fill huge reactors ten times taller than us with chemicals to make Agent Orange. The US is using it in Vietnam to kill plants, spreading in from the air. It makes makes my eyes water," Brandt said, after taking a drag on his cigarette.

"Ya, it dyes your skin," Stretcher said. He pointed to a large orange spot on his arm.

John said, "I saw that in Vietnam. Nobody wanted to handle it, but soldiers take the duty that is ordered. You don't have to work at Skinner." John said.

"We have to work there. It is the only job in town. Neither

of us have any money. We barely got through high school in town here," Brandt said.

"Most of the maintenance guys in the plant are in the same boat as the Calders, with health problems," Stretcher said. He took a big swig of beer.

John said," It must be nice to work on the Corn River. You can sit outside and have a pleasant lunch."

"Are you kidding? That river is so polluted by Skinner that you could almost walk on the water. Also, all of the municipal shit and upriver chemicals float by us. We don't even drink the water in the fountains at Skinner since it comes from city wells. The only water that is safe to drink is in these beers," Stretcher said.

"Ya, and the stuff we dump into the river is enough to poison every fish down-river," Brandt said.

At this point, John just waited for either of them to fill in more details.

Stretcher said, "We open a sluice gate and all them by- products from the reactors slip into the river with a hissing noise. A chemist at the plant told me that the water just neutralized acids in the waste." They both laughed as if they didn't really believe it. Stretcher continued, "If you drink that stuff, even in small amounts it will kill you. We think the water down river with waste chemicals from making Agent Orange made the Calder women sick, poisoning their well."

Brandt said, "Supposedly what is put in the river water is safe. Some of the by-products from the chemical reactors are so bad they put them into fifty-five gallon steel drums. They store them on farmland north of Greenburg surrounded by a wire fence topped with barbed wire. The by-products are so corrosive that they dissolve the steel and leak out in a year. A sign says Danger Poison. I wouldn't eat anything from anywhere near that farm."

After taking a long pull from his bottle, John said, "Sounds like you guys have pretty dangerous jobs. What happens if you are hurt?"

Brandt said, "We have Workman's Compensation as a last resort, but no health insurance. We had a health insurance company come interview us, but they determined that there was too much risk."

We do OK, making seven dollars an hour and sometimes time and a half overtime," Brandt said, as if resigned that was the best he could do.

"That's a lot of money for two guys who didn't graduate from high school," Stretcher said.

"What about you John? Are you going to take the Calders' case?" Stretcher said.

John said, "We are going to represent the Calders with your help. Here's one of my cards."

They shook hands with John and slapped him on the back, saying, "It was a pleasure meeting you", and then dropped a few bucks on the bar for Bess, who smiled in appreciation. Stretcher said, "I hope you can help the Calders. They are family."

When he left the Hamburger Palace, John felt more confident about suing Skinner Chemical Company. John speculated that their leukemia was caused by the tap water supplied from wells near the Greenburg River. No other plant in Michigan produced Agent Orange and dumped the chemical waste into Corn River.

The next night, John secretly photographed Stretcher in color with a full moon as he opened the gate to the sluice into Corn River. This became Exhibit A in the Complaint he had filed in the circuit court in Grand Rapids. He photographed the iridescent orange liquid flowing like a snake into the water and the burst of bubbles as it boiled angrily in the flowing water until the river water diluted it. After flowing about one hundred feet downriver, the last traces of orange were gone, as if death slid into hiding from its victims. As he watched, the scene made John feel physically ill as he thought about the horrible deaths from cancers for the people living downriver from the Skinner Plant.

After reading Rachel Carson's *Silent Spring* while he was an undergraduate chemistry student in college, John decided to go into environmental law. His old, retired chemistry professor was incensed about the book, denying that that any chemist would be polluter.

Clearly, that teaching had not reached Arnie Skinner, a PhD

Chemist and President of his company or any of his Board of directors. Certainly the message had not reached his shareholders, who saw only the bottom line profits on the financial statements and thought they were terrific. Business was so good for Skinner Chemical that there were rumors of the sale of the company to an unknown chemical company out in Washington State for a very handsome profit on the sale of the company stock. This would make Skinner and the shareholders rich. The new site was on a river.

CHAPTER 15
SKINNER
October 1970

John filed suit against Skinner personally and his corporation for polluting the Greenburg River, thereby causing the leukemia of his clients. The suit was in Kent County Circuit Court. Unfortunately it was assigned to Judge Zimmer, who was known to favor corporate businesses, something to do about American enterprise. John heard this from other plaintiffs' lawyers.

During preliminary proceedings in court, John had a chance to observe Skinner. Skinner was a few inches taller than five feet, but what he lacked in height he made up in sartorial splendor and self assurance which radiated to observers. He wore a white silk shirt every day with a black bow tie. His shoes were black and so shiny that John would swear that one could see his reflection in them. He was possessed such a high level of confidence that taller men from his company in court appeared to bow in his presence.

If one of his executives had a tie knot out of place, Skinner would straighten it and appear to suggest that the miscreant try harder. In the final analysis, John learned that Skinner was a bastard of the first order to work for, who would not hesitate to fire anyone who disagreed with or crossed him.

His lawyer, Rush Ready, was a Charles Dickens character, like Uriah Heap, with an oily obsequiousness that made you want to wash your hands after meeting him and shaking hands. In fact, he was a powerful force in court and had a reputation amongst lawyers for being as mean and sneaky as any lawyer in Michigan. Skinner did not try to straighten his tie. He always wore a rumpled suit and shirt. There was a stale sort of smell when near him.

John was certain that lawyer Ready was well aware of Skinner's operation. He would try to destroy anyone to protect the company, especially since he had a large number of original shares of stock, based upon public information john obtained from the State of Michigan.

John did not get any favorable press about the lawsuit. For weeks after the lawsuit was filed, articles appeared in the *Grand Rapids Press* pointing out what good citizens Skinner and his company were and that they were falsely accused of polluting. The journalist noted that the company had a spotless record as far as the state inspector was concerned. John believed the inspector must have been bribed to look the other way. Written reports about diseases caused by Agent Orange never made the news!

It seemed to John that it was unlikely that any of the jurors in Kent County could have missed the newspaper stories, unless they couldn't read. John thought, I will have a difficult time selecting a jury at trial.

Rather than file an Answer to the Complaint, Ready filed a Motion to Dismiss the Complaint to be heard in two weeks before Judge Zimmer. Skinner alleged that only tepid, cooling water from the reactors was going into the river. Attached to the Motion were affidavits of Carl Brandt and Richard Stretcher, who affirmed it was just water. Both said they were drunk and pulling John's leg at Hamburger Palace.

John filed a Reply to the motion, stating he believed the waste from the manufacture of Agent Orange dumped into the Corn River by Skinner produced the leukemia of the plaintiffs based upon scientific papers describing cancers caused by dioxins in Agent Orange. Unfortunately, he could not use the tape recording, but it wouldn't have helped anyway. John subpoenaed Carl and Richard as witnesses at the hearing.

———

JUDGE ZIMMER MADE IT CLEAR that Friday when motions were heard that he was not interested in anything but the facts of the case. He told Ready to make his argument and he walked to the lawyer's podium with his head bowed down at a respectful position, almost like genuflecting.

"May it please the Court, Your Honor I am here to rid your docket of a frivolous lawsuit against my esteemed client and his company. No basis exists for the assertion that my client dumped dangerous chemicals into the Greenburg River. The affidavits from Carl Brandt and Richard Stretcher attached to the Motion show that only tepid cooling waster was discharged into the river.

"The by-products from producing the Agent Orange are placed in sealed drums for later safe disposal. Also, even if there was some small discharge of Agent Orange in the waste for some reason, it would be negligible. Finally your honor, no evidence exists showing that the chemicals supposedly released by Skinner could have caused the Plaintiffs' leukemia's."

"Therefore we request that the complaint be dismissed with prejudice so that the plaintiffs can't sue my client again. Thank you Your Honor."

"Mr. Gooding, do you have any reason why this case should not be dismissed?" asked the Judge.

John approached the podium and paused to gather his thoughts.

"In the first place your honor we have evidence the dioxins in Agent Orange were released by Skinner Chemical in the Greenburg River. I have subpoenaed the two men, who swore that only water is discharged, into court today. I request that they be put on the stand under oath so that they can testify as to the veracity of the Affidavits. I believe they have been forced to lie."

Ready said, "I object, your honor."

"On what grounds do you object Mr. Ready? The plaintiff has the right to question the veracity of the affiants before I make a decision. This court will not tolerate lying. We will hear the rest of Mr. Gooding's argument first."

———

"YES, YOUR HONOR, I ACKNOWLEDGE this is a difficult case for the plaintiffs. We will prove the chemicals in the Corn River came from Skinner Chemical by an analysis of the land adjacent to the sluice gate at the plant. We will show that these chemicals cause cancers including leukemia in humans from publications in recognized journals. I know firsthand that soldiers in Vietnam are becoming sick from this product, which the Army may not want to admit. The jury can then decide if the Skinner caused the leukemia.

"Do you mean that you can't prove the dioxins in Agent Orange caused the Calders' illness?" Zimmer said.

"At this time we can show a pattern of various cancers in individuals along the Corn River where the plaintiffs live. We are obtaining medical histories for the last twenty years in that area," John said.

Judge Zimmer said, "Enough argument. I am not going to dismiss this suit at this time, but you will need to prove specific injury to the plaintiffs caused by the defendant. Otherwise, you must consider a class action identifying all of the people alleged to be injured."

"In the matter of the two affiants, the court will hear their testimony next Friday at nine o'clock."

The judge banged his gavel and said, "Court is adjourned." Without another word, he got up from the bench and the clerk said, "All Rise."

Judge Zimmer then left the courtroom without a backward glance.

John turned and started to go over to explain what had happened to the Calders who were sitting on benches in the back of the courtroom. Skinner got up and walked over to John before he got there, without his lawyer who was still sitting at the defense counsel's table stooped over.

Skinner said, "I'm a generous guy and I want to help the Calders and I have a suggestion for settlement.

My offer is two hundred and fifty thousand dollars to each of the plaintiffs for a complete settlement, without any admission of guilt and the absolute silence of the Calders about Skinner Chemical. In return, the case will be dismissed with prejudice by the two plaintiffs, so that it could never be brought again.

Any research on health issues of other people in Greenburg will be destroyed."

John said "Make it $500,000 for each of them and I will recommend it." Skinner agreed.

Standing next to John, Skinner straightened John's tie, smiling about the publicity he was going to get as newspaper photographers took their pictures.

John walked back to his clients and then explained Skinner's offer.

"Skinner offered to settle the case after the Judge's decision if you will accept five hundred thousand dollars each. Also, they do not want to have the possibility of your bringing the lawsuit again or working with others to do so." Our fee would be twenty five percent.

"Well, John, what do you think we should do?" Wendy asked.

John said, "If you dismiss with prejudice, you could never bring the lawsuit again. The settlement terms are to be confidential so you could never discuss them with anybody."

John continued, "Even if we try to gather evidence of leukemia or other cancers in your neighborhood, we might not be able to prove that Skinner Chemical caused them. Because of your financial circumstances, I recommend that you accept the offer. The apparent reason they want to settle now is because I said we were going to conduct a study on cancers in your community. It would be an important study, but expensive."

The Calders accepted the offer and the settlement which was sealed in Kent County Court. John received the settlement payments from Skinner.

The Calders now drank bottled water and were even hesitant to wash their dishes or bathe in the well water. They did mention to their neighbors that they thought the well water was unsafe to drink, but nobody listened.

John and Shamus split the fees equally, pleased with the way he handled the case. Ann was thrilled that John received one hundred and twenty five thousand dollars as his share. Ann did point out that Shamus hadn't done anything to earn his share.

John said, "Shamus earned that fee for his confidence in me. He is the best lawyer I have ever met."

CHAPTER 16

WASHINGTON D.C.

May 1971

John was lecturing at a three day lawyer's conference on litigating personal-injury cases involving chemical pollution, which was exciting for him but boring for Ann.

The cherry trees were blossoming pink along the Potomac River as John walked near the Lincoln Memorial. The monument made no impression on Ann.

For John, this was the best time to be in the Capitol. He was particularly looking forward to visiting the Supreme Court. Ann was talking about shopping at Union Station and the dinner dance coming up on Saturday at the Mayflower. John thought, It will be boring.

The Mayflower was infamous because one of John F. Kennedy's paramours stayed there and Ann was interested in that story. Herbert Hoover had lunched there every day in the Town & Country room before he died. The Hotel was built in 1925 and John liked the feel of the old building.

Breakfast in the restaurant was a treat for John. He had eaten grits and gravy there for the first time and liked them. They gave John the feeling of the old South. On the other hand, Ann felt the room was small and antiquated. She said it smelled musty, like people had died there.

Later, as they walked past the Lincoln memorial, John only half listened to her chatter about shopping as he thought about the lecture that morning by Professor Easton from West Virginia University in Huntington about strip mining of coal. The pictures were tragic. Whole tops of mountains in West Virginia and other Appalachian states were cut off to remove the coal, then, left to erode. Overburden and coal tailings from washing the coal were dumped into the valleys, rivers, and lakes. John thought, The interest of those attending the lecture besides me is low. Public opinion is that coal is essential for keeping the country strong.

Easton said, "The mercury from the coal ends up in the fish in the lakes where the coal tailings are dumped." John was very interested since there was a health issue for the people eating the fish, linked to the strip mining. John thought, This looks like a great opportunity for litigation by a lawyer who takes cases on a contingency. The coal mine operators are very rich.

John lectured about taking cases on a contingency. He said, "There is no regulation of chemical waste. Toxic chemicals are dumped in waste sites in steel barrels which corrode and leak chemicals into the ground. The aquifers used for drinking water around the dumps are contaminated. The resulting illnesses are not always the same, but patterns of cancers are developing. Worst yet, the chemical companies are dumping toxic chemicals directly into the rivers and contaminating drinking water. Usually this is done at night so the chemicals are diluted, undetectable to the naked eye."

John told the audience a story about how a retired PhD chemist, who worked for a plating company in Ohio, describing the dumping jokingly.

The chemist said to me. "Hexivalent chromium was dumped into the Ohio River at night by Shine Chemical, reduced by the river water into trivalent chromium, which was an iridescent red until it was diluted by the river. One night the workers dumped it too close to morning and the bright red plume was visible for hundreds of yards down river. We were reprimanded by the state, and we promised not to do that again. From then on we had a regular schedule for the dumping around midnight. We never had a problem after that. He laughed while pointing out how dumb the workers were."

John observed, "There seems to be patterns of serious diseases from drinking well water near chemically polluted rivers."

A member of the audience raised his hand and John said, "Yes".

How do you prove that a particular chemical causes a particular disease?"

"To begin with, there are large numbers of publications describing diseased caused by a particular chemical. For instance, mercury is a well known poison. It is well known that the herbicide Agent Orange causes disease. You then look for patterns of disease in the polluted area where the victim lives or works."

John said, "In conclusion, it appears that the general population and politicians do not care about pollution as long as it wasn't near them or they can't see it. The illnesses in the animals and humans caused by chemical waste dumping is just becoming recognized. Thus this is an important conference for lawyers attempting to obtain money damages on a based upon a contingent fee. Most judges think like the PhD chemist and dismiss the case for lack of proof of injury. Finally, the decision is in the hands if a jury, and the result is totally dependent on us. We end up with nothing or one third of large judgment."

John noted at the end of his lecture that the purpose of the conference was to discuss litigation strategies that worked, but he concluded that these were hard to find. He closed with, "You damned near have to prove that those injured were drinking the pollutant from the drum to show that there is causation."

CHAPTER 17

LESTERS

May 1971

After the conference lectures, John met Frank Lester a DC lawyer and a sponsor for the reception at the Mayflower. Frank said he was lobbying for legislation to regulate various forms of chemical pollution, but he had been unsuccessful thus far.

Lester invited John and Ann to dinner at his home in nearby McLean, Virginia, one of the best suburbs near Washington. He met them at the Mayflower Hotel and drove them in his new four-door 1971 Cadillac Coupe Deville. His home tucked into the side of a steep hill, with a view of the valley, was a very large and impressive two-story colonial in one of the best suburbs around Washington. D.C. John wondered how a lobbyist could have afforded the home and the car. He decided that Frank's family must have money. Ann nudged John and smiled approvingly.

She immediately warmed to Frank. "You certainly must love your home. It's a beautiful neighborhood," she said, turning on her most accessible smile as they walked to the front door.

"Thanks, Joanne and I am very proud of it and glad that you could see it." Frank said with a small catch in his voice as if he was out of breath. He glanced at her breasts.

Joanne met them at the door and invited them in, sounding glad they could visit their home.

John smiled and said, "We're glad to be here. Thanks for inviting us."

Joanne was about thirty years old, slightly on the plump side. She did not seem to match Frank who was handsome with black hair. He was polite, with old Southern manners.

Over cocktails the conversation revealed that Joanne's parents were Irish. She came from a humble background in a small coalmining town in Maryland. Frank's family came from North Carolina, and no suggestion of serious money in what they said.

John saw Ann flirting with Frank. This did not seem to bother Joanne as she talked with John until dinner was ready.

The meal of roast beef, peas and potatoes was served by a maid who Joanne said acted as a nanny for their two children, pointing out to her guests while she served that good help was hard to find.

They drank two bottles of a very expensive French Cote' De Rhone red wine with dinner and ate apple crisp for dessert. All of them were a little tipsy, particularly Ann, as Frank led her into the living room. John could see her breast rub against Frank's arm. Frank leaned into her. John was fed up with her antics.

Frank shared stories about his unsuccessful efforts to get into Congress to pass legislation stopping chemical pollution. "It's obvious that the polluters have deep pockets. Most of the Congressmen are receiving gifts of money, travel and most likely sexual favors from the companies and would not even consider introducing any legislation regarding pollution.

John said, "President Nixon, just created the Environmental Protection Agency in the US by executive order this year. The U.S. was dumping tons of Agent Orange on Vietnam. The contract manufacturer for Agent Orange is dumping dioxin from the by-products of the manufacture of it into the Corn River in Michigan. Barrels of toxic military wastes were routinely dumped offshore into the Pacific and Atlantic Oceans, poisoning the sea life, particularly the dolphins and seals. Maybe that will change."

Frank said, "Every time I broach the topic of chemical pollution with a congressman, he says that it is too expensive to fix. It will cost jobs, which would be very unpopular with their constituents. Besides, no proof is available showing that the chemicals that are dumped injure people." John started to argue with Frank.

At this point Ann restlessly said, "It's time to talk about something besides work." Joanne agreed. Frank and John agreed reluctantly.

For the rest of the evening, they talked about the people who would be at the dinner and dance at the Mayflower after the meeting the next day.

Frank said, "I have a summer home on Deep Lake next to a mansion owned by Charlie Webber. I invited him to the dance on Saturday evening. Charlie is visiting D.C. to promote more coal usage. He's a very wealthy coal mine owner. I invited some congressmen as well, but I doubt if they will show up. Anyway, Charlie is a very interesting person."

John said, "What he does to the mountain tops is tragic."

At the mention of money, Ann smiled. "Well, I'm looking forward to meeting him. I've never met a coal mine owner." John could almost see her ears perk up at the mention of money. John sensed her anticipation of another flirtation.

"Webber's hoping to convince you that coal is good for the country," Frank said. "Nobody has ever been successful in obtaining damages from the coal industry for environmental damage."

As they rode back to the Mayflower Hotel with Lester, Ann quizzed Lester about Webber. He said, "Webber is a terrific guy." John sensed Ann's new excitement about the dance and her anticipation of another flirtation.

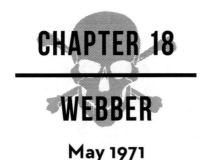

CHAPTER 18
WEBBER

May 1971

The ballroom Saturday evening had a twenties feel to it. In truth, Charlie Webber never paid much attention to such things, and the point was to meet Ann Gooding. Frank said she was a real looker.

Environmental lawyers were the enemy, and he believed in knowing what they were thinking. To be precise, he hated lawyers in general, except when he needed one and then he hired a crook.

Webber dined with an environmental lawyer by the name of John Gooding. The evening will not be a total loss. This is another chance to get laid, he thought.

Webber thought. I forty years old and women are attracted to me. My appearance attracts woman as much as my money. I have a wiry muscular body, no bulges of fat. I am well-hung. I brag to women about it. U.S. Senator Wallenby's wife, Evelyn, couldn't get enough of me. She has a face like Ingrid Bergman and is great in bed, but I can't afford to antagonize the senator, who is my friend. I am going to have to end the relationship. I will not miss her. She is too clingy.

Before Webber arrived, Frank thought, he is a hard man in a cruel business. He succeeded by being meaner than all of the other mine owners in the state of West Virginia and was at least as tough as any of the miners he employs. People mostly notice his eyes, which narrowed to slits when he is mad, accompanied by thin-lipped smile.

A worker discovers his life is in jeopardy when this happens, which is frequently. They learn never to cross him for fear of a beating by one of his goons or worse. Workers are expendable to Webber since there were always more. Miners are known to disappear if they are involved in attempting to form a union. For 150 years, Webber and his family prevented the formation of any mine unions.

Webber arrived a little late to the party and Frank introduced him. He shook hands with John Gooding and, in a quick assessment, determined he was just a lawyer who never stepped out of the bounds of etiquette and wouldn't be any trouble in the unlikely event they were adversaries.

Webber thought, Lester is right about Ann Gooding sensing an easy conquest. She made no effort to conceal her admiration of him when they shook hands and their eyes met. He felt that Ann was a woman who could take care of herself. Her hands lingered in a firm grip a little longer than necessary for a polite introduction. Frank made certain Ann sat next to me.

Dinner was served, and Charlie had the halibut. He said, "Some of the best fish in the world were caught in the Atlantic Ocean. There are terrific bass in Deep Lake, West Virginia, where my summer home is located."

John said, "Aren't you afraid to eat the fish because of the pollution from strip mining coal?" Ann frowned.

Narrowing his eyelids to slits, in a thin-lipped smile, Webber started to respond.

Ann said, "That's impolite." She raised her hand up to silence John.

Charlie ignored the comment. "Deep Lake is about one hundred miles South of Charleston, where I live most of the year. It's about two miles long and fed by a river coming down from the mountains. I have eaten the fish all my life."

Ann said, "Sounds beautiful. I'd like to see it."

Ann and Charlie spent the next hour talking, their bodies close to each other. Charlie quickly was drawn to her.

After a while Ann left the ballroom, saying she was going to the powder room. Webber also left a few minutes later, saying he had to make a telephone call.

Webber took her up to his hotel suite. They stripped naked. Ann said, "That's incredible, let's see how it fits in me." She reached over and stroked his erection and guided it into her as Charlie climbed on top of her. She came and then he came immediately thereafter. The whole affair lasted only ten minutes.

"That was fun," Ann said when Webber rolled off her. "We need to get back to the party. Sometimes a quick one with a stranger is just the best." She kissed him on the mouth and dressed quickly.

"I want to arrange to get together again with you," Webber said.

"Ann said,"Well let's just savor the moment."

When Ann returned to the ballroom, she said, "I sat in the powder room feeling ill. It must have been the white fish. When they returned to the ballroom Ann said," I sat in the bathroom feeling ill."

Charlie said, "I resolved a problem at one of my mines on the phone."

Webber and Ann danced a slow dance with their bodies in close contact. Ann said, "John is engaged in a conversation with Lester about chemical pollution, ignoring what you and I are doing."

Webber whispered in her ear, "Are you going to attend my party next July at my summer home?"

Ann replied, "I wouldn't miss it."

Charlie felt her body melt into him. He thought, I want to see her long before the party this summer. Something is different about Ann.

CHAPTER 19

GETTING BACK AT SKINNER

May 1971

Brandt and Stretcher, the employees at Skinner Chemical, telephoned John to complain that they were sick from handling the Agent Orange.

Brandt said, "Skinner fired us after your lawsuit. We need to get Workman's Compensation. Nobody will hire us now."

Both Shamus and John met them in their office. When they arrived, they were both rolling tanks of oxygen and using clear breathing masks.

Between gasps for breath, Stretcher said, "John, we're sorry about what happened. Skinner said he would fire us if we didn't sign the affidavits his lawyer prepared for the hearing on that Motion."

John said, "You guys need to realize your affidavits w weren't the most important problem. Skinner knew you would tell the truth under oath in Court. We needed to prove that Agent Orange caused the Calders' leukemia's. It all worked out very well for the Calders in the end when the case was settled."

"What happened to your jobs?"

Brandt said, "Well, we were fired for drinking on the job. The real reason is that both of us are sick," Brandt said as he lit up a cigarette after turning off a valve on the oxygen tank. Stretcher could not breathe well enough to turn off his oxygen.

"Ya, our beers are the only thing that kept us going. Our doc says we have emphysema, forces us to carry an oxygen tank for the rest of our lives. We will never be able to work again. Skinner never objected to our drinking a few beers before. Nobody drinks the water in the plant."

John picked up the doctor's reports for the two of them, passed a copy to Shamus, and read them. He thought, Clearly these two guys were telling the truth. They are not dumb enough to lie now.

John guessed their life expectancy was numbered at a few years, at best, based on the reports. He felt sorry for them. They were both only in their forties. John thought, In view of the money we made in the settlement, we need to represent them.

"Did you give the doctor's reports to anyone at Skinner's?" Shamus asked.

Brandt said, "We gave the reports to our supervisor."

"Have you heard from Skinner's Workmen's Compensation insurance carrier?" John asked.

"Someone from Michigan Liability Insurance called and asked us to fill out a claim form and we did," Stretcher said as he handed copies of the forms to John and Shamus.

John said, "It looks like you filled them out correctly. From what I see so far, payments for permanent disability will be made for the rest of your lives."

Shamus said, "You need an attorney to help you because of the issue regarding the beer. Many simple claims are settled without an attorney. When an attorney is required, the fees are regulated by the law. In any event we will take only the fee from the settlement. If you agree, we will talk to the carrier to find out how they want to handle the case."

Shamus handed them a representation agreement. They signed and dated without reading them. Neither of them was conversant with the written word.

Brandt and Stretcher shook John's and Shamus's hand and scraped their shoes, walking out of the office dragging their oxygen tanks. John wondered if they would be able to do anything but drink beer and watch TV. He felt sad. Nobody was going to hire disabled hourly workers with emphysema.

JOHN AND SHAMUS ARRANGED TO meet with the insurance carrier, whose offices were in Lansing. The representative of the carrier, Tony Romano, said the lawyer for Skinner, a man named Rush Ready, would be there as well. John told him they were asking for a finding of permanent disability and lifetime monthly payments or a lump sum. Romano did not comment either way wanting to appear impartial.

John and Shamus entered the park like campus of Michigan Liability. The employees sat near a pond with large Koi in it. Old elm, chestnut and oak trees stood, like umbrellas, over well-manicured lawns. Cattails surrounded a larger pond where ducks and geese waddled back and forth in the water. Workers were strolling in pairs on pathways around the building.

———

SKINNER AND RUSH READY RODE down together from Greenburg Rapids, driven in the company limousine to attend the meeting at Michigan Liability. Skinner thought, I regret the decision to fire those two bozos. I could have paid them a settlement. Lawyer Gooding is certain to be looking for my blood.

Skinner said, "We need to make this case go away quickly. The company offering to buy Skinner Corporation is not going to stand for this risk," Skinner warned.

Ready said, "Well you knew the risks that making

Agent Orange posed. Anyway the manufacturing is going to be in Washington State when the company is sold."

"We're going to have to put money in escrow for possible health care costs and legal fees. Is there any company or personal liability after the sale?" Skinner said.

"We are okay as long as there is no intentional harm, such as knowingly placing workers in a dangerous environment, so that they are likely to be injured. Just between us, this could be the case. You need to maintain that you took every precaution to protect your workers. You were also unaware of risks if the masks were worn properly," Ready said.

After they arrived at the Michigan Liability office, Romano's secretary showed all the participants into a large conference room overlooking the pond. They all introduced themselves.

Romano said, "Thank you, gentlemen, for attending this meeting. I am hoping we can make some progress today on these claims.

"Can you tell us anything about the toxicity of the chemicals that are used in the process?" Mr. Romano said.

Skinner said, "Agent Orange contains dioxins which might have caused Brandt's and Skinner's condition. We are very careful in the plant. All of the workers use gas masks when they are introducing chemicals into the reactors."

"Did Brandt and Stretcher use the masks?"

"Yes. Everyone in the plant has to wear masks. They were ordered to do so, with signs all over the reactor room."

"Have there been any injuries from Agent Orange in your plant?"

"Yes, there was one recently, where the worker was in the hospital, but he is back to work now."

"Have there been any other injuries from the Agent Orange?"

"No! It is produced in the plant and then shipped to the military in sealed barrels," Skinner said.

"How about the chemical waste pumped into the Corn River?" Gooding asked. He thought, I want to needle Skinner and his lawyer.

"We were involved in litigation with Gooding about that," Ready said. "It was determined that the only liquid pumped into the river was water."

John said, "That's untrue. Mr. Brandt and Mr. Stretcher said to us that the Affidavits were false and that you forced them to sign them or lose their jobs," Gooding said.

"I object to this line of questioning! There is no reason for this line of inquiry in this case." Ready said.

"This is not a court of law, Mr. Ready" Romano said. "We are just trying to outline the problems. My company can investigate this matter." Romano said.

John knew that was unacceptable to Skinner.

Skinner asked, "Why don't we assume that Brandt and Stretcher could have been exposed to chemicals in the plant, in some manner we don't understand, to see if we can reach a resolution?" Skinner asked.

"At this point we can assume exposure. The question then is did it produce the emphysema?" Romano asked.

"Dr. Skinner, are you aware of any cases where Agent Orange produced this type of disease?"

"I have read that workers in other plants that produce Agent Orange have suffered difficulty in breathing," Skinner said.

"Is it possible that this could have happened in your plant?" Romano asked.

"We are very careful to prevent any exposure. Brandt and Stretcher were fired for drinking beer on the job," Skinner said.

"Were the supervisors in your plant aware of the beer?" Romano said.

"Brandt and Stretcher were warned several times," Skinner said.

"So, Dr. Skinner is it your claim that Brandt and Stretcher caused their own injuries in some manner?" Romano said.

"No, for the purpose of settlement of this case only, we can assume they were injured by the chemicals in the plant. I note that they are heavy smokers, which could easily been the cause of their disease," Skinner said.

Romano said, "Legally we don't regard smoking as a health hazard."

So, we come to the central issue which is should these men receive compensation for the rest of their lives?" Romano asked as he turned to face John.

"It is the doctor's opinion that they are both going to be on oxygen for the rest of their lives and thus permanently disabled. The doctor's estimate is that they will live only for seven to ten years," Shamus said.

"Dr. Skinner, do you accept these estimates?"

Ready said, "We accept these estimates, but only for the purpose of settling this case."

Romano said, "We do have a settlement of this matter. I note that their wages were seven dollars an hour before taxes. Michigan Liability will continue to pay their medical expenses. We need to arrive at a temporary bi-weekly payment to these men based upon eighty percent of their wages. We can assume two hundred working days in a year and an eight hour day." By my calculations, this is about $8,000 dollars per year or about $180 per week. They should be able to draw disability social security as well. Are you agreeable?"

They all nodded their heads yes.

"Thank you, gentlemen. We can consider a lump sum payment based upon each of their expected life spans, if that is your clients' wish, Mr. Shamus and Mr. Gooding. Thank you for coming." Romano said, shaking hands with each of them.

———

SKINNER LAUGHED HAPPILY AS HE climbed into the limousine with Ready. "That was easy. The purchaser of Skinner Chemical will be satisfied with the result. I can remember only five people who worked routinely in the reactor room. That son-of-a-bitch Gooding has interfered with our business for the last time," Skinner said.

That was not to be. John, as a last shot at Skinner Chemicals, had a meeting of five hundred residents around the barrel farm. He told them to stop drinking their well water because of the leaking barrels. He sent copies of the letters to Skinner and would have loved to see his face.

He went over to the barrel farm a week later, the barrels were gone, and so was the fence with dirt gone three feet below where the barrels rested. A farmer whose property was adjacent to the barrel farm said that workers on four large tractor trailers arrived and removed the barrels over a period of two days. The workers were encased in yellow hazard suits with masks and oxygen tanks.

Skinner Chemical closed its doors the day the trucks left the barrel farm. The *Greenburg Press* said that the business was sold and the Editor said the workers were sorry to see the company leave and the workers go on welfare. He said Skinner moved to parts unknown as soon as the deal was closed.

John speculated about where the barrels were dumped. He thought, Probably poisoning people in another state.

CHAPTER 20

CLEM BLOCK

June 30, 1971

Webber's party was on July 4th, when he distributed bribes to the politicians. Clem Block chauffeured the Cadillac limousine with license plates spelling Clean Coal, brooding about how much he hated his boss, Charlie Webber, who sat in the backseat smoking a fat cigar, with large alligator leather bound suitcase on the seat beside him. Fortunately for Block, they were nearing Webber's summer mansion on Deep Lake, since the smoke was searing his throat and lungs.

His mind circled back to how he bowed and scraped afterwards, like the servant he was, supposedly grateful for the work that paid far less than what he had made in Webber's mines.

Block saw Webber, in the rear view mirror, deep in thought. I'll get that son of a bitch and he will never know its coming.

Block was injured five years prior in a methane gas explosion deep in Webber's mine. Afterwards breathing was difficult, but he began jogging to expand his lungs and it helped. He worked out lifting stones until his strength returned. Almost six feet tall with a well-muscled body, he was close to his fitness level following his tour in Vietnam. Black hair and bushy eyebrows lent a sinister look to him: and he was as evil as he looked, as he relished orders to torture North Vietnamese prisoners for information.

Block had shared his wartime experiences with Webber when

he applied for the job. This expertise caused Webber to hire him, along with the fact that he had no qualms about killing people. One of the miners picked a fight with Block while trying to organize the miners to form a union. Later he snapped the miner's neck like a stick. Webber concealed it as an accident caused by a falling chunk of coal in the mine. There was no investigation, since such accidents were so common.

Webber hired Block as a bodyguard to kill or maim those who crossed his path. Block considered this to be a perk of his job. Webber was himself an accomplished killer and participated for the pleasure of making the kill. The other mine owners told Webber about problems with union organizers and workers. Webber was always ready to provide the ultimate solution for them, which to date involved five killings by Block and Webber, the bodies dumped down in an abandoned mine shaft and covered with lye. Chauffeuring Webber was just his day job.

As soon as they arrived at the mansion at Deep Lake, Webber dismissed him. Block knew that the suitcase Webber carried into the mansion was filled with money which Webber would distribute at the weekend party and he didn't want him to steal it. Webber no doubt thought that Block could kill him for the money. Block would have been happy to do it if he could have gotten away with it.

"I'll visit my brother in Treadwell, so I'll only be about ten miles away if you need me," Block said.

"I won't need you until tomorrow morning to help set up for the party," Webber said, turning away from Block, thereby exposing a shoulder holster holding his Colt 45semiautomatic, as he carried the suitcase into the back door of the mansion.

Block knew that Webber was sending a message about the danger of attempting to steal the suitcase. Webber was a first-class shot with that pistol, and at twenty yards he could put all of the shots in a two-inch circle. They had been shooting at targets every month. He thought, I'm not going to get at Webber by shooting him, as he motored to Treadwell.

On the way to Treadwell, Block listened to a speech by Nixon promoting the idea of ending the Vietnam War with honor and saying the protests should end. Block viewed the protesters with scorn. He would have still been there if he hadn't been discharged for a mental disability, which was that he liked killing too much. He was suspected that he had killed his own lieutenant, which was true. The discharge was less than honorable.

Nixon's Committee to Re-elect the President appeared on the lists in the ledger Webber kept in his Charleston office. Webber planned a very large donation to the Committee this year. The ledger also contained the names of politicians who received annual payoffs at the summer parties at Deep Lake. Block reveled at the thought that he had made copies of the lists which he planned to use at an appropriate time to destroy Webber.

Block reflected on how he had come into possession of the list. The ledger was kept in an old safe in Webber's Charleston office. One afternoon Evelyn Wallenby, the young and supple wife of senator Wallenby, a very important West Virginia Senator and friend of Webber's, showed up at Webber's mansion demanding to see him. Block brought her in as Webber was working on the ledger. She entered and sat on Webber's lap. She whispered in his ear and then kissed him on the mouth. She reached down below the desk and stroked him. "I want to go upstairs right now," she said.

Webber got up and closed the ledger. "Put the ledger in the safe and lock it," Webber said as they left the room and went upstairs. Block walked over to the book, examined it and started towards the safe with it as he listened to them go up the stairs. Instead, Block walked over to the copying machine and reproduced ten years of records, about twenty pages in a few minutes and then placed the ledger in the safe, closed the door and spun the dial. To cover his use of the machine, he copied several centerfold pages of Webber's Playboy magazine.

When Webber returned to the office an hour later after the senator's wife had left, Webber saw Block outside the office looking at the photocopies. Webber didn't comment except to smile and suggested that Block needed to get laid more often. Block knew if Webber found out about the copies, he would suffer a terrible death.

When Block arrived at his brother's home, he gave them food, corn whiskey and hard candy for the kids. Hank invited him to have a beer.

Hank was younger than Block and worked at Webber's strip mine on Mt. Hope above Treadwell. At least the open pit strip mining was safer for Hank and Clem made sure he had a safe job driving a coal truck. Nobody on the crews at the mines even argued with Clem when he said, I want this taken care of right now" to a driver. Block knew the driver had heard stories about what happens to people who didn't agree with him.

As they sat on old chairs, made by their grandfather, on the porch, with the sun setting, the weathered pine siding creaked in the gentle wind, and Clem felt a sense of ease. Hank's hardworking wife had born him two children, who Clem loved, even though they were afraid of him because of his appearance. The beer had been cooling in Deep River behind his brother's home and tasted good.

While they were alone, Clem asked Hank to keep an envelope without opening it in a safe place. Hank said he had an old lockbox buried on the property and would put it there. He put it under a cushion on his chair so that his wife wouldn't see it.

Clem said, "Webber would kill your family and you if he knew you had these papers. I want you to promise never to open it unless something happens to me. I will let you know who to send it to when I figure it out. Don't tell me where the box is located."

They sat on the porch and finished off a six-pack of beer. Hank's wife, Jennifer, dressed in faded blue jeans and a denim shirt, served them fried chicken and fried potatoes followed by pie for desert. A good wife, she sat in the kitchen with the children and ate dinner, leaving them to talk.

Clem thought it might be nice to have some home life, but he knew that few women who could tolerate him. He told Hank that Webber provided whores for him once a month along with his paycheck and they did whatever he asked. "The girls are skilled at their trade and rarely complain if I get rough with them."

After dinner, they drank corn liquor as the frogs croaked.

About nine o'clock Hank said Clem could use the sofa in the living room to sleep on, as usual, and went to bed in the next room. He could hear Hank making love to his wife. The liquor and their conversation about whores must have made him horny, he thought.

———

AFTER BREAKFAST THE NEXT MORNING, he thanked Hank and his wife for their hospitality. He promised to bring food, beer and whisky again on his next visit and drove back to Deep Lake. He felt rested when he reached Webber's mansion.

Block helped set up the security for the party, which included local cops from all around Deep Lake and West Virginia State Police from Charleston. He knew from past years that certain politicians would have police escorts take them home because of the large amounts of cash dispensed to them by Webber during the party.

By Friday morning all was ready for the party. Webber told Block he was pleased. Block mumbled, "Thanks Mr. Webber."

CHAPTER 21
CHARLIE WEBBER
June 30, 1971

harlie Webber walked briskly from his limousine after dismissing Block, carrying the large suitcase into his summer home on Deep Lake. Above the entry door was a plaque with Respite on it. He easily climbed a wide spiral staircase to his second floor office. Nobody would come up these stairs without his permission.

Working for his father as a young man in the family coal mines gave him muscles like the coal miners he now employed, and he still lifted heavy weights to maintain his body. He never wanted to mine coal down shafts deep in the earth again, expecting to die in an explosion or cave in. This was the reason when he began strip mining, tearing off the tops of mountains for coal. Besides it was a more economical way to mine the coal.

Lining the walls were pistols and rifles of many vintages, and trophy heads of the game animals he had killed. He felt comfortable and in control in this room, which reflected his prowess as a hunter.

The suitcase which he carried was covered with the skin from a twelve-foot man-eating alligator he had killed in Florida with his favorite 45 caliber Peacemaker Colt.

He hunted people when they interfered with his coal mining operations. They met the same fate as the animals, usually without much sport. The one exception was a tough union organizer who attacked Webber with a knife, slashing his side before gunning him down. At least he put up a fight, Webber thought.

Flipping the latches and opening the suitcase, he took out fat envelopes of money and put them into an old floor safe, which was a family heirloom and had been used by his father. As each envelope was nested in the safe, he listed the contents in the bound ledger and detailed the recipient, the amount of money in the envelope, and the date. The list in the ledger included the names of all the politicians he had bribed for years to prevent legislation, state or federal, from being passed to regulate coal mining in West Virginia. The payments protected his strip mining, and allowed him to blast off the tops of mountains, leaving a giant, pitted landscape, dumping dirt and coal tailings into rivers which flowed into lakes. The profits were enormous and the bribes were a small part of the cost of mining his coal in open pits.

As he sat at his desk, he stroked the cloth cover of the book almost lovingly, feeling comfort in the names and dates and amounts of cash payments recorded there. There were many pages and years with total payments amounting to tens of millions of dollars. The list was his insurance should any of them decide to change their mind about regulation.

Closing the ledger, he placed it in the safe with the envelopes, shut the door and spun the dial, thinking he was invulnerable from any criminal charges for bribery. I am prepared to eliminate anyone, including the politicians, who change their mind about strip mining.

The money for the bribes came from members of the Coal Mine Operators Association of which he was the permanent president. They knew that the bribes worked very effectively year after year. The members of the CMOA were content with his efforts, like well-fed carnivores that kill without warning. These were fiercely independent, hard and cruel men, who were exactly like Webber, and he had no doubt they would turn on him if something went wrong. The profits they made from strip coal mining over the years, enabled by the bribes, had made them all extraordinarily rich.

Webber was the meanest of this group with eyes that signaled, with the thin-lipped smile and a nod, sometimes with a slicing movement of his index finger across his neck, the mutilation or death for anyone, particularly the miners and union organizers, who crossed his path. Two of the organizers disappeared as a result of his murders in the last five years. The bodies were dumped, with the help of Block, down an abandoned 1860s mine shaft, hundreds of feet below ground level on land owned by Webber Mining. They also threw down bags of lime to stimulate rapid decomposition.

For years, Webber and his goons beat miners who met with the organizers until effectively they didn't even try any more to form a union. Other men who crossed Webber's path with various complaints about his coal mining operations vanished down the mine shaft. Webber did not see himself as a serial killer, but rather as a businessman protecting his coal mines in the family tradition.

The members of the CMOA, appreciative of Webber's efforts, showed their gratitude by paying him a large sum of tax-free cash each year. In turn, he helped them dispose of people who were interfering with their operations without any additional payment. In fact Webber liked hurting people and was very good in taking care of this part of the coal mining.

All during the war in Vietnam, Webber said to news reporters in frequent interviews that West Virginia coal produced electrical power in generating plants all over the United States, and this electricity was essential to the strength and defense of the country. In truth, Webber thought, The war is merely a means for making more money, and I am completely in favor of it for that reason alone.

Webber had his picture taken with Mr. Nixon. The picture was on Webber's desk in his office. He was singularly proud of this moment in his life.

Webber moved in the best social circles in Charleston, where the family mansion was located, and Washington D.C. These were friends who did not care where his money came from. His money and power enabled him to preserve this position. He believed no force on earth to keep him from what he wanted. It was as if he was a feudal baron in the Middle Ages and the miners were his serfs. He reveled in this thought.

The politicians, like Senator Wallenby and his wife Evelyn, and his rich friends were like servants at his beck and call for whatever purpose suited him. He particularly enjoyed the young wives and daughters for sexual encounters and many were excited by the prospect of bedding such a notorious and rich man.

The mansion he lived in most of the year was 150 years old and was built in a red brick Federalist style. It had been occupied by his father, grandfather and great grandfather on his father's side of the family since 1853. His great grandfather supplied coal to the Union army, the history of which Webber was justifiably proud. His parents and grandparents were deceased and he had no brothers or sisters. He felt compelled to marry and produce a son to carry on the family business, but not right away.

Respite was his playground. He came as close to loving it as he could anything on earth besides himself. His father had built the home in the 1930s as a retreat. Mt. Hope was located behind the home, and one of his strip mines was on the back side of the mountain out of sight. He heard the dynamite blasting the mountaintop to reach the coal daily except on Sundays. To Webber, this sounded like the bell on a cash register. His father would have approved.

After Webber mined the coal off the tops of mountains, it was too expensive for him to restore the land. The depleted mines remained a deep scar on each mountaintop, a wasteland of coal dust and dirt blowing in the wind. The soil overburden and coal tailings from washing the coal before rail shipment were dumped into Deep River, which had a dark brown color. The mountain residents said the color was from tree tannins that dropped into the river, ignoring the truth. Webber laughed at this explanation whenever he heard it—as if the speakers were too stupid to know the truth, but he never corrected them. Wildlife, especially ducks, geese, and swans, died from drinking the river water, but Webber knew that only the birdwatchers cared and nobody paid any attention to them.

When miners died on the job, which they did every year, Webber provided a decent burial and one thousand dollars in cash to help the family. The children would die of starvation or sickness if they stayed in the hollows around Deep Lake, or the family could take the money and move away. He strongly encouraged the latter.

Webber knew there was always another miner to replace a dead one. Injured workers became beggars and were on their own to forage for food and a place to sleep. Webber had no mercy for them. As far as he was concerned, they were as expendable as the mining machinery, which had worn out from use. The only exception was his driver, Clem Block.

Many times women who met Webber were interested in him. Their body language left no doubt as to what they wanted. He particularly liked women with blond hair and creamy skin. The wives of the miners and the politicians were a particularly well-populated and fertile field for him. They were attracted by his good looks, money, power, and legendary prowess. He couldn't get enough of them in numbers and variety. He likened himself to the mythical satyrs.

At forty years old, he never had established a relationship with any woman for more than a few weeks. He was not inclined to marry and even the possibility seemed remote to him now. He'd have a child later. His father was fifty when he was born.

Webber was looking forward to seeing Ann Gooding again when she visited Deep Lake with her husband. Webber ordered Lester to house the Gooding's for several days at their cottage for his party.

From his last meeting with Ann in Washington, D.C., Webber was certain she would be willing to slip away with him from the party. He basked in anticipation of having sex with her again.

His former paramour, Evelyn Wallenby, had become too clingy. She talked about divorce from Senator Wallenby, one of his major supporters. Unfortunately, she would be at the party. He planned to ignore her.

Webber was aware during the ride in the limousine that Clem Block was becoming more unpleasant and gruff by the day. He had developed a curt tone of voice which Webber disliked. Soon he thought I'm going to dispose of Block and dump his body down the mine shaft.

Webber knew it wasn't wise to keep drivers too long. Plenty of my miners wanted the cushy job driving me, but he's got to be a murderer. I'll wait until I find the right person.

CHAPTER 22

GOLF

July 2, 1971

Before the party, on Wednesday, John and Frank Lester played golf on a nine-hole course, bulldozed into the mountain and maintained by Charlie Webber's employees. Mostly they lost balls in the rough mowed grass that passed as a fairway. The greens had grass long enough to consider chipping rather than putting.

Frank volunteered that a "nature boy" ran naked in the woods, a teenage imbecile, by the name of Billy. Later, while they golfed, a boy streaked across the fairway while they were on the seventh tee.

Frank said, "The boy's family is very poor and they let him roam wild, buck naked, in the summer. Apparently he has a skin disease of some sort. In the winter, he stays inside a rundown shack with his mother and father."

Lester speculated that "nature boy" was the product of incest between closely related family members, although he had never met the boy or his family. John thought, This might be an explanation even though this is Bible country.

Frank said, "Charlie told the boy to stay off his golf course or he would 'kick his bony ass from here to Sunday.'" He did beat up the boy when he caught him once. Charlie bragged about putting the fear in the imbecile. Lester said, "It would not be a good idea to mention seeing him to Charlie, since it will only cause trouble.

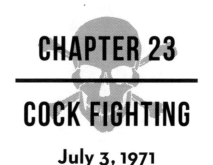

CHAPTER 23

COCK FIGHTING

July 3, 1971

The next day, John said he was interested in seeing how the hill people lived. Frank took John to see fighting roosters on a farm in the back mountain country. A friend of Frank's, Bob Harrington, the county prosecutor, said he wanted to come along to deliver a warning about illegal cock fighting.

The only knowledge John had about cock fighting was that the sport was popular in the nineteenth century, but had been outlawed, along with dog fighting, in West Virginia and throughout the country.

Harrington was dressed in blue jeans and a red-and- blue checked shirt so that he would look like one of the hill people. He ambled over to the car his belly bouncing and huffed for breath.

In the car as they drove, Harrington said, "I don't care if there is cock fighting in other counties, I just don't want it in my county. Jess Black needs another personal warning," he said with a smile.

When they arrived at a shack on a mountain top, John saw that Black had tethered the roosters on long ropes so each bird could move in a wide circle. Black was dressed in raggedy clothes, and his face showed too many drinking bouts, with a chaw of tobacco in one cheek. Occasionally he spat some out and then inserted some more.

THE PLACE SMELLED LIKE CHICKEN shit. The circles were separated to keep the roosters from killing each other, although they tried over and over again, struggling against the tethers, with wings carrying them into the air. Black said he was particularly fond of a very large rooster that had successfully fought many battles, although one eye had been pecked out in a fight. The bird turned his good eye towards John and crowed with its wings spread, which seemed to be menacing.

At Harrington's request, Black went inside his shack of a home and brought out shiny steel spurs, which he strapped to the birds feet like claws. They curved down from the back of the leg to above the foot.

"The object is for the bird to kill his opponent by flying up and spiking it with the spurs. I have a set of long spurs and a set of short spurs, depending upon how long the fight lasts. The short ones kill faster and are more commonly used. The spurs come in a purple felt-lined case with individual pockets. They are polished from use at least once a month. Returning the spurs to the case, he said, "They have been in my family for hundreds of years"

John could not understand how it was sporting to have two birds fight each other to the death of one of them. However, he learned that the loser's neck was wrung to be certain it was dead and then ended up in soup which was cooked for a long time to tenderize the meat of the tough birds. In the normal course of killing chickens, their heads would be chopped off so that they flew around headless until their blood drained out. Maybe this was a more valiant way to die. They were allowed to breed with hens to produce more of the birds.

To John and Lester, Harrington said, "Betting keeps the sport going. It has been around since before the founding of our country. Webber is a big fan of the sport, so I can't press too hard to stop it." John thought, He's probably killed people who get in his way, so why would he care about chickens or any other animal, for that matter?

Harrington warned Black about fighting the birds in his county. He'd been convicted previously of cockfighting and spent thirty days in jail on an occasion when Webber was not gambling on the fight. Webber always had an invitation to every match.

A woman named Rebecca, probably Jess's wife, poked her head out the door and said dinner was ready. So as not to offend, they ate chicken soup with home baked corn bread. John wondered about the fate of the bird in the soup, but decided not to ask. In fact the soup tasted very good and each of them told Bess so, which pleased Black, who asked John to come and see a cock fight sometime.

John politely responded, "I'm only here for a few days." This was not sport and had no intention of ever watching a fight. You have to admire the rooster's courage, forced to fight to the death, he thought.

CHAPTER 24

WEST VIRGINIA

July 3, 1971

Driving back to Deep Lake, John asked Harrington about the history of coal mining. Harrington said, "Well, it provides a lot of jobs for the Appalachian mountain men of West Virginia. They live in poverty, since the pay is low and the work is very dangerous, but it's better than nothing. These are some of the most backward, uneducated people in the country here, isolated by language, geography, and poverty, but they are proud people of Scottish descent and generally refuse help. They die of black-lung disease from the coal dust, cave-ins, or explosions. It's a very hard life.

"Charlie Webber and his forbearers have gotten super rich off these coal mines. He owns the mineral rights for coal mining for hundreds of miles around this region. Any side of the mountain he sees from his compound on Deep Lake is safe, at least for now. Eventually this whole region will be strip mined, as long as coal is in high demand."

"Don't you think it is a bad idea to destroy the mountaintops?" John asked.

"What choice do the miners or we have? The mountain people need to earn a living. Webber as good as owns us all," Harrington said, not getting a further question from John.

John wondered for the first time what it would be like if he lived and practiced in West Virginia. Webber would be a very rich target for big fees, winning for a plaintiff on a contingency. Certainly coal mining pollution must be a problem, he thought.

John observed the shacks as they drove down the mountain back to Deep Lake. Unpainted and gray, with rust covered metal roofs, they would have been condemned in another part of the country. Children played in dusty, dirt yards, worn by generations of poverty. They dressed in a patchwork of rag or were naked, since it was the middle of summer and hot. He could only imagine what it would be like for them in the cold West Virginia winters. They would burn coal stolen from Webber's mine or falling from his box cars. Most of the trees were cut down and burned long ago, since John could see only a few.

CHAPTER 25

THE CLIMB

July 4, 1971

John climbed Mt. Hope to see Webber's strip coal mine. Wiping the sweat off his forehead as he paused after the steep climb, he saw a large red-tailed hawk circling above him rising on the thermals in the morning sun. Suddenly the hawk folded its wings and rocketed down towards the ground. At the last moment it extended its wings to level off as his talons grasped a light brown rabbit, screeching to immobilize his prey with fear.

With the rabbit struggling and bleating and shrieking, the hawk climbed back into the sky and then dropped to the ground, blood staining the rabbit's fur, and started tearing the flesh into strips with its talons, as john watched. The rabbit bled out on the rocks. John's heart muscles tightened, sensing the ferocity of the attack. Then he turned his head away from the hawk and resumed his climb up the mountain. The hawk must feel anger for the loss of his hunting ground because of Webber's strip mining, he thought.

John pulled up the collar of his blue denim jacket feeling coolness in the air as he climbed the rocky slopes. Bees were swarming around him. He felt for the epi pen in his pocket to use if he was stung.

Sighing, he thought, These are incredibly backwards people. It seemed to be right out of Taylor Caldwell's book, *God's Little Acre,* with a father telling his daughter dressed in rags that he wanted to get down on his knees and lick her like a hound dog.

The sun rose yellow and soft in the east, against a purple and white dawn sky above the peaks of the distant mountain ranges. This omen promised fine weather the rest of the weekend. He was thinking unhappily about having to go to the party at Charlie Webber's house that night.

John had seen before and after pictures of the tops of mountains which had been strip mined, leaving nothing but a gutted pit of blowing coal dust. In the Charleston Gazette John red that Webber said that he invented this method of mining coal, and it was rapidly replacing downshaft mining all over coal country. Webber stated that he owned the land and he could do anything he wanted with it.

John climbed easily upwards using an experienced mountain climber's hesitation step, with his uphill leg straightening to rest his muscles with each stride. Flat stones ground down by the glaciers and large boulders littered the path in front of him. Grasses and wildflowers grew where dirt had accumulated in the nooks and crannies.

He had a spiritual feeling and reverence for Mt. Hope.

It had been named with the thought that the spirits of the dead former inhabitants could look at the face of God as they rested in their high graves, in hopes of salvation.

A hard, gritty taste of coal dust drifted into his mouth from above him, driven by the wind. He knew he was nearing the top of the mountain.

John thought about Ann. They were married in Grosse Pointe, Michigan, after a few months' courtship with a full scale, eight-bridesmaids wedding in the Episcopal Church. The reception was at the Yacht Club on the Detroit River, with over two hundred guests. They had come a long way since.

A light breeze washed against his face, which evaporated the sweat and pushed away the ugly thoughts. The further up he climbed, a sense of calm and focus evolved, like from jogging at home, as he watched his breath come in and out of his lungs. Steadily he climbed towards the peak over the rocks for an hour without meeting another hiker.

When he paused to rest before his final assent to the peak, he saw Deep Lake a crescent between surrounding mountains below fluffy clouds. White capped waves, whipped by a west wind, flashed in the sunlight. The lake reflected a deep blue, conveying a sense of purity, which John knew was an illusion. Coal strip mining on Mt. Hope sent tailings from washing the coal into Deep River until they settled in Deep Lake.

Without proof, John believed the coal tailings caused illnesses from mercury in the coal. He thought, Most of the evidence regarding the safety of coal mining is from the coal companies and unscrupulous men like Webber who would never let any hint of poisoning leak to the public.

Beside Deep Lake, John saw clearing for Webber's house, an ugly gash in the landscape on the lake. A helicopter pad was located beside the lake and now stood empty. A three-story house, with shiny white siding stood out against a manicured lawn. Conifer trees lined the lake shore except for Webber's patch of land.

John was not looking forward to Webber's party which promised to be a late-night drinking bout with people he did not know. Those he met he didn't like. This was corn mash whiskey country, sometimes up to 150 proof, which John had to dilute to prevent burning of his throat. He was of the opinion that men, and many women, drank this water clear whiskey every day of their lives to the point of drunkenness, and tonight would be an example. John thought, Maybe the harsh whisky washes away the coal dust in the throats of the miners and the pain of coal mining as the whiskey burns its way down their throats and is absorbed into their blood.

Abruptly, John's thoughts were interrupted by the sound of a string of explosives detonating in the mine ahead of him. The sounds echoed off the mountain and made John's eardrums sore.

He reached the top of Mt Hope a few minutes later. Towards the east was a deep valley, as far as he could see, with roads snaking around mounds of coal tailings. Giant dump trucks were waiting to be filled with coal by gigantic power shovels that scooped up a truckload of coal at a time. The shovels were like long-necked dinosaurs relentlessly devouring the earth. The wind whipped up the coal dust to create a haze over the scene. The mine had come as near to the mountaintop as possible. There was an untouched wall of coal facing the valley below and Deep Lake. It was as close as Webber could get to the top of Mt. Hope without destroying his view from Respite.

John involuntarily uttered "shit" as his mind absorbed the scene in the mine pit. There was no strip mine on the very old trail map he got from Lester. The old cemetery a little bit down the mountain was gone. This was where the remains of Scottish immigrants who settled this region in the late 1700s and early 1800s were buried. They mined the coal, some by hand with a shovel, and carts to take the coal to the bottom valley.

In front of him there was a sign which read:

PROPERTY OF WEBBER COAL MINING

TRESPASSERS WILL BE PROSECUTED

DANGER! HIGH EXPLOSIVES

CHAPTER 26

THE MINE

June 30, 1971

On top of Mt. Hope, John found a dusty path into the mine pit. He thought, Probably the top part was beaten down by generations of hill people and Indians. Further down in the pit where the coal was exposed, John saw four men standing at the deepest part, which was hundreds of feet below the peak of Mt. Hope. Webber was there, pointing to various parts of the mine.

John decided to go down a truck road path into the pit in order to speak to Webber. After about a half hour, he came upon a miner covered with coal dust who asked John what he was doing there.

"I'm going down to talk to Charlie Webber. He knows me. What's the best way of going down without getting blown up?"

The miner pointed to a road that switch-backed down into the pit and said, "Follow the road. Is Mr. Webber expecting you? If you were not invited, you need to go back. He doesn't take kindly to trespassers, and usually he has them arrested and thrown into jail for a week."

John said, "Thanks for the advice. I'll take my chances." He descended to the group of men.

Webber turned and glared at John as he walked up to him. He did not introduce John to the group. "You're not supposed to be here. I can have one of my men drive you back to Frank's cottage."

From newspaper articles in the *Washington Post*, John recognized

Senator Wallenby. He had been invited to the conference in D.C. but did not attend.

"Thanks, Charlie, but I'll walk back. You want to introduce me to your friends?"

Webber hesitated a moment and said, "These are U.S. Senator Wallenby, and State Representatives Lundener and Samson. They wanted to see a strip mine. They are going to be at my party this evening."

John shook hands with each of them and said, "Nice to meet them. I will have an opportunity to talk to them."

John turned to leave and then turned back to Webber and said, "What are you going to do to fill up this hole in Mt. Hope when you're finished mining the coal?"

Webber's eyes narrowed to slits and said, "It's too expensive to fill it in. We will just let it return to its wild state. Eventually, we will not strip mine the side you hiked up."

Without another word, John turned and started up the mountain without looking back. If he had, he imagined he would have seen a very angry Webber. John was certain Webber was going to humiliate him tonight with Ann.

The sun warmed the black coal and the coal dust in the air and he was sweating through every pore when he reached the top of Mt. Hope. His lungs felt like they were coated with coal dust. A helicopter circling to land in the middle of the pit stirred up the coal dust even more.

Facing Deep Lake, he felt better because of the pleasant view and descended the mountain. As he descended, he twirled his wedding ring on his finger a few times. It was loose and he made a mental note to have it fixed. He thought about how the ring represented a happier time when he was first married to Ann. She didn't care about the issue of pollution or anything else John did. Instead Ann was primarily interested in money, something Webber could supply in abundance.

CHAPTER 27

COTTAGE

July 4, 1971

When John arrived at the cottage late in the day, he found Ann in the bedroom, dressed in a white skirt and matching blouse. She sat on the bed waiting for him to get dressed.

Ann, sounding irritated said, "Finally you made it back. You need to get ready right away. You stink of sweat and are covered with coal dust. I laid out your clothes on the bed. You don't have much time."

Ann was used to having her way in all social matters and about how he dressed. He thought, Usually she is right about what I should wear.

"Well, we don't have to be right on time." Lots of people will be at the party there. I guess the whole of the United States Congress is invited." John said. He remembered that Webber said that members of congress would be at the party.

Ann gave him a very cross look. "Charlie wants us to come early."

"So when is *Charlie* expecting us?" he asked sarcastically.

"In about an hour. Now get ready," she replied, unruffled.

Ann flounced out of the room leaving him to get ready alone before he could tell her to go to hell.

When he entered the living room, properly dressed, Ann was chirping to the Lesters about how great it would be to meet the important West Virginia and Washington politicians who were going to be at the party. John did not care for politicians, whom he thought were generally bloated with their own self importance.

John understood that it was patronage, in the form of campaign contributions from Webber, that attracted the politicians, like flies to sugar water in a jar. He thought, This party will be my first chance to see this interaction." John had a sense of foreboding.

He said nothing to Ann or the Lesters about his feelings concerning the strip mining on Mt. Hope or his conversation with Webber in the mine. He thought, This trip to Deep Lake is really giving me a very uncomfortable feeling about what might happen.

CHAPTER 28

THE PARTY

Saturday, July 4, 1971

John felt like he was dressed to watch a regatta at a sailing club with white pants, a white shirt, and tennis shoes. He thought, At least Ann approves of how I am dressed.

Also, the thought of the wealthy and powerful was making him increasingly uncomfortable. He wished they had never accepted the invitation to visit Deep Lake, but Ann insisted to the point that she threatened to come alone.

Ann and John walked with Frank and Joanne down a dirt access road in the fading sunlight to Webber's compound. A police guard admitted them after saying "Good evening Mr. and Mrs. Lester." John could tell by the smile on Ann's face that she could hardly wait to get where Webber was greeting guests.

Webber's summer home was enormous, at least eight thousand square feet on the three floors, with red roof tiles white wood siding, pretending to be rustic, but clearly grandiose in an ostentatious way. It seemed to John that almost every light in the house was lit. Outside floodlights illuminated the grounds, so that it was almost like mid day.

A long and wide pontoon boat was docked on a pier that extended into the lake. Tulip-shaped lamp shades mounted on poles with a green brass patina were standing every ten feet on the pier. The helicopter was on its pad, surrounded by lights on the well-manicured lawn pointed at the fuselage. Painted royal blue, the helicopter conveyed Webber's great wealth. The setting sun illuminated the aluminum hull of the boat and the helicopter, highlighting the scene.

John saw Webber standing on the long porch in front of the house facing the lake. A young woman stood beside him, whispering into his ear as the guests arrived, certainly feeding the names of each of the guests to him. Frank pointed out and named several state representatives and congressmen who were responsible for coal policy in West Virginia while they waited in line.

Ann was excited. She said, "This is going to be a once-in-a-lifetime evening."

Webber shook hands with John without emotion. Then he turned and smiled broadly at Ann. "Hi Ann It's very good to see you again." He gave her a hug and held her hand.

She beamed at him in a way that made John certain that Ann was falling for Charlie, who commented on how beautiful she looked. The nipples on her breasts were erect. Charlie's eyes slowly and obviously drifted down to look at them.

Webber turned to John. "I see that you made it back safely from the mine. I delayed explosions until you were down the mountain," he said, implying that John had interfered with his operations.

John said, "That was the first time I've seen a strip mine. I understand that before you started mining, you removed some cabins and a small cemetery on the mountain."

Webber said, "Those rickety houses were torn down, and I had the coffins in the cemetery moved to the valley below for reburial. We even provided new coffins, since some the graves were over one hundred years old. The old wooden coffins disintegrated."

Ann looked at John, pursed here lips in disapproval, and said, "Let's enjoy Charlie's party and not talk about business. I'm going to have a good time."

Webber smiled at her and said he would talk to her some more in a little while and let her hand slide from his, as if it was a caress. He turned to greet more of his guests standing in line, dismissing John without further comment.

John observed Webber carefully and thought his face in profile looked a lot like that of a ferret with shiny black hair, smoothed back. He wore white pants and shirt like Johns. Webber's eyes seemed to glitter in the fading sunlight. John sensed that no person could stand in the way of what Webber wanted without suffering pain and possibly even death. He realized Ann would never leave the party early with him if he went back to the Lesters cottage.

At dinner, it was apparent that Webber had employed a very tough looking bodyguard. The bodyguard periodically whispered in Webber's ear and he nodded once, 'yes' or shook his head. He was a big man, taller than Webber or John, with well-developed muscles, dressed in blue jeans and a white T-shirt He did not smile or converse with the guests.

Webber explained to his guests that Clem Block was his personal bodyguard. He said that the necessity of moving the families from their homes in the mountains and their kin from their graves produced a lot of anger. John could only imagine the fate of those to whom the shaking of the head was directed and he did not want to be one of them.

Webber said, "Many of the families had lived in the mountains for over one hundred years and didn't want to leave."

John asked, "And what happened if they didn't leave?"

Charlie snapped his head around and stared into John's eyes and said, "I'd step on their necks with my mining boots. Of course, they most wanted the one thousand dollars I paid them to move since they are dirt poor. There was rarely an argument."

During the rest of the dinner, John talked to a number of politicians and lobbyists for the coal mining interests at his end of the table, which was opposite of Ann who was sitting next to Webber. She ignored John. Ann did not look towards him once during dinner. She was clearly focused on every word Webber said.

All of the politicians at the table were in favor of strip mining as a way to reduce foreign oil dependence. Not one of them suggested that coal mining was polluting rivers and lakes or harming people in West Virginia. John didn't argue the matter since he likely would have been escorted out of the house by Clem Block. Ann would not leave.

THE DINNER WAS PERFECT, FILET mignon and apple pie with ice cream, with French wines and cigars afterwards. Young women dressed in black pants and white blouses uniforms served the food. They looked worn out like they were from the vallies around Deep Lake.

Webber excused himself after everyone was finished with dinner and climbed the staircase to the second floor. Probably to his office, John thought. One by one the politicians followed. Afterwards they came down the staircase, smiling with a bit of a jaunt to their steps. At this point it was clear to John that almost all of the politicians received payoffs.

Three hours later, Joanne staggered drunkenly up to John. Frank said, "I want to stay at the party. I would like you to escort Joanne home." John was reluctant, but he did want to leave the party. He agreed after trying to find Ann. Nobody volunteered any information.

As Joann and John moved through the woods to her cottage, she leaned on him, slurring her words and kissing him on the cheek. In the distance, he heard Webber's helicopter taking off. The sound of the beating rotors echoed off the still surface of the lake. He wondered about the helicopter leaving at night.

Back at the Lester's house, John took Joanne up to her bedroom and helped her to bed with her clothes on. After removing her shoes, he covered her as she looked up at him smiling with her lips parted, her arms beckoning him.

John hugged her and then said, "I'm very tired from hiking and need to go to my own bed." He thought, I have no interest in sex with a woman who is too drunk to consent.

John went to his room and collapsed on the bed. He was upset by the encounters with Webber in the mine and at the party. He was sure that Ann was with Webber. He tossed and turned for hours, finally deciding to divorce Ann. He could not stand the images of Webber making love to Ann.

CHAPTER 29

MORNING AFTER

July 5, 1971

In the morning, John awoke with Ann sleeping beside him, smelling of liquor and musk, like after they had sex. Her cheeks were unnaturally red, as if from whisker burn.

She woke up long enough only to tell John that she had come in late and needed more sleep. Reminding him of the pontoon boat trip on the lake scheduled for that afternoon, she rolled over to go back to sleep, her back to him. John had no chance to ask her when she came home.

Around eleven in the morning, Ann came downstairs dressed for the day in a string bikini and a white linen jacket. Her hair was damp from showering, and the redness on her face was now camouflaged with makeup.

They ate brunch with Frank and Joanne. No one mentioned the party. For now, John kept his mouth shut.

———

ABOUT TWENTY PEOPLE BOARDED THE pontoon boat that afternoon, and Webber began a slow tour around the shores of Deep Lake. Clem Block came along, presumably to protect Webber.

As soon as they left the dock, Webber played twangy mountain music on the sound system which annoyed John, who put his hands over his ears. The large speakers facing out from the boat on each the four corners made certain everyone on the lake heard the music too.

"Nobody around the lake complains about the sound," Webber said with a slight smile. The locals like it.

John asked Webber to turn the music down, which he did with his fingers remaining on the volume control knob. Everybody on board was quiet, listening.

With a pleased look on his face, Webber said, "You know, Gooding! I took Ann on a helicopter ride last night all around the lake. We landed on the top of Mt. Hope by a cabin I keep there. We enjoyed the view. We had a wonderful time." He smiled at John.

John looked at Ann with a flash of anger. She was afraid to fly, deciding to drive here rather than fly, but apparently not enough to turn down the ride. Webber displayed a big shit-eating grin and turned up the music again full blast.

John walked over to the edge of the deck. Clem Block walked over near John.

John threw his wedding ring into the water. The people on the boat said, "Oh!" In a quiet voice only to John, Clem Block said. "Good throw, Mr. Gooding. Revenge is best served cold."

John said, "Good advice"

A strong swimmer, John took off his shirt and shoes, preparing to jump off the side of the boat and swam towards the pier. Before he jumped into the water, he saw that Ann was still smiling, apparently enjoying her conversation with Webber.

John did not talk to Ann at all when she came home or when they went to bed. The following morning John and Ann left Deep Lake for home.

In addition to disposing of his wedding ring, John knew he was finally going to divorce Ann. It was going to be very messy and involve Webber as the reason for the divorce. Fault was still a big deal in dividing up the assets of the marriage in Michigan. As far as he was concerned he didn't want to pay her anything. John wanted revenge against Webber as well.

John thought, West Virginia is a great place for a profitable legal practice dealing with coal pollution and injuries caused by mine owners. He thought, I hate Webber and his strip mining.

CHAPTER 30

ANN'S STORY

July 6, 1971

Driving home to Lansing, Ann was thinking about a story to tell John about her tryst with Charlie Webber. Just the thought of him made her go moist, as she felt the warm seat of the car, aching for him to be inside her again. Her knees spread to allow the blast of the air conditioning to cool her off.

She thought back to the party. Charlie had walked up to her after he came downstairs from meeting the politicians and kissed her on the lips as if they were old friends. She returned the kiss and smiled. In a very good mood after meeting with the politicians, Charlie grabbed her hand and led her out to the garden in front of his house.

"I want to make love to you again. The first time was not enough," he said guiding her with his arm so that they were facing each other.

"I want to kiss you all over your body."

Ann eagerly put her arms around his neck with her body pressed against him and kissed him.

Charlie smiled and asked her if she wanted a ride in the helicopter, saying that he had a pilot's license and would make certain she was safe. Ann hesitated and then said she would go on the ride, even though she was afraid of flying.

"Charlie, I assume you have taken women for rides before."

"Just for sex. This is different. I feel like I might be in love for the first time in my life."

After taking off and flying for a few minutes, the helicopter landed on a pad beside a small log cabin overlooking the strip mine. She saw that all of the equipment was at rest and there were no miners.

In the cabin, Charlie pulled her down on a large bed and took off her panties. His beard alternately rubbed against her face and then her breasts and clit. As his tongue searched for the opening between her legs, Ann took his hardness in her mouth, tasting his readiness. He moved on top of her, thrusting hard against her body.

After Ann came the first time and they were resting in each other's arms, Charlie said, "I want you to be with you again and again."

Ann said, "I feel the same. I feel like I could love you."

Charlie said, "I'll arrange for you to come to Steadfast, my home in Charleston. You'll like it."

Ann agreed right away. She was excited, but she did not know whether she would hear from him again.

————

RETURNING TO THE PRESENT IN the car, Ann knew there was one important problem. She had forgotten to take her birth-control pills on the trip and had been without them for five days when she made love to Charlie. Anxious now she thought, I hope am pregnant with Charlie's child. I'll have an abortion if Charlie doesn't work out.

Concocting the story to tell John, Ann thought, I believe John is afraid of Charlie. Maybe I can work with the fear, telling him that Charlie forced her to have sex with him or Block would beat up him. Given what Charlie said about stepping on the neck of people who get in his way, this story could work.

John was pretty gullible when it came to her sexual activities, and probably he would believe her. If he only knew how many men she had screwed during their marriage, he would have been shocked. They were good looking and powerful, they just had to ask nicely, as they did more often than not. She would be very contrite in asking for forgiveness for going with Charlie.

————

HOME FOR THEM WAS A modest two-story colonial with four bedrooms. Ann was sick of taking care of their home. It would never be like Respite. Her life with John was, a middle class home lodged in a middle class neighborhood in a middle class marriage. She hated her life in Lansing with John.

Ann, in a pleading voice said, "John, I hope you are not mad at me about the party."

"You humiliated me in front of Webber and his friends on the pontoon," he said, clenching his fists on the steering wheel.

His reaction was worse than Ann imagined. There was anxiety because her marriage was ending and she didn't know whether she would hear from Charlie again. John was driving so she couldn't use her body as a negotiating tool as usual.

The idea came to her that this was like writing a play, and she needed to come up with a plot that would work. This would be the first draft, which she would refine over time to fill in the details, making it more plausible.

"Charlie threatened to have Clem Block beat you up if I didn't have sex with him. I asked Joanne to take you back to their cottage so you would be safe. Your pride would have forced you to defend me, which could have gotten you killed. Charlie mentioned a coal truck could run over you or a load of coal might bury you or you might drown accidently in the lake from drinking too much Scotch." The thought sounded very funny to her, since she would be rid of John and own everything, but she managed not to crack a smile.

Ann was warming up to her story. John's hands had slowly unclenched, and she felt some of his anger slide away. She saw that maybe he was buying his story.

Ann continued, "Charlie asked me if I wanted to go for a helicopter ride in a way that I couldn't refuse. You know how frightened I am of flying. I was frightened the whole time. When we landed, he tried to have sex with me, but he couldn't get an erection. He slapped me twice on the face making my cheeks red. Afterwards he warned me not to tell anyone about what happened, threatening to kill me."

John said, "Your story is just that. I don't believe you. I'm leaving you and getting a divorce."

Smiling, Ann said, "I will agree to the divorce providing we can work out a large settlement."

————

AT HOME JOHN SLEPT ON the couch.

As Ann lay down in bed, she thought, Charlie is a man and not a wimp like John. He said," I like killing and skinning coyotes, bobcats, black bear and gray fox. I am an excellent marksman and have killed animals at five hundred yards using a varmint rifle with a telescopic sight." His cabin had the trophy heads in the walls.

Ann said, "I love the fact that you are a hunter."

She remembered that john used guns in Vietnam. It had been a sunny afternoon last year when they went to the Handgun Emporium outdoor shooting range in Lansing. Along the firing line people were shooting at human outline targets 30 yards away. John was wearing a cowboy holster nesting a 45 caliber, single action Peacemaker Colt revolver, the holster strapped to his leg. John placed six bullets into the center of the human outline target, fanning the hammer cowboy style with his left hand.

Ann thought, Shooting at targets is a stupid sport, because, there isn't the challenge of stalking and killing a game animal.

Ann fell into a deep and calm sleep.

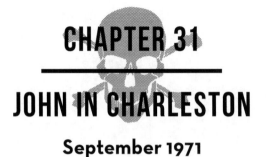

CHAPTER 31

JOHN IN CHARLESTON

September 1971

After the trip home from Deep Lake, John searched the advertisements in his law journals and in *Martindale and Hubble,* a lawyer directory, for a law firm in West Virginia that litigated plaintiffs' cases against coal mining companies. He found Mayfield and Masters in Charleston where Webber had his home. The head of the firm was Jason Mayfield, a graduate of Harvard law school about thirty years ago, and a highly regarded general litigation specialist. Jake Masters graduated from Yale Law School and was a litigator as well, specializing in coal mining litigation. Jake represented the West Virginia Coal Workers Union.

John telephoned Jake Masters and asked if they might discuss his joining their firm.

After some preliminary discussion, Jake said, "Send me your resumé so I can review it with Jason."

"I'm interested in handling pollution cases, particularly litigation against the coal mine operators for injuring people," John said.

"That type of litigation, especially class actions by a group of plaintiffs, is of interest to us. We do not represent any coal mining companies and we never will, so there can be no conflicts of interest." Jake said.

John told Jake about some of his contingent fee cases. Jake

said he would talk to Jason to arrange a meeting in Charleston. He called the next day and invited John to visit the firm the following week and asked him to bring his resumé.

John did not tell Ann that he was interviewing at a firm in Charleston. He told her he had to go out of town for a few days on business and that he had hired a divorce layer.

Ann said, I'm going to meet my divorce lawyer while you are gone."

John said, "That was a very good idea."

John arranged to visit Charleston on a flight leaving from Detroit. It was only an hour's ride in a small twin turboprop airplane. He drove to Metro Airport in Detroit and parked in airport parking. A van took him to the McNamara terminal where he boarded his flight. The flight bumped along and landed at the small regional terminal in Charleston, carved out of the top of a mountain, as if a giant knife sliced off the peak.

It was a short cab ride to the Hotel Charleston in the center of the city. After checking in and settling into his room, he decided to tour the city where he would likely be spending the next several years of his life.

Charleston looked rundown to John as he had ridden in a taxi from the airport. The buildings were blackened with coal dust blown by the wind from the mines. Coal barges motored down the Kanawha River to docks for unloading the coal into rail cars. Black soot from the power plant streamed out of a tall smokestack. A river water whirl pooled in black circles and there were no wild ducks or geese on the water. He thought, If there are fish in the water, they are loaded with poisonous metals, such as mercury, from soot in the air from the coal fired power plant and the coal tailings from mining the coal upriver.

The Charleston Gazette, which he picked up at a grubby newsstand on a walk around Charleston, applauded the coal companies for keeping the power plant operating economically. It was evident to John that coal was "King" in West Virginia even though he thought, Coal mining is poisoning the environment and the people here on a massive scale.

Hearing voices singing as he walked down the street, John tracked the sound to a large Methodist church. He entered and sat in a pew. A black men's choir was practicing *Amazing Grace*. The music echoed off the stones of the vaulted ceiling. It had been years since he had been in any church. He felt at peace and thought, Charleston is revitalizing me.

The next morning he arrived at the offices of Mayfield and Masters on the top floor of the First National Bank, the tallest commercial building in the city. Jake Masters greeted John in the office lobby after his receptionist had announced him. They met in a large conference room with windows overlooking the city. John saw the West Virginia State Capitol, which was the highest government building in the city. The golden dome shone dully in the sunlight. It looked a lot like the National Capitol in Washington, D.C.

Jason Mayfield and Jake Masters came and greeted John. Jason was tall with a gray beard and looked to be in his late fifties. Smiling, he shook hands with John with a crushing grip. Jake was muscular and lean, in his late thirties, John guessed, and also gripped John's hand firmly. After they were seated and discussed the hot weather, they talked informally about John joining their firm. They reviewed his résumé, which included his degrees in chemistry and chemical engineering. He told them details about his current cases.

Jason said, "Why would you move from Michigan?"

John said, "I went to a party at Charlie Webber's home on Deep Lake this summer and saw the desolation of Mt. Hope as a result of strip mining by his company. I decided that I could do something important with my life in West Virginia.

Jake's body stiffened and his face and eyes hardened with his lips pinched together as he said, "Charlie Webber is a very powerful and dangerous man. People disappear when they cross him. How did you happen to be at the party?"

In order to be truthful, John explained how Ann, his wife, and he had been invited and explained what had happened at the party that finally resulted in his deciding to divorce Ann and relocate to work in West Virginia. He didn't go into any great detail about Ann's affair with Charlie Webber. They both said that Webber had lots of affairs with married women.

"Are you trying to get even for what Webber did with your wife?" Jason said.

"My marriage to Ann ended before the trip to Deep Lake. This move transpired because I could not stand by and watch the likes of Webber destroy the peaks of such beautiful mountains. I believe that coal mining is killing people with the mercury from the coal. If somebody doesn't stop the strip mining, there will be nothing left of the mountains but pits which erode every time it rains, poisoning the rivers and lakes with coal tailings. I want to live here and start a new life. I want to be at the forefront of the movement to stop what is happening in this beautiful state."

Jason said, "We admire your fervor."

John was sure they had reservations about his ability to win these cases, producing large contingent fees for the firm.

John continued, "In the meantime, I can handle cases involving black lung disease caused by coal or any other litigation you ask me to work on."

Jake said they had two associates who had been with them for three to five years. He said that one of the associates, Ward Temple, was involved in current litigation with Jake against West Virginia Power for the loss of fish, ducks, and geese from coal pollution of the Elk and Kanawha Rivers downstream from the plant. Jake said, "It's not going very well. Nobody can touch West Virginia Power for the coal ash and smoke it spews from burning coal, which results in acid rain."

Jason said,"Only Federal legislation can stop the pollution."

Jake said the other associate, Jane Seymore, worked for Jason. Jake said that she could work for Jason and for John at first.

They agreed that John would join the firm as a partner. He would pay for his interest in the firm as a partner. A percentage of the revenue he brought into the firm would be paid to Jake and Jason, which seemed more than fair to John.

John liked these two men. He said, "Together, maybe we can make a difference for the people of West Virginia against the likes of Charlie Webber."

John said, I will apply for admission to the West Virginia

Bar on reciprocity from the Michigan Bar and be here by the beginning of 1972, if not sooner."

Before he returned to Michigan, John had dinner at the hotel with his new partners including the associates. He found that Ward was a very bright lawyer, but he was especially struck by the intellect and personality of Jane. She was twenty-eight years old, single and a graduate of Harvard Law.

Jane's red hair and green eyes lingered pleasantly in his thoughts as he flew back home. He was going to have to deal with divorcing Ann which would be a bitter fight over the division of their property and alimony. It was nice to be able to think about a beautiful woman who would be close by him as he worked.

CHAPTER 32

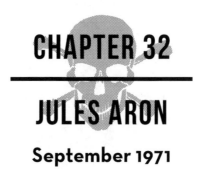

JULES ARON

September 1971

In Lansing, John met with his friend and fellow attorney Jules Aron to discuss his divorce from Ann. He knew and respected Aron as a divorce lawyer, who labored in a field where lawyers used every dirty trick they could to advance the interests of their client and their own fees. Honest lawyer is a joke when it comes to divorce, he thought as he sat in front of Aron's desk.

Aron was about six feet tall and thin with a scholarly look. John imagined him teaching a class in Domestic Relations Law, rather than practicing law.

Aron said, "You can expect to transfer fifty percent of your assets to Ann, including some present value of your law practice. Since the profits are taken out of the practice every year for tax reasons and clients are not assets, the value of the practice will be low. The value of your home would go to Ann as part of her share.

Aron said, "An appraisal of your home by a professional is required. You can expect to pay alimony for about five years, so Ann can train for a job and you will make the mortgage payments on the home."

Lastly Aron said, "Michigan is a no-fault state, meaning that the divorce is certain, but fault is important to the percentage of your joint estate Ann might get."

As Aron had requested when he made the appointment, John

handed him a list of all of his assets. He agreed in principle to a settlement on this basis, which Aron outlined, and agreed to Aron's billing rate.

John said, "I just want to end the marriage as soon as possible. Any reasonable settlement is fine with me."

"I'll talk to Ann's lawyer and see how close we are to settlement. Ann will get less if you could show fault. I have heard rumors about her relationship with another lawyer in Lansing over the past year or so."

John said, "I have a suspicion she was unfaithful."

"Recently, Ann had sex with Charlie Webber, a wealthy coal mine owner in Deep Lake, West Virginia, when we were there two months ago. I don't want to use it in the divorce, unless it is necessary."

"If we did need to use it, we would have to depose Charlie Webber in West Virginia," Aron said.

John said, "He has a home in Charleston. The deposition could be taken at my new law firm there."

Jules said, "I will prepare a settlement proposal and, after you have reviewed it, send it to her lawyer, who I understand from the rumors is Jack Staple. He is a pit viper of a divorce lawyer. You need to stay away from a new relationship with another woman for now."

John said, "There is no problem with that."

John left Aron's office feeling better than he had in years, quickness in his step, as if he was moving rapidly in a whole new direction in his life. He would finally be rid of Ann.

The next day he met with Shamus and resigned from the firm. John explained everything that happened in West Virginia. Shamus said "I understand vengeance, but you are in a fight which will likely cost you your life. You would be better off here and forgetting about Charlie Webber and Ann. You know that the Lord said,"Vengeance is mine."

John said, "I know your advice is right, but I can't stop what is going to happen. I have no idea."

They shook hands and John left the office for the last time. He felt a tinge of regret and fear of the future. Quickly he put this aside.

CHAPTER 33

ANN'S DIVORCE LAWYER

September 1971

Jack Staple met with Ann in his office to discuss the divorce. Her face was flushed as she described how she wanted to get as much as she could get from John. Staple had seen her temper before, when he cut off a sexual relationship with her last year because he had taken a lover who was single. He decided the relationship with Ann was too difficult in a town where lawyers gossiped about other lawyers they had seen with a married woman.

He wanted her now though, since she was so sexy and beautiful and going to be divorced soon anyway. This divorce will make a lot of money for me, he thought.

"Ann, here is the settlement proposal. I think we can squeeze a lot more out of John, since he is anxious to have the divorce finalized."

Ann looked at the papers and kept shaking her head, her lips curled in disgust. Jack saw this as a good sign.

"I'm going to make that son-of-bitch pay, this is nowhere near enough. I want lifetime alimony and certainly more than fifty percent of the assets."

Staple smiled, "No way that John will accept that. If you insist, there will have to be a trial."

"I don't care. John will have to pay your fees one way or another."

Staple figuratively licked his lips and thought, There is no way for me to lose at my billing rate of three hundred dollars per hour.

Staple was determined to make John's life miserable until he extracted the most money he could. He wrote Aron a letter and said the offer was unacceptable and that Ann wanted far more than the offer, including lifetime alimony amounting to about seventy percent of John's income. He filed a Complaint for divorce, thereby beginning the battle.

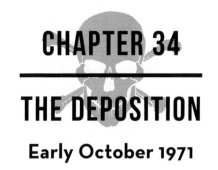

CHAPTER 34

THE DEPOSITION

Early October 1971

No settlement was possible. Jules arranged to take the deposition of Charlie Webber at the offices of John's new law firm in Charleston. John asked his new partners to attend along with him and they reluctantly agreed. They arranged for a court reporter.

Jack Staple was present. Charlie was there with his lawyer, Rex Reed, an old lawyer who quickly tried to establish he was the toughest lawyer and best trial lawyer in the room. He stated that Webber's deposition was merely harassment.

Reed looked a lot like a bulldog with hanging jowls and pinched lips, thin nostrils flaring. He said for the record that the deposition was irrelevant to the divorce proceedings.

After Webber was sworn to tell the truth, Aron asked the usual slow-pitch questions about his background and his business. He then launched into his relationship with Ann.

"Do you recall having met John and Ann Gooding?"

"Yes, so what?"

"I ask the questions, and you get to answer them."

"Do you know that they are involved in a divorce proceeding?"

"So I heard. I understand this happened after I met them at my home on Deep Lake."

Reed whispered in Webber's ear with his hand over his mouth.

"I hope your lawyer is not answering the questions for you, Aron said. When were the Gooding's there?"

"Last summer."

"Can you tell us how you came to know them?"

"They were friends of the Lesters' who have a cottage next door."

"Where did you meet them?"

"In Washington D.C. at a dinner meeting in the spring and at a party at my home in July."

"Who attended the party?"

"Objection, this is the irrelevant to the divorce proceedings and I instruct my client to refuse to answer," Reed said.

"That is none of your business," Webber said.

Jules said for the record, "The observations of the other guests as to the goings-on at that party between Ann Gooding and your client are highly relevant to this divorce proceeding and I intend to depose every one of them to find out. My understanding is that there were a large number of politicians who met and talked to Ann and John Gooding. They also saw Ann and you alone outside your home on Deep Lake and fly away together in your helicopter."

"Like hell you are going to get away with deposing my friends," Webber shouted raising his fists, his face red and his eyes closing to slits.

John's law partners were visibly upset.

"Let the record show that Mr. Webber yelled and raised his fists at me."

Aron continued, "Mr. Webber, I am informed that you took Ann Gooding for the helicopter ride to a cabin on Mt. Hope the evening of the party, is this correct?"

"Yes."

"What happened there? Aron said.

"We fooled around a little." Webber is smiling now, as if he was having fun.

"Mr. Webber, if I told you that Ann Gooding told her husband that you forced her to have sex, but it wasn't significant because you had a very small penis, how would you respond?"

Before his lawyer could object, Webber stood up and dropped his pants to show his penis, hanging about six inches down even though it was flaccid. Webber would have been thrown in jail if he had done that in court.

"Let the record show that Mr. Webber has a long, non erect penis," Aron said.

"Now, Mr. Webber, do you have any problems getting an erection?"

"Listen, you son of a bitch, it grows to ten inches. I screwed her twice and she came both times, moaning for more. She sucked my cock in between to make me hard again. She was a great lay, and I am going to arrange to see her again. She is well rid of that husband of hers who is a pussy, in my opinion. He better hope that I never see him again in private. I will kick his ass for doing this to us."

John Hated Ann and Webber. He thought, Somehow I am going to get even.

Aron said, "I believe we have heard enough. Mr. Staple, do you have any further questions? I expect we are no longer talking about lifetime alimony or any alimony at all."

"No, I think this deposition is concluded."

"For the record Mr. Aron, do you intend to depose any of the other guests at the party?" Reed asked.

"If John settles this case with Ann, there will be no more depositions of people at the party. Clearly, on this record, Ann Gooding was unfaithful." Aron said.

Webber gave Aron a hard look but said nothing.

Aron thought, I'm glad I live in Michigan.

Aron said to the reporter, "Miss Stewart, please prepare a transcript for Mr. Webber's signature and filing in the Court."

Staple said, "Let's defer that until I talk to my client. We don't want this on the public record."

Aron agreed on the record to hold the preparation and filing of the transcript in court for two weeks.

A day after the deposition was finished, John met with his partners and Jane in the same library. He said,"Ann has agreed to the divorce on my terms."

Jane looked at John as if she was particularly happy. The partners congratulated him on ending the divorce before getting Webber more involved. John thought, Clearly they are afraid of him.

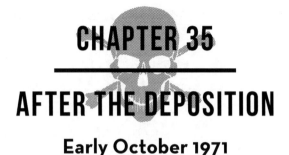

CHAPTER 35

AFTER THE DEPOSITION

Early October 1971

Shortly after Webber's deposition, Staple reported to Ann. She was sort of upset at Charlie's performance, but it was funny.

Ann said, "Didn't you attempt to stop him?"

"I couldn't, he just kept going as if I wasn't there. I repeated 'Mr. Webber several times."

"There must have been something you could have done."

"I almost said, put a sock in it. That was a bad idea."

Jack, I want out of this marriage as soon as possible."

Jack said, "Let's see if their original offer is still good. If you approve I'll call Aron now."

Ann agreed.

Aron answered the call, "Hello Jules this is Jack. I have Ann Gooding in the office with me and we are on speaker. Is your offer is still good."

Aron said, "Yes. Both parties are anxious to end the marriage. That's great Jack. I will draft the final Settlement Agreement, I believe we can have the formal hearing and enter the divorce decree in the near future."

Staple said, "Our only condition is that all copies of Charlie Webber's deposition in Charleston be destroyed, including the reporter's machine transcript taken at the deposition."

Aron said, "Yes," again.

Staple said, "That's great Jules, and thanks."

Ann thought, I have no intention of having Webber's transcript become a part of a public record in a contested divorce. My relationship with Charlie would be aired in Court. Lawyers like Staple are very talkative. I need to make certain he was too frightened to say anything about us in the future.

Ann said,"Staple your need to keep your mouth shut about me."

Staple said, "I'm a gentleman and would never tell on a lady."

You need to check the malpractice cases. It can be very expensive for you."

Staple said, "My lips are sealed."

Ann turned and left without another comment.

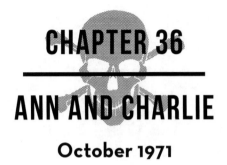

CHAPTER 36

ANN AND CHARLIE

October 1971

Right after his deposition, Charlie telephoned Ann to tell her what had happened. When he told her, she laughed so hard her stomach muscles hurt. Charlie was laughing too.

"You should have seen the look on the stunned faces of the lawyers and court reporter when I dropped my shorts. Your lawyer was speechless. I guess you didn't tell him about us."

"The reason I called, Ann, is to make sure your divorce doesn't reach the point that John's lawyer decides to depose some of my political guests who were at the party. This would prove to be a problem for them and me."

"Charlie, my love, you needn't worry. I have settled by taking John's original offer. He is as egger to escape from our marriage as I am."

"Terrific! On a different topic, come visit me in Charleston next week. I will send my chartered plane to pick you up."

"Charlie, I want to visit you. I need to know that the invitation has nothing to do with John's not deposing the people at the party."

"Believe me. This is about my needing to feel your naked body and to see you again. I have thought about you every day since the party." Ann thought, Is this lust or love? Probably there is a lot of each.

CHAPTER 37

THE FLIGHT

October 1971

Ann arrived at General Aviation at the Lansing airport on Wednesday morning. The weather was clear and sunny and the temperature was in the eighties, according to the radio station to which she was listening. She was very frightened about flying in a small plane for the first time, but she desperately wanted to spend more time with Charlie.

She dragged luggage containing dress clothes and two negligees and carried a cosmetic case into the terminal.

"I'm looking for a plane that has been chartered to take me to Charleston, West Virginia."

The guy behind the desk, with Mac labeled on his shirt, said, "There's a Beech Bonanza on the tarmac that just flew in from Charleston. The pilot is refueling. His name is George Papolis, and he said you were coming. Your name is Ann Gooding?"

"Yes, this is the first time I've been here and I am nervous about flying in a small plane."

"The Beech Bonanza has twin engines and can fly with only one engine. It is one of the most reliable airplanes ever built. It can land and take off almost anywhere there is a flat field."

Ann saw George Papolis finish fueling the airplane and then he came in the building. Mac introduced Ann Gooding. "Hi Ann, I am pleased to meet you," Papolis said with a broad smile. "I'm

Charlie's pilot from West Virginia Airlines. Charlie said you were easy on the eyes."

George carried her luggage to the plane and put it into a hold behind the passenger compartment. Her cosmetic bag went into passenger cabin beside where she was to sit. From the wing of the plane, gave her a hand so she could climb into the passenger compartment. Ann picked a rear seat next to a window on the opposite side of where George was seated.

George climbed into the pilot seat and put on earphones and started talking into a handheld microphone. Then George explained that he obtained clearance to get into position to take off. The engines started and were brought to an idle. She could feel the fuselage of the plane vibrate which made her more uncomfortable. Soon the plane taxied toward the runway and George turned to see that her seat belt was fastened. At the end of the runway he throttled up the engines and told Ann they were taking off. Ann felt the power of the engines pushing her back in her seat as they became airborne. The wheels retracted into wells in the wing with a thump and she gasped. George gave her a thumbs up.

After they leveled off, George handed her a set of earphones so that he could talk to her about the flight.

"We've leveled off at ten thousand feet, which is about the maximum altitude we should fly, since the cabin is not pressurized. You're going to feel bumps as we fly but there is nothing to worry about. Also you may feel the plane drop hundreds of feet because of the warm weather in West Virginia. This plane can handle that without any problem. You can just relax and enjoy the flight. There is unlimited visibility today. We are going to fly over Lake Huron and you will be able to see the beautiful mountains in Pennsylvania and West Virginia."

Ann thought, I just want to get through this flight. I am not interested in a travel log.

Ann finally settled back in her seat and listened to the music of James Taylor and Karen Carpenter that George was sending through the earphones. She closed her eyes when they reached the shore of Lake Huron and slept.

When Ann awoke, she could feel the plane rising and falling.

George said, "This is normal in the West Virginia mountains. We will be in Charleston shortly. Charlie will be at the terminal to meet you," George said.

Ann was still tense. It seemed that the airport was postage stamp in size and was cut into the top of a mountain. It became larger as they descended to land. The flight controller told George where to land, which he did smoothly. They taxied to the terminal and George cut the engines and the propellers came to a stop. Ann breathed a sigh of relief.

Ann saw Charlie standing near the plane. Clem Block was behind him. Helping her out of the passenger compartment onto the wing, George said good-bye to her. Charlie reached up and lifted her down. He held her in his arms and they kissed for several moments, their bodies molded together.

"Welcome to Charleston, Ann. I'm really glad to see you."

Charlie said that his car and driver were waiting for them. Ann and Charlie said good-by to George.

"See you on Sunday Ann. Have a good time," George said.

Charlie and Ann left for the waiting car. He said, "Ignore Clem Block. He's surly and probably will dislike you on sight He doesn't like women."

Charlie showed Ann the sights in Charleston as he held her hand, including the State Capitol building. Ann thought, The town seems to be a little dirty.

Charlie closed the divider behind. Clem smiled slightly as it closed.

Charlie began to put his hands on her breasts. Ann said, "I feel stinky from sweating on the plane. I want to wait until I've had a shower and a change of clothes." I don't want Block anywhere near us. Charlie pouted slightly and then said that was OK and told Clem to head home using an intercom beside him.

Along the way, he told her some of the history of Charleston, which centered on coal mining and shipping. Ann could tell that he was proud to be a leading member in the community.

Charlie's home was in the heart of town and was a Federalist style two-story brick mansion. He bragged that Abraham Lincoln had stayed there overnight during the Civil War en route to

Gettysburg to give his address for the soldiers who died in battle. Charlie said the coal for the president's train came from Charlie's great grandfather's mines.

Inside the front door, Ann viewed a large tiled hallway with a curved staircase to the second floor. A large room on the right was big enough to be a ballroom. On the left was a living room, next to a library with books on shelves ranging from floor to ceiling.

Charlie said, "This was my family's collection of rare books." The rooms were filled with early American antiques, which conveyed great wealth.

Charlie said, "The mansion is named 'Steadfast'. It has been in my family for over 150 years."

Ann wondered where this was leading, beginning to hope Charlie was serious about a relationship with her-even marriage.

Charlie led her upstairs to a large bedroom with a huge four-poster with a canopy bed.

He said, "I want to make love to you now, but I can wait until after you have showered." He smiled at her.

Ann smiled. "Give me about thirty minutes to get ready, Charlie." She kissed him on the mouth and he left her alone.

Ann took a shower, humming some of the songs she had heard on the plane, taking care not to get her hair wet. She dried herself and put Estee Lauder dusting powder between her breasts and perfume on her neck. She found that men were really turned on by this scent. Charlie had said he liked it when they were making love in the cabin on Mt. Hope. As she finished, Charlie knocked on the door.

Although she was not dressed, Ann enthusiastically said, "Come in Charlie!"

He entered, dressed only in a velvet maroon robe, and closed the door. Ann walked over, naked, and helped him discard his robe. She led him by the hand to the bed.

Charlie made love to her with his hands and mouth on her breasts and between her legs before he mounted her. Again Ann felt the rush as they came together. He was insatiable and made her come again and again.

At last, they rested side by side, and Charlie held her close and stroked her backside. She felt that Charlie seriously cared for her by the way he was treating her. She thought, On the other hand, it might just be an interlude. God I love this man.

CHAPTER 38

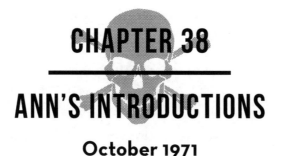

ANN'S INTRODUCTIONS

October 1971

Charlie took Ann shopping for evening clothes in Philadelphia. He said, " I've planned parties for the end of the week. You will get to meet some of my closest friends." Charlie drove. Block did not seemed pleased that he was left behind. Charlie said, "I know Block is a bit creepy," as they drove.

Several thousand dollars were spent on dresses and shoes. He even helped her pick them out, which Ann found charming. Charlie seemed comfortable in this setting which surprised her. She thought, Charlie really knows how to please a woman.

Ann was surprised that Charlie did all of this for her. She thought, Maybe there is a chance he will marry me. In any event the clothes and shoes are stunning and worth the trip.

They stayed three nights in a fancy hotel and wandered around the city, tourists absorbing Revolutionary war history. Surprisingly, Charlie knew a lot about the battles. They saw the Liberty bell and museums, including the Benjamin Franklin exhibits. Charlie continued to be loving and kind.

On Thursday and Friday evenings, Charlie introduced Ann to his friends in Charleston, small parties at Steadfast. Charlie said, "You will fit in well with my friends. They have money and are the powerful elite in West Virginia."

At the second party, Ann was introduced to State Senator Nick

Wallenby. He observed, "You look like you could get old Charlie to settle down and have some kids."

Ann politely smiled. "He hasn't asked me yet, Senator, but I thank you for thinking of me."

Mrs. Wallenby, standing nearby, gave Ann a look that said, "Good luck with that". Ann recognized that she must be one of Charlie's past conquests, and just smiled.

Later Charlie said, "You held your own very well at the party. My friends said they like you very much."

Maybe I could become Mrs. Webber, Ann thought. I hope he asks me.

The next day Charlie took her to see his strip mining operation on Mt. Hope. Block drove, somber as an undertaker. He hasn't forgiven me for leaving him behind for the trip to Philadelphia, she thought. Charlie gave Block a couple of days off to visit his brother.

————

IN THE MINE, GIANT MACHINES carved away the mountain in large bites. Again, Charlie said, "We do things on a grand scale. Coal produces the electric power which makes the economy grow. We are performing a public service."

Ann thought, A massive amount of coal is mined from Mt. Hope. That means lots of money for Charlie, maybe for us.

They stayed overnight at Respite on Deep Lake and went fishing and caught some smallmouth bass. Charlie said, "I stocked in the lake over the years."

Ann said, "I've never fished.

Charlie said, "They're fun to catch. They fight hard before they are netted."

Charlie cleaned and fried the fish, and they ate them for dinner, accompanied by an expensive bottle of French white wine. The lake surface shimmered as the sun set in the west across the Lake.

Ann said, "This is a beautiful place, Charlie""

"I'm going to have you visit me as often as you can. I want to have you all to myself. Is that clear?"

Ann smiled. "Yes, as long as you agree that there will be no other women."

Charlie said yes, and they held hands on the porch until the sun set over the lake. The trees were taking on shades of yellow, red, and brown. Ann and Charlie made love on the porch lounge by the light of a full moon.

Sunday morning as they drove back to Charleston, they rode past shacks where his coal miners lived. Children dressed for church were running around in the yards.

Ann asked about the politicians she had met at the July party. Charlie bragged about controlling the politicians.

Ann asked, "How is that was working out for you?."

"They do what I tell them to do. I have been able to stave off ridiculous environmental complaints about strip mining. In any event, Ann, you must never say anything about the people at the party."

"Charlie, I will never say anything about the people at the party. You can count on that."

Charlie turned and smiled and kissed Ann. He said, "Sealed with a kiss." He raised the divider window.

"How do you feel about children, Charlie?" Ann thought, I am almost certain I am pregnant. This is likely to be a problem for Charlie.

"Well, that came out of the blue, Ann. I haven't thought about that much-maybe."

"Wouldn't you like to a child so that you can pass on the business?"

"Maybe now," "Charlie said. Ann smiled and breathed out slowly.

———

WHEN THEY REACHED STEADFAST IN Charleston, Ann went upstairs to pack. Charlie said, "You can have half the closet for the dresses and shoes. I'm sure you will be back."

While Ann was packing, downstairs Block asked Charlie if he was concerned that Ann knew about controlling the politicians at the party.

Charlie thought a moment and said, "No, Ann is different. You are to protect her with your life, the same way you do me. Is that clear?"

"Yes sir."

In that instant, Charlie knew he held Ann's life in the balance. Block would have killed her if he had answered differently. He thought, Block has to disappear.

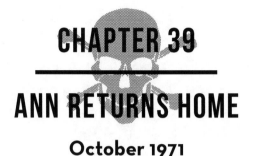

CHAPTER 39

ANN RETURNS HOME

October 1971

At the end of the week, George was waiting for Ann beside the Bonanza. Charlie kissed her good-by at Steadfast. He said, "I have a bad accident in one of my mines and the Bureau of Mine Safety is threatening to close the mine."

———

AT THE AIRPORT, BLOCK TOOK her luggage from the trunk of the car and her cosmetic case and carried them to the plane. Ann saw that they were in the plane the same way as when she arrived.

Block turned and walked to the car without looking back. Ann felt a chill, sensing evil. She would talk to Charlie about getting rid of Block. Ann saw the cosmetic case was on her seat, so she would have it during the flight.

George helped her up and into the plane and she sat in her seat, moving the case next to her. He said, "We've clearance to take off, Ann. Are you comfortable? The flying weather is perfect," anticipating her next question.

"I'm ready to leave, George. I was just thinking Block gives me the creeps."

"Everybody has that feeling. He's a mean son of a bitch. Rumor has it that bad things happen to miners when Block is around. Not to worry though, he would never do anything to you without Charlie's permission. Charlie is obviously very taken with you."

The plane taxied to the end of the runway and took off. Again the weather was clear and the plane easily climbed to ten thousand feet. Ann relaxed a little.

They flew for about two hours until they were over Lake Huron again. Ann fumbled opening her case to put on some lipstick, to ease her chapped lips. It slipped and fell onto the floor, spilling the contents. A small piece of brown plastic with a clock mounted on a board fell out and was on the seat beside her. Ann showed it to George.

"Shit, Ann that looks like plastic explosive with a timer!"

"George! It has a stop watch that has only thirty seconds left," Ann screamed.

George grabbed it, opened the small window beside him, and threw it out the window, climbing to the left as steeply as he could. In less than fifteen seconds, a huge fireball with an explosion erupted. This forced the plane to spiral down until they were heading nose first into the lake. In the last few seconds, George was able to level the plane enough for a rough water landing, skidding across the surface.

He slipped off his safety harness and reached back to unbuckle Ann's seat belt. She was stunned, but alert. He kicked open the door and pushed her and two life jackets through the door into the water. He jumped into the water with her. Then he slipped one jacket on Ann, pulled the inflation cord and it ballooned out. He then put one on.

"Ann! Where do you hurt?"

"My ribs hurt, and I'm having trouble breathing," she gasped.

Just then they heard the gurgling sound of the airplane beginning to sink. In a minute it was gone. The lake was calm, but the wind seemed to be picking up.

"The plane had a transponder flashing a signal that was on before we crashed. The Coast Guard will find us right away. My company and the Capitol City Airport in Lansing will report us as overdue in less than an hour," he said in a calm voice.

Ann could only nod her head, crying. She was thinking about the bomb. Why would Charlie do this to her. She thought back to her conversation with Charlie about the politicians in his pocket. Is he trying to kill me?

"Ann, do you have any idea of how the bomb ended up in your case?"

"Well it wasn't there when I packed. It had to have been put into my bag by Block. Charlie had an important call at the last minute. Maybe that was a ruse."

George held her tightly he said to keep her body heat from draining. She was comforted by the warmth of his body.

In about an hour a Coast Guard rescue crew with swimmers found them, jumped from the helicopter, got Ann and George into harnesses and lifted them from the water. The crew covered them with blankets and gave them some hot coffee. They headed for the heliport on the roof of the Cleveland Clinic and landed. Ann was taken to the emergency room. After an hour and an X-ray, the doctor informed her she had cracked ribs, which would heal in a few weeks. He said George was cold but otherwise uninjured. In an hour he visited Ann's room and made sure she was out of danger.

Ann telephoned Charlie at Steadfast to tell him what happened. Then she demanded, "Charlie, did you have Block plant a bomb in my case?" Charlie said, "Please let me talk to George." She handed the phone to George.

Ann heard George explain to Charlie in more detail what had happened. Then he turned to Ann and said, "Charlie asked that we not mention the bomb to anyone. He is going to buy me a new plane. He wants to handle this his own way. He said you can be certain that you would never have a problem again with Block or the person who had him do it. He wants to talk to you again."

"Ann, the next time we meet, I was planning to give you a very large diamond ring and ask you to marry me. I'm flying to Cleveland to pick you up and get you home to Lansing. Ann fell asleep thinking about Charlie.

The next afternoon Charlie arrived in Cleveland by commercial airplane. Ann told him that she would be discharged at noon. He was there early within a few minutes of the time. He drove a new Cadillac sedan, rented for the trip.

On the way to Lansing, They held hands with Charlie driving with his left hand.

Quietly, barely over the car sounds, Ann said, "Charlie the doctors said I'm pregnant. It happened when we were on Mt. Hope. I haven't had any relations with John or anybody else."

Charlie said, "Ann, I am not certain I want to have children, but if I did it would be with you. We can wait and see what happens for a few months."

Ann said, "I want to have your baby. He will be handsome and strong like you."

Charlie drove Ann to her home and spent the night. They made love carefully.

Charlie said, "I still want to marry you Ann." He gave her the engagement ring with a headlight of a diamond.

Ann smiled and said, "I accept, Charlie."

In the morning they said good-bye and Charlie dropped off the car at the Capitol City Airport and flew back to Charleston.

CHAPTER 40

BLOCK'S END

October 1971

Charlie called two of his employees in one of his mines who handled dirty jobs when Block was not available. They were ordered to come to Charleston to have a "heavy conversation" with Block about a problem that had arisen. They were to fly over in the company helicopter and be there within two hours.

Sam Cutler and Luke Sharpe arrived on time and went into Charlie's office and closed the door. The first thing Charlie asked was if they had their pistols. Each man pulled out a pistol from his shoulder holster and showed it to Charlie.

"A serious problem has developed with Clem Block," he said giving them an abbreviated version of what happened to Ann's plane and the bomb. He's too stupid to do this on his own and I need to know who paid for it. I want him eliminated, but not before you discover who put him up to this.

"You will to work him over in the old basement prison chamber without killing him. Make him suffer as much pain and fear. Use everything you know. When you are done, I will kill him."

Sam and Luke were artists at torture, having been military interrogators in Vietnam. They told Charlie over beers about some of their captured NKVD interrogations following some of the CMOA meetings.

They found Block polishing Webber's limousine. He knew that there was no place for him to go where Charlie couldn't find him.

Sam walked up to him and pushed the muzzle of his pistol into his back while Luke stood with a pistol aimed at his head. Sam jammed a needle into Clem's neck and pumped an anesthetic into a vein in his neck.

Block swore, "You motherfuckers," and passed out.

Sam and Luke supported Block on each shoulder and dragged him into the basement. They walked into a small red brick walled room. A refrigerator was stocked full of beer, like they would be watching football on TV.

Sam said, "This is going to be like the old days. I want to drag this out as long as possible with this asshole."

They clamped Clem's wrists with handcuffs to the arms of a straight backed steel chair bolted to the floor. After removing his shoes, they also clamped his ankles to the legs of the chair. They lowered a metal cap to cover the top of his head, connected to an electrical panel, and then cut away his clothes. Satisfied, they decided to have a beer before Block woke up. They needed to have Block awake.

They arranged a set of tools, which were duplicates of those they had used in Vietnam, so Block could see them. They hoped they would be able to use every one of them.

Soon Block started to wake up and struggled without success to get out of the chair. Sam and Luke said nothing and waited for him to start talking. At first he just looked around as Sam and Luke finished their beers.

"What in hell is going on here? Charlie is going to cut off your heads and shit down your necks for this, you motherfuckers."

"Well Block, it's like this, Charlie wants us to investigate a little matter involving your loyalty to him," Sam said.

"I've always been loyal to Charlie."

"Well, I'm glad to hear that lie, because you will tell us everything we want to know." Sam fastened a blood pressure cuff around Block's arm. This will help us to know you are alive as we work on you.

"Let me tell you about this chair, Block. It is part of the history of this house. It was used to torture Confederate spies and soldiers during the Civil War to discover information about troop movements. In a way, Block you are going to become part of the history of the chair and you will go into the log books. It is an honor for you to sit there," Luke said.

"Block, see all those volumes on the shelf over there? Those are the records of people who were tortured in that chair before you," Sam said.

————

CLEM FELT HIS ANXIETY TIGHTEN the muscles of his heart. He said nothing. He strained against the cuffs on the chair as a jolt of electricity went through his body. The room smelled of singed body hair, as the electricity entered his body where it touched the chair, including his pecker.

Luke said," We're going to find out about the bomb you planted in the airplane."

Clem thought, Even if tell them, I will die anyway. My brother and his family will die. I hate Charlie for the broken bones and weak heart when methane had exploded in a mine. My son and friends died in that blast, all because Charlie was too cheap to buy breathing equipment and sensors for the gas.

Clem did not know who paid him to get rid of Ann Gooding. His contact, Abe, who looked like a spy, said some people were very concerned that Webber told Ann too much. She had to be taken care of right away. Abe gave Clem the bomb to plant on the airplane and ten thousand dollars.

————

"WELL CLEM, WE NEED TO know about the bomb which you planted on Mrs. Gooding's plane," Sam said. He reached for a pair of pliers and pulled off the nail off Clem's left index finger.

Clem howled in pain, which brought a smile of satisfaction to Sam and Luke's faces. It was clear to Clem that they were going to enjoy every minute of his pain. Methodically they pulled off the nails on the rest of the fingers, as Clem screamed.

"So Clem, I hope you're not ready to tell us what we want to know. The fun is just beginning." said Luke.

And so they started on the toe nails. All the while Clem thought, I just need to die to save my family.

As Sam held up Clem's penis with the pliers, for Luke to cut off, he screamed and said that he didn't know who his contact was.

"He acted like a federal government employee," Clem said.

"Now we're making progress," Sam said, reaching for the electrical switch.

This duration of the current was much longer and Clem felt his heart explode in his chest and the room went black.

———————

"AW SHIT. DIDN'T LAST VERY long," Luke said after he listened for a heart beat using a stethoscope.

"Charlie is *really* going to be pissed," Sam said.

They turned away from Clem's body and exited, locking the basement door behind them. They walked around to the front of the house and entered.

Charlie was waiting for them. "So what did you learn?"

"The only thing that asshole told us before he died was that he had gotten money from a person who looked like a government employee," Sam said.

"Funny though, Clem looked like he would be a lot tougher," Luke said.

"What in hell did you do to him?"

"We gave him a light shock for a minute or so. Shouldn't have killed him," Sam said.

"You guys knew he had been injured in a mine explosion. Didn't it occur to you that you had to be a little less rough? Anyway, dispose of the body down the mine shaft as usual."

Sam and Luke rolled Clem's body in a rug ready for that purpose and carried it to Webber's car. They drove up to the old mine shaft surrounded by a barb wire fence with razor wire on top. The mine was abandoned well over 125 years ago. They dumped Clem's naked body into the shaft and watched it fall out of sight and then threw in some quick lime.

Sam said, "Clem's body dropped one thousand feet to rest with dozens of others. This is the burial ground for those who got in the way of Charlie or his ancestors."

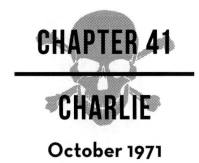

CHAPTER 41

CHARLIE

October 1971

Webber sat in his office in Steadfast and attempted to figure out who would have had a reason to kill Ann. Repeatedly the answer arose that the attempt was related in some way to one of the congressmen he bribed. He could not think of a person who would benefit from her death. It bugged him to the point of losing sleep over the matter.

The question for Webber was would the killer make another attempt on Ann? Importantly, they might try to get rid of him as well. He was driven to at least find and punish the bastard who built the bomb and possibly find out who ordered it.

After he returned to Charleston and met with Charlie, George's said, "The bomb was not made by an amateur, since it was made with plastic explosive. There is a professional behind the design of the bomb." Charlie bought him the new airplane as promised.

Afterwards, in a meeting with Charlie, Sam said, "There were only a few professional assassins in the country who use plastic explosive in bombs. We knew men in Vietnam who were experts."

Sam and Luke agreed that they would ask around to see if they could locate somebody who fits the profile.

Webber said, "I hope the search goes well," implying that Sam and Luke might not survive if it didn't.

"Don't screw this one up and, if you do, you two may be the next ones dumped down the mine shaft."

"Understood, Charlie," they answered in unison and turned around and left.

Webber concluded that these two guys were not experts in the torture of men like Block. The subjects in Vietnam were just in better physical condition and braver and tougher than Block.

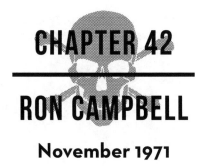

CHAPTER 42

RON CAMPBELL

November 1971

Ron Campbell was at home in San Francisco the day Clem Block died. He was paid fifty thousand dollars, the price of an expensive car, to build the bomb that Block placed on the airplane in Charleston.

Feeling bad about his job and the outcome was not part of his make-up. After all, he made about a million tax-free dollars a year. He thought, Failure on the other hand is not tolerated by my clients.

Campbell informed a very unhappy bag man, Abe, that he would kill Ann himself this time.

Abe said, "My sponsor does not want another missed attempt. The bomb should have been made to look like something else. We were fortunate that Webber covered up the fact that the plane was downed by a bomb, even though he had nothing to do with it."

"This was not my fault. Of course you have every right to be unhappy, but remember, you hired Block to place the package. This time I will do the job myself. By the way what happened to Block?"

"He has disappeared. I expect Webber took care of that problem."

Campbell thought, I wonder if Webber might try to come after me. He dismissed the thought because Webber would not be able to locate him.

"You need to let me know when you need my services. They will be free of charge," Campbell said.

CHAPTER 43

SAM AND LUKE SAN FRANCISCO

November 1971

With the help of some friends from Vietnam, Sam located Ron Campbell as the likely bomb maker. Sam and Luke flew to San Francisco after finding out where he lived.

A M-16 sniper rifle with night scope waited for them at their hotel. The rifle was stolen for them from a nearby armory by the soldier who sold it to Sam over the phone.

The rifle was capable of killing at one thousand yards. They knew they would be unable to get closer than five hundred yards to Campbell.

Sam and Luke took up a protected position on the roof of an abandoned building near a bar after watching Campbell go in. At closing time, Campbell exited the bar with a blonde. Sam whispered to Luke that she was a real looker.

Luke only said, "Collateral damage. She's probably a hooker anyway."

When Campbell moved under a street light, Sam fired two shots, killing both of them. No trace of the bullets would be found. They were designed to fragment, making bones into secondary projectiles.

They quickly vacated their position and headed to Campbell's apartment. On the way, Luke called Webber from a phone booth. Webber answered on the first ring.

"We delivered the package and the problem is neutralized.

We are going to check out the apartment and then come back to Charleston."

Webber said, "Good," and hung up.

Sam and Luke entered the apartment cautiously, expecting it to be wired with explosives. They checked every inch of the place, but did not find a bomb. They then moved to Campbell's computer. They touched a key, and a message came up on the screen. It read, "If you are reading this, you are dead."

In a flash, both Sam and Luke died in the blast.

The next day Webber read in the *San Francisco Chronicle* that two people were killed, Ron Campbell and an unidentified woman, by an unknown shooter. It went on to say that there was an explosion at Campbell's apartment where two unidentified men died.

CHAPTER 44

JOHN IN CHARLESTON

November 1971

John rented an apartment in Charleston near the Kanawha State Park, so he could hike. He walked the trails that wound through hemlocks, a translucent green in the sunlight, clustered along a creek. Dead trees on the ground, covered with a dark green moss, slowly decayed to sawdust. He felt that God resided in this place, a cathedral with the trees forming the arches and prayed for his success. A sense of calm descended over him.

On Monday morning, John went to work at his new law firm. Jane showed him how the firm operated and told him about the current coal-related cases. Standing close to her he was attracted.

When lunchtime approached, John asked, "Why don't we have lunch together and talk about West Virginia?"

"Sure. I know a noisy restaurant where we can eat without being overheard."

Jane took him to Gino's and they sat in a back booth. Nobody seemed to be interested in them.

"So John, how is the move progressing?" Jane asked.

"I've found a house near Kanawha Park. Maybe we can go hiking there."

Jane said," That would be nice."

Jane talked about West Virginia and its history in the Civil War and the Reconstruction.

"During the Civil War, West Virginia was in the Union, but

a lot of Confederate sympathizers lived here. After the War, a strong Ku Klux Klan membership arose. A lot of Klansmen are still active. They are a dangerous group and have a wide following in the hills. You have to be careful there," Jane warned.

"How do you find out who they are?"

"I have no way of knowing for sure, but many prominent people in West Virginia are secret members of the Klan- particularly in Charleston."

John wondered if Webber might be a member of the Klan. He did not mention this to Jane to avoid explaining Ann's and his involvement with Webber. Also, he did not want to place her at risk because of him.

"I'm very interested in what the coal mining industry has done to the environment in West Virginia," John said.

Jane said, "Coal is king in this state. For over one hundred and fifty years, we have been a primary source of coal used for making steel and producing power for the country. Hundreds of mines are operating throughout the state. State and Federal regulation of coal mining is limited. Strip mining is virtually unregulated.

"The mines are dangerous, and every year they kill at least one hundred miners. Periodic mining disasters kill whole families with explosions, poison gasses, or floods. The pay is poverty level.

"The mining industry has almost all of the state and federal representatives on the take from the coal mine operators. This problem is not going to be cleaned up anytime soon," Jane said.

"I'd like to try," John said, with a quiet voice and Jane nodded in agreement.

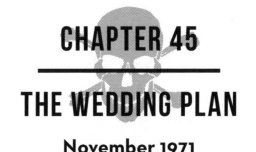

CHAPTER 45

THE WEDDING PLAN

November 1971

Ann was excited about her wedding to Charlie set for December. It would be the largest and most elaborate event held in Charleston for many years. Charlie gave her fifty thousand dollars, all of which she intended to spend. She wanted Charleston society to take notice.

She planned expensive engagement parties in Lansing and Charleston for friends. The first was a dinner dance at the Gross Pointe Country Club overlooking the Detroit River, an old-style club with light oak floors and art deco furnishings. Her mother and father paid for it.

As guests arrived, attendants, wearing blazers with the club initials, parked their cars.

Ann invited all of her Junior League friends. As they arrived, she introduced them to Charlie. Her friends told her later in the evening that he was handsome and a wonderful man, so strong. Some of the ladies were a little too friendly to Charlie and Ann deftly steered him away from them.

Charlie was a skilled ballroom dancer and invited some of the ladies to dance. He told Ann that as a child of a rich family in a city that held cotillions each spring, he had taken dance lessons when he was young. He danced foxtrot, swing, cha-cha, waltz and rumba with the ladies and each of them came away smiling after their dance. Charlie charmed them with his Southern accent and wonderful manners.

Ann thought, There are going to be a lot of husbands taking ballroom dancing after tonight. I'm going to have to watch Charlie around other women. She was happy and pleased that her friends seemed to like Charlie. She thought, Rich people see to make friends easily. My family is only middle class by comparison.

At the end of the party, Charlie made a short speech. "I am pleased to meet you all and look forward to seeing you again at our wedding in Charleston."

After the party, Charlie and Ann sat in a hotel room and talked about the party.

"Ann, that was a well-planned party." I really liked your friends."

Ann and Charlie made love that night with candlelight around her childhood room. She did not feel any sadness about her divorce from John. She felt her body beginning to move towards maternity, as if her baby was talking to her. Everything is working out perfectly, she thought as she fell asleep beside Charlie.

In two weeks, there would be the Charleston engagement party, which would be a gala in the tradition of the Old South. She basked in the anticipated splendor.

CHAPTER 46

CHARLESTON GALA

December 1971

Ann was ready to impress Charlie's social circle. She planned the party at the Charleston Hilton Hotel ballroom, using a list of three hundred guests that Charlie had given her. The list included politicians, wealthy friends, mine owners, most of the social register of Charleston and those who had any influence on coal mining. Ann understood that the party was partially for business and some of the people on the guest list had been at Charlie's place on Deep Lake in July.

Wanting to make a good impression, she purchased a very expensive designer gown. Charlie gave her a fifty carat, multiple diamond necklace to wear which belonged to his mother.

Ann and Charlie greeted the guests as they arrived. The men were cordial to her and the women smiled at Charlie. They were respectful to Ann, but she felt a reserve, particularly from some of the politicians, as if they did not approve of her.

Evelyn Wallenby said, "I see that you were able to finally pin Charlie down. This has been a long time in coming. I didn't think Charlie would ever stay with one woman. I hope you have completely recovered from the plane accident. I read the story of your accident in the newspapers."

Ann said, "I'm fully recovered, Mrs. Wallenby. Thank you for asking. It makes me even more apprehensive about flying in small planes."

"Please call me Evelyn."

She smiled at Ann with a slight upward turn to her lips. Ann saw the glance at Mrs. Wallenby from Charlie, his eyes sharply focused even as he smiled. She suspected that Evelyn knew a lot about Charlie. She thought, I will not be inviting her to the house for a chat anytime soon.

Charlie's guests danced counterclockwise around the ballroom to the music of a large society orchestra that played music from the forties to the sixties. For a Viennese Waltz, the dancers moved as if they were in a precision routine.

The guests ate, drank, and socialized, many of whom had known each other all their lives. Ann discovered in conversations with them that they felt as if they owned West Virginia. They made Ann feel like an outsider by very subtle changes in their voices or body language. Fitting in with some of them is going to be difficult, she thought.

One young woman insulted Ann when she snidely said, "Charming dress. A good copy."

Ann replied tartly, "Well, at least it doesn't does not make me look pudgy. I'd refrain from wearing ruffles next time."

Ann talked to almost all the politicians. They all were tied to coal mining in some way. Senator Nick Wallenby bragged about his ability to block coal mine safety reform legislation in the national committee that he chaired.

"We don't need any more laws regulating safety. The mines are safe as can be. The miners understand it is a dangerous job. They have to consider the money they earn for their families."

Ann smiled, moved closer to him to lower her voice to a whisper, and asked, "How does one block such legislation, Senator?"

"Well it's not too difficult. We amend a bill to include something unacceptable, like taxes on the coal to fund a federal agency to regulate the mining operations. Nobody wants to see their utility bill rise. Works every time. Governor Blanding vetoes any state legislation regulating coal mining," Wallenby whispered in a conspiratorial voice to Ann.

She touched him on the arm and said, "That sounds very clever,

Senator. Maybe we could visit Washington and you could show us the Senate."

"Be pleased to do that, Ann. You will have to put up with Vietnam War protestors. Also people are planning a large gathering for civil rights, which you'll want to avoid. Those people don't know when they are well off. Pretty soon they will want to marry white women, and that is going to produce mixed race babies, which is contrary to God's order. We have to prevent that."

"How can we do that, Senator?" Ann asked in a low voice.

"Well a group of us here are committed to teaching the civil rights people about the error of that type of thinking."

Ann said, "You'll have to tell me more about that later, Senator."

"It has been my distinct pleasure to speak with you." The Senator bowed slightly to her as several people watched. After that, she noticed that the men and some of the women became a lot friendlier.

As the evening came to a close, Charlie took her by the hand, and together they thanked the guests for coming. He said, "We are both looking forward to the wedding and the reception," and kissed Ann lightly on the lips. Her cheeks flushed in pleasure and the guests clapped. She noticed that some of the women clapped more enthusiastically than others. Evelyn Wallenby didn't clap at all.

————

CHARLIE SAID LATER, AS THEY lay in bed after making love, that she was a great hostess. He said, "Senator Wallenby was very taken with you."

Ann refrained from asking Charlie about the name of the group dealing with civil rights.. She was confident he would tell her about it eventually. It really didn't make any difference to her life with him. She loved him regardless.

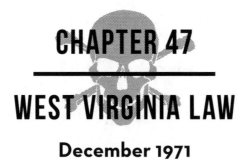

CHAPTER 47

WEST VIRGINIA LAW

December 1971

John litigated a lot of *pro bono* cases against the mine companies for injuries from explosions or gas exposure in the mines. Jane assisted him. At most, minimal damages were paid by the mine operators, who avoided or ignored safety equipment because the cost was too great. He found that the operators considered miners an expendable piece of equipment.

Soon, the mine operators learned to hate John, as a result of his handling these cases. When he called one of the mine operators to the witness stand, the man said, "Mining is dangerous work, and the miners know the risk. I'm providing the coal that is needed to keep the United States strong during the war in Vietnam."

John thought, All the jury hears is the American flag snapping in the breeze.

John's client, a young widow with three children, was awarded ten thousand dollars for the death of her husband in an explosion caused by inadequate ventilation of a mine shaft. His body was never recovered, because the operators said the shaft was buried too deep to retrieve the bodies.

John had a feeling that coal was a hazard to the heath of the people around Deep Lake. University of West Virginia analysis of the coal-tailing sediment on the bottom of Deep Lake by the University of West Virginia showed very high levels of mercury.

He brought the finding to the attention of his partners in a meeting in the library where the firm had lunch catered once a week. Associates Jane and Tom were invited to attend.

John said, "I want to bring a case against Charlie Webber and his company for damages for dumping coal tailings into Deep Lake and for the cost of remediation of the site." He heard a quick intake of breath by Jake and Jason, sitting on either side of him.

Jake said, "I want everyone to stop taking notes and give me what you have right now! This conversation cannot leave this room without my permission. Understand that your lives might be at stake. Charlie Webber is a very dangerous man. John has some experience in this regard."

John related an abbreviated story about the plane crash involving his ex-wife. "Webber's driver, Block, has disappeared, probably on Webber's orders," he said. "In my opinion, Webber is indeed dangerous."

"We need to decide what kind of proofs would be necessary for the case," Jake said.

John said, "Mercury from the coal tailings has ended up in the fish in Deep Lake. I know that the presence of the mercury is not enough. We need to show an injury was caused by the mercury."

Jane said, "If we had a sick individual with high levels of mercury who had contact with the lake over a long period of time, we might have a case."

John said, "I know of a local a teenager the locals call 'nature boy' I saw last summer. He wanders naked in the woods near Deep Lake. If we could test him and find high mercury levels, we might have a case. We would have to obtain his parents approval. It would be a private gesture on my part to help a mountain child."

His partners agreed reluctantly. Jake cautioned, "This is a fishing expedition and there are nothing but sharks around us."

After more general discussion concerning upcoming trials, Jake dismissed the associates.

Jake said, "John, I want you to obtain a permit to carry a pistol, at least in your car. Charlie Webber will go after you as soon as he discovers your interest in Deep Lake."

CHAPTER 48

ANN'S MARRIAGE AGREEMENT

December 1971

Just before the wedding, Charlie's friends were only tepidly friendly. Only two wedding showers were held for Ann. She had Charlie, and she thought, They are just jealous.

As she sat in the library thinking about Charlie, he came in carrying a bundle of papers and sat down next to her and gave her a hug and a kiss.

"My lawyer has recommended that we have a premarital agreement. It protects you in the event we are divorced. It provides for a payment to you of three hundred thousand dollars a year for life."

"That seems very generous Charlie, but we are not going to be divorced. I'll sign it," She thought, I've got nothing to lose. It will be enough for our baby and me. I love him. Excited, she kissed him, wet in anticipation. They climbed the stairs to their bedroom once again.

CHAPTER 49

THE WEDDING AND HONEYMOON

December 1971

Ann and Charlie were married in the Episcopal Church in Charleston. Charlie said,"I don't care much for churches." Ann said a large church wedding was required given his social station and then he agreed.

Ann said, "I feel like I am marrying a member of a royal family." as she walked down the aisle with her father.

He said, "He's just a man with a lot of money. You need to be watchful with him."

Charlie was dressed in a black tuxedo with a jacket with long tails. Senator Wallenby was the best man.

Ann wore a white French designer wedding dress. Five months pregnant, she was beginning to show, so the dress was loose at her waist. A college friend was her bridesmaid.

The wedding service lasted over an hour and was captured on film by a professional movie maker.

Before the wedding, Ann said,"Charlie, I want to remember this day as long as I live." Charlie smiled.

The Charleston Gazette sent a reporter with a camera man to interview Ann and Charlie before the wedding for publication in Sunday's supplement the day after the wedding. Afterwards, Ann said, "I can hardly believe that our wedding has attracted so much attention."

A RECEPTION WAS HELD FOR four hundred guests at the Charleston Country Club which was set in a pine and spruce forest which lined the fairways. All of the members of the staff were white. Many of Ann's friends, all white, flew to Charleston to attend the wedding and reception. Ann danced with her father, who proudly handed Ann over to Charlie to finish the dance.

Charlie and Ann danced to the Tennessee Waltz counterclockwise around the dance floor and Ann once again felt his strong and confident lead. She said, "I am as happy as I have ever been in my life at this moment."

————

AFTER THE WEDDING, ANN AND Charlie honeymooned in Jamaica at a Sandals Resort for two weeks, a very happy couple and amorous on the beach and at dinner. They made love every night to the point of exhaustion. Every once in a while, Charlie left Ann to make a private telephone call. He told Ann this was just business.

As they flew home in first class, Charlie told Ann about his idea to run for governor of West Virginia. She was excited about being a governor's wife and hugged and kissed him. They talked about organizing the wealthy families to donate money for the campaign, and Ann volunteered to be the chairwoman of the drive.

"I have the support of many of the politicians in the legislature. I have asked Senator Wallenby to head up my campaign and he is going to talk to our congressmen and President Nixon to get endorsements. Vice President Agnew has already agreed to endorse my campaign, and he promised that the president will be behind it."

"Charlie, this is a wonderful idea. The people of West Virginia will finally have a governor who cares for them. What about Governor Blanding?"

"He has decided to retire at the end of his term," Charlie said.

"My friends encouraged me to run. They said we need a governor who is clearly against changing the laws governing coal mining. I have pledged to do just that. Last year Blanding started a program to clean up the mines and make them safer. There are safe enough already."

Ann thought, I will be First Lady and live in the Governor's mansion. She felt the baby move and wondered if her pregnancy would affect Charlie's campaign.

"Charlie, I felt our baby move," placing his hand over her stomach.

He smiled slightly at her.

————

THEY ARRIVED IN CHARLESTON AFTER transferring to another flight in Atlanta, Georgia. Ann was relieved to be back at Steadfast. The campaign for governor would begin in January 1972 and go until the election in November. It would take up a lot of Charlie's time, but he said the effort was worth it for the Coal Mine Operators Association.

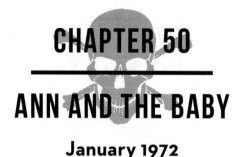

CHAPTER 50

ANN AND THE BABY

January 1972

Ann was seeing Dr. Samuel Kruthmer, recommended by Charlie, for the first three months checkup. Charlie said he was the best obstetrician in West Virginia and a friend.

Ann had developed confidence in the man. Over six feet tall and about forty five years old, Dr. K., as he was called by his staff, had a handlebar mustache which made him look like a late 1800s cowboy, except for his short cropped hair.

This time he said, "Ann, I am sorry to have to tell you this. Your fetus has a very irregular heartbeat. In my opinion your baby will not make it to nine months. You don't want to listen to it."

Ann cried and he waited until she had time to wipe her tears away with a tissue he had ready and recover her composure. His face was emotionless, and his lips were turned down.

"Tranquilizers that will help you cope with the loss. I also have vitamin pills for you."

"Are you sure, Doctor? Charlie will be very upset."

"I'm certain that you will miscarry in the near future when the heart stops beating. If you want, I can do a safe abortion in my clinic, even though it is illegal, since Charlie is my friend"

"Thank you Doctor. I want to think about this and discuss it with Charlie."

After she left the office, she wondered why Doctor K had not let her hear the baby's heart beat. She decided that he did not want to upset her any further.

————

AT HOME, SHE TOLD CHARLIE, and he seemed to take her news calmly. He said that Sam was a fine doctor and that she should take his advice.

"It's all for the best, Ann. We wouldn't want to have to go to the hospital. Arrange the abortion with him." She was used to Charlie not showing much emotion, but she thought he should be more sympathetic. She was not going to give up her baby without a fight.

Ann decided to get another opinion from a doctor Charlie did not know, without telling him. In the telephone book she saw the name of a doctor who had offices in the poorer section of Charleston. She called and arranged an appointment through the receptionist for two days later.

————

DR. GEORGE BRUSH'S CLINIC WAS crowded with patients, both black and white. He was an older doctor with a general practice that handled all sorts of medical conditions.

Ann checked in with the name, "Barb Dell." The receptionist told her to find a seat. She squeezed in between a little black boy and a pregnant white woman who looked like she was ready to deliver twins.

"Hi, my name is Ruth, what's your name?"

"I'm Barb," she said.

"This is your first time here?"

"Yes, I'm new in town."

"Well, you picked a wonderful doctor. He has been in the city for many years, and he lets you pay when you can. I can see that you are pregnant."

Ruth looked at the way Ann was dressed, as if wondering about the expensive clothes. Ann decided to dress down if she came back.

"I'm from out of town. I thought I should dress up in my Sunday go-to-church clothes. I can see that it wasn't necessary, which is great."

"What church do you go to?" Ruth said.

Ann said, "I've attended protestant churches, but I don't have a church here."

"Well my church which is downtown. First Methodist is a beautiful old church with a wonderful new minister. You can call me to go together." She wrote her name and telephone number on a slip of paper from her purse, just as the receptionist called her to see the doctor.

Ann waited for over two hours to see Dr. Brush. The little boy next to her said he had a cut in his finger and showed it to her. His mother smiled at Ann and told her boy to mind his manners. Ann smiled and said it was all right.

When the receptionist called her name, she did not respond at once. The receptionist came over to where she was sitting and directed her to a room in the back of the clinic. She told her to undress and put on a gown. After about fifteen minutes, while she sat reading a two year old National Geographic magazine, Dr. Brush came in and introduced himself.

"Well, Mrs. Dell, I'm told you are several months pregnant. How are you doing?" he asked in a soft, clear voice.

Dr. Brush was a short man with dark black skin, white hair, worry lines on his forehead and creases lining his cheeks. He had a nice smile, and she felt at ease with him. Charlie would be furious if he knew about this, she thought.

Ann paused briefly, as if catching her breath, and then created a story about being unmarried. Dr. Brush asked her to lie down on an examining table and place her feet in the stirrups so he could examine her. He said his nurse, Miss Higgins, who came in as if on cue, would help her.

He listened to the baby's heartbeat and measured her stomach. The vaginal exam was careful and took several minutes. Finally he said, "You're in fine condition with a fetus of about five months."

"How does the baby's heart sound?"

"The heart sounds normal. Here, you can listen."He placed his stethoscope around her neck and in her ears.

Ann listened for a few moments, "Doesn't it sound a little fast to you?"

"No, it's normal for the fetus to have a rapid heartbeat. It sounds very good to me. Your blood pressure and pulse are a little high, and I want you to walk each day and drink lots of water. No drugs of any kind, except aspirin occasionally. You need to be careful how much you eat and avoid coffee and alcohol. If you smoke, I want you to quit for the rest of your pregnancy. I'll want to see you once a month until the eighth month and then every week."

Ann said, "Should I take vitamins?"

"Yes, we will give them to you for free."If there are no problems, I can deliver your baby here in this clinic, which is cheaper, if there are no problems. If there are problems I can deliver your baby in Charleston General. Nurse Higgins will set up the appointments, removing his rubber gloves and discarding them." He smiled, shook her hand, and hurried out.

Ann was shocked and furious at Dr. Kruthmer. He was either incompetent or lying. Ann decided he was lying. She then decided that Charlie had something to do with the lie. She thought, Maybe he did not want a pregnant wife or a baby that was premature. In any event, she was going to have to a way of convincing Charlie to keep the baby alive. She was not going to give it up.

Ann decided that she would be against abortion on religious grounds but would offer to give the baby up for adoption. She would tell Charlie that she wanted to join the First Methodist church and also consult with the minister about a private adoption. Telling him that she had gone to another doctor under an assumed name as an unwed mother was going to be difficult. He would be certain that she could not have another child if she told him she would arrange to have her tubes tied after the birth of the baby.

————

AFTER TELLING CHARLIE THE STORY about having the baby and the adoption, he agreed. He seemed to Ann to be relieved not to have a baby at Steadfast.

"I'm surprised that Dr. Krutmer told you to have an abortion. You should not go outside Steadfast, until you deliver the baby. I will announce that you are having difficulty with the pregnancy and that you spontaneously aborted in the eighth month. Dr. Kruthmer will corroborate the difficulty of the pregnancy. This will produce sympathy for me, and help my nomination for governor."

Ann thought, I am going to have my baby and I am not going to put him up for adoption, even if I have to leave Charlie.

CHAPTER 51

ANN AND CHAS

April 1, 1972

Ann's boy was born about nine months from the date she had sex with Charlie on Mt Hope. Charlie came into Ann's hospital room. He said, "I want to make certain that you have no intention of keeping the baby. I don't want a baby around making noise, crying and taking up your time. I'm not even sure it is mine."

Ann said, "That's nonsense Charlie, he looks just like you, even the smile."

The nurse came in with her baby for breast feeding. At Ann's request, this was the time Charlie was visiting. She said, "I have no intention of giving up my baby. Even if it means our marriage is over."

Charlie stood and stared at the baby.

Ann said. "He's too much a part of us. If I have to, I will go home to Michigan to my family with him." Her maternal instincts were in full force. The baby was sucking vigorously on her nipple.

Ann saw that Charlie was backing down, a confused look on his face

Charlie said, "The baby looks good, except his skin is very red."

"That's the way babies are born Charlie. He has your nose and eyes," she said firmly.

The baby fell asleep.

"Do you want to hold him?" She held the baby out to him.

"I don't know how to hold him. I might injure him."

"Just cradle him in your arms and support his neck."

Charlie lifted the baby and held him close. He said, "I'm surprised how tiny he is." Just then the baby opened his eyes and seemed to smile at Charlie.

"I've thought of calling him Chas. What do you think Charlie?"

In a reversal Charlie said, "I don't want to lose you Ann. I am enjoying holding him. I trust and love you."

Ann said,"Thank you Charlie. We will have a great marriage."

With a catch in his throat he said, "I want to keep him. I need an heir to pass on the business to anyway. I like the name Chas."

The nurse took Chas to the nursery.

Ann said,"Come over and kiss me."

He came over and kissed her and then cuddled up to her on the bed.

———————

WHEN THEY LEFT THE HOSPITAL the next day, Charlie carried Chas, and an orderly pushed Ann in a wheelchair. In his limousine, driven by a new man, named Alfred, Charlie sat in the back seat with Chas, holding him.

For the next weeks Charlie spent a lot of time taking care of Chas. He even changed diapers and talked baby talk to him.

A shower was planned for Ann and the baby. All of their women friends came to see Chas. They remarked how handsome he was, like Charlie. The gifts were enough to keep Chas in clothes for months. Evelyn Wallenby did not attend although she was invited. Ann dismissed this as pique.

Ann was very happy and her hormones told her that she wanted to make love to Charlie again. This time, she went on birth control pills so she wouldn't become pregnant again. She could not bring herself to have her tubes tied. I don't want to risk a problem with Charlie by getting pregnant ever again, she thought.

Charlie told her of his plans to teach Chas about hunting

and sports. He sat in front of the television set and explained baseball to Chas as he made gurgling noises.

Ann heard Charlie say to Chas, "You are my heir, I will teach you to be as tough as me." Ann shuddered at the thought of Chas being as mean as Charlie.

CHAPTER 52

THE RUNOFF

On Mt. Hope, Webber watched the rainwater gush down the slopes, sending coal tailings into Deep River. Webber's company did not make any effort to trap the tailings from washing the coal down in the valley. The tailings were just coal dust. As far as Webber was concerned, trapping the tailings was too expensive for the inconsequential amount of sediment going into the River.

Webber fired an overly careful assay firm, which listed the mercury content of the coal, as the highest in the country. Mercury was not required to be reported by the state and Federal governments. It occurred in very small amounts and was not considered a health hazard. The assay firm reported that mercury in high doses could produce brain damage, referred to as Mad Hatter's Disease. The report further said that there was evidence that mercury in tailings could be polluting the rivers and end up in the fish. It suggested that the tailings could also be responsible for other diseases.

Webber told them to destroy every copy of the report, and based on their fear of Webber, they did. Webber also verbally warned the other members of the Coal Mine Operators Association, at their next meeting, not to report on the mercury content of their coal.

At the meeting, Webber said," Earthen dams are trapping tailings in a huge ponds. There could be a disaster if a dam fails." They ignored his advice.

As far as Charlie was concerned, a dam was too expensive for the amount of coal tailings going into Deep River and then drained into Deep Lake. The tailings just settled at the bottom of Deep Lake where, in his mind, they would cause no harm. Webber knew the mercury was bound up in the coal tailings as mercury pyrite, which did not dissolve in the water.

"My summer home, Respite, is on Deep Lake. It does not show the coal sediment on the surface and the water looks clean. "I swim in the lake, and I have eaten the fish I catch all of my life, as did the children of my employees, their relatives and other homeowners on the lake. We are all in good health."

He thought, My family had been mining in West Virginia this way for over one hundred and fifty years. I am not going to change the way I do business because of traces of a metal that concerns nobody but the environmentalists. If by some remote chance, a few mammals, birds or fish are poisoned, that is just the price of doing business.

People had always died from coal mining. Cave-ins, black-lung disease and poverty were historically a part of the miner's daily life. That coal mining was harmful to people was of little consequence to Webber. After all, he paid for their funerals and provided a suitable headstone of polished granite. The undertakers and the firms who carved the monuments were more than happy to provide a volume discount, since the business from Webber Mining was consistent year after year.

New coal mining companies that took care of their miners by providing health and life insurance benefits did not remain in business very long because of the Association. Equipment failed, explosions happened and workers died, and all because a new company did not want to adopt the established business practices. Association members stuck together to make things happen their way.

At a steak and corn whiskey dinner, fellow mine operator, Bob Plant, had the right philosophy, Webber thought. Plant said, "Coal is what drives the engine which is West Virginia. Above all else, we have to continue to power that engine." Plant, with a nondescript pudgy face and body and a snub nose, was also out to get as much money from his mines as possible, without regard to the workers.

They drank toasts to the huge annual profits they made from ripping the coal out of the mountains and leaving a giant hole. They toasted Charlie for handling the donations to the politicians.

Someday West Virginia will erect a statue of Plant with his motto, Webber thought. Charlie decided this was a really good idea for favorable publicity, and he would raise the matter at the next Association meeting.

CHAPTER 53

THE TEENAGER

May 1972

John arranged to visit the small town of Treadwell near Deep Lake. Webber's friend Frank Lester shared the name of the boy's parents, McLeans, and how to find their cabin. Lester located their home through the Prosecutor, Bob Harrington, whom John had met when they visited the man with the fighting roosters. To allay any suspicion, John told Lester that he wanted to help the boy get some medical attention as a charitable gesture.

Old worn blue jeans and a red flannel shirt that had seen better days seemed appropriate to John for visiting the family. He wore his scraped and battered hiking boots and a denim hiking jacket, which was faded to gray from multiple washings and exposure to the elements. John drove his car to Tredwell. At John's request, Harrington, who lived in Treadwell, accompanied him to visit the boy's parents.

"These people do not take kindly to strangers," Harrington said, as they drove near the town of Treadwell in his ten-year-old Jeep mud spattered and tired looking. "They are very proud and independent, even though they are poor. They believe that every word in the Bible is true. You have to make treating Billy appear to be a mission of yours."

When they arrived, John saw that the McLeans lived in a wood shack with a metal roof. It looked as if it would blow away in a strong wind from a summer storm. They were sitting on their front porch waiting for John and Harrington, dressed in their Sunday best.

Mrs. McLean was in a rocking chair, moving back and forth and holding an old Bible. After introductions, they exchanged pleasantries about the fine weather. To John she looked like a Norman Rockwell painting of an elderly woman; the wrinkles in her face were deeply grooved, as if she had lived a hard life.

"Lawyer Gooding has visited to see if he can help your son, Billy. John saw him running naked in the woods last summer, and he is moved to try to help him," Harrington said.

"We don't have much to do with lawyers, Mr. Harrington, but we are willing to listen because we know who you are," Mr. McLean replied.

John said, "I want to help Billy, and possibly any others around Deep Lake, to find out what is wrong with him. I have been praying on the matter for the last year and feel called to help."

"Are you a Christian man, Mr. Gooding?" asked Mrs. McLean.

"Yes ma'am, I belong to the Methodist church in Charleston and I am a Protestant and a Christian man," John said. He thought, I haven't been to church in years. It is fortunate I'm not a Catholic.

"Do you believe in Creationism?" Mr. Mclean asked.

John recognized that this was a critical question and answered, "I believe the bible says the truth." He thought, That is, the truth that the writers of Genesis believed.

"How do you figure you can help our son, Mr. Gooding, when nobody has been successful in the past? We believe that the devil has gotten into Billy," Mr. McLean bluntly stated.

"I believe that your son is afflicted by a particular kind of poison from the fish in Deep Lake. It is possible this poison might be washed out of his system. I will pay all of the costs for the clinic. Both of you can stay with him during his treatments. I promise you that nothing will be done to Billy without your approval. I would like to meet Billy, assuming you give me your approval."

"He is down by the lake fishing as he does every day. I cook the bass from Deep Lake for him, which is all he really likes to eat except for my bread and pies."

Mr. McLean reached over to a side table and put an old military bugle from World War I to his lips. The sound echoed off the forest around the cabin.

"He'll be here shortly. He will be naked. Don't make nothing of it," Mr. McLean said.

When Billy came home, his mother draped a sheet around his naked body, which was covered with sores. She said, "That helps keep flies off the sores. When they are bad, he has to wear it in the woods." The sheet made him appear like a ghost.

Billy's father introduced John and Harrington formally. "This is Prosecutor Harrington and his friend Lawyer Gooding, who want to get doctoring for your disease."

"Billy has had some home schooling and he is a quick learner," Mrs. McLean shared with pride in her voice. "He is not an ignorant boy. A retired teacher from down the road taught Billy reading, writing, and arithmetic until she passed away."

Both John and Harrington shook hands with Billy as he trembled under the sheet. Billy was about eighteen years old with long brown hair and brown eyes like a deer. In a different setting and dressed, he would have been described as good looking.

John said, "I would like to arrange to have some doctors in Charleston examine you to see if they have a treatment that can help you get rid of your sores."

Billy said, "I believe I am possessed by the Evil One and nobody but Jesus can help me."

John said, "Billy, I believe you have a poison in your body from the fish in Deep Lake that is causing your sores. Do you go naked for a reason?"

"Clothes make my skin itch so badly, I can hardly stand it. My bed is covered with sheepskin fleece which is all that I can sleep on."

In the end, Billy and his parents agreed to accompany John to the clinic. At dinner with Harrington, John said, "Hopefully Billy can be cured."

CHAPTER 54

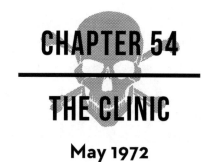

THE CLINIC

May 1972

The next day John drove Billy and his parents to an appointment at the West Virginia Children's Clinic in Charleston. They brought some clothing. Billy brought a guitar and told John that he played and sang on occasion.

Renowned for high-quality medical care, the clinic was established by the state legislature. Numerous businesses supported it, including a few thousand dollars from the Coal Mine Owners Association.

Doctor Ronald Richards was Chief of staff and he greeted them at the lounge. The welcome seemed to John to be more apropos of a private hospital for wealthy patients. Richards shook hands with Billy, his parents and then John.

Dr Richards examined Billy in one of several examining rooms adjacent to the lobby, with Billy's parents and John watching. He said, "Well, Billy, I hope we can cure you. We're going to try to discover what is causing your skin condition. You'll need to stay here in the clinic for a couple of weeks for tests."

"We are going to draw blood from you. We will take X-ray pictures of the inside of your body. We will extract some bone marrow from your hip to see if bad cells are there. Your colon and your stomach will be examined to make sure they are in good shape. When we have completed the tests, we will explain the results to your parents and you as well as to Mr. Gooding, with your permission. His firm is paying for all of these tests. Nothing will be done which is painful or will cause you discomfort, without my telling you beforehand. Is this all right?"

Billy and his parents agreed. They gave permission for John to get the results as well.

Dr. Richards talked about the weeping lesions all over Billy's body. He said,"Billy must have had this disease for a long time."

"Those sores began many years ago," Mr. McLean said.

Billy asked a lot of questions about the tests, and each time, Dr. Richards explained in detail. Billy's parents only asked if all of the tests were needed. Dr. Richards said, "Yes, certainly."

Dr. Richards reassured Billy that pain medication would be administered when necessary. He told his parents that he would not treat Billy for the disease without their permission.

————

AFTERWARDS, JANE TOOK BILLY SHOPPING for inexpensive clothing. She bought clothes that were loose fitting to reduce the irritation of his skin.

Billy said, "I know I have to keep my clothes on here. I've read about large cities and the people who live there."

John arranged for Billy and his parents to stay at a Howard Johnson's hotel near the clinic. There was a restaurant for their meals.

Billy's parents had never eaten in a big city restaurant. They were uncomfortable being waited on by a waitress in uniform. Billy, on the other hand, was at ease and talked to the waitress, who was only a year or so older than him.

While Billy was not undergoing tests, Jane took a day off to show Billy and his parents the sights in the city. They were awed by the Capitol building, which Jane told them resembled the one in Washington. They watched airplanes take off from the West Virginia airport, turboprops screaming.

Jane said," Maybe you will be able to fly on one."

Billy's parents replied, "We will never get on one of them. If God wanted us to fly he would have given us wings."

Billy on the other hand said, "That would be great fun."

————

AT THE END OF THE second week, Dr. Richards met with Billy and his parents. He was not smiling.

"I am sorry to have to tell you, Billy, that you have mercury poisoning. Mercury is in your blood and the cells of your body, which is causing your disease. Currently there is no known effective treatment for your disease. There is an experimental treatment called 'chelation therapy', which might be partially effective, but it will be impossible to totally remove the mercury from your body because it is in your tissues. I can give you some drugs to make you feel better and reduce the itching."

With tears streaming down her cheek, Mrs. McLean said,"That is terrible news. How did this happen?"

"It's likely that the mercury is from the fish in Deep Lake. John showed me an analysis of the fish in the lake and in the river where you live. The fish in Deep Lake contain high levels of mercury and Billy has been eating them for a long time. The one thing that is clear is that all of you have to stop eating the fish."

Billy said, "If I can't eat the fish I catch from Deep Lake, I'll starve. My father can't work in the mines, because he was injured in a mine accident at Webber's mine. There are no jobs for women in the mountains. I can't do anything but sing mountain songs and play the guitar a little. Treadwell hosts performances twice a year where I perform for free."

John said, "I'll arrange an account for you at the local store so you can buy fish and other staples. You can stay in Charleston until we develop a plan."

The McLeans and Billy, with long faces, thanked John. They wanted to know why he would do all of this for them.

"I want to start a lawsuit on Billy's behalf against Webber Mining and Charlie Webber personally for damages because of Billy's condition. I expect there are other people on the lake who have mercury poisoning."

Mr. McLean said, "If this is Webber's fault, damn him to Hell." He stood in a posture like a boxer with his fists closed as if to strike Webber. That man hurts everybody who comes into contact with his doings."

Billy said, "If Charlie Webber is responsible for my being the way I am, I want him punished."

Mrs. McLean said, "Remember father, we should turn the other cheek. You should not get so riled up. You might have a heart attack. We know Webber is a very dangerous man. He might stomp on us."

Billy said, "We know what Charlie Webber will do to people who cross him. They end up missing."

John said, "I'm going to arrange for publication of an article in the *Charleston Gazette* after the lawsuit is filed. This should stop Webber from attacking you, because the publicity will point to him as being the culprit.

"The pleadings we prepared will be filed tomorrow. I have asked the judge for an injunction against any representative of Webber Mining coming anywhere near any of you."

Obviously afraid, the McLeans agreed. Mrs. McLean said, "It sounds like Billy is dying from the mercury. I want Webber to be punished for that."

Billy asked, "How long will I live, Dr. Richards?"

"Billy, I guess you will have six months to a year without treatment. The mercury will affect your mind. This type of poisoning is fairly rare, based upon the readings of published reports, only a few people in the world have been exposed in the way you have. I'm going to learn more about a treatment which will wash at least some of the mercury out of you."

John said," Dr. Richards will do all he can for you."

Dr. Richards said, "We will admit him tomorrow afternoon into the hospital."

————

AT THE HOTEL WITH THE McLeans and John, Jane asked Billy to play the guitar for them. He played songs that laid bare the hardships of living in the Appalachian Mountains. He sang in a beautiful, clear tenor voice. They could feel his pain in his singing. Afterwards, they ate dinner there. Billy ate salmon from the Pacific coast and said it was better than the bass.

CHAPTER 55

THE LAWSUIT

The next day, John filed the legal pleadings in court, seeking damages for personal injury to Billy McLean in excess of one million dollars. He served Charlie's attorney, Rex Reed, by taking it to his office. Within half a day, he heard from Reed by telephone.

Reed's language was filled with expletives and anger. However, the clear suggestion was that if the lawsuit was suppressed, a settlement could be made. Reed said, "After all, how much is the life of a deranged, asshole hillbilly boy really worth?" He offered twenty-five thousand dollars to make the lawsuit disappear, without admitting fault and with a secrecy order against any disclosure of the details of the settlement.

John said, "I'll convey the offer to my client and let you know." He thought, Not nearly enough.

Reed said, "This is a lot of money. If your client refuses, we will fight until your firm has so much time invested, you will not be able to financially afford the lawsuit."

John knew this was no idle threat. John said, "There will be a lot of bad publicity for Webber. Others may have mercury poisoning."

Reed said, "The public has a very short memory and they will lose interest in Billy's problem quickly," as if he was hoping John was bought off in a settlement.

AT THE MOTEL JOHN TOLD Billy and his parents about the offer from Reed.

"What do you think we should do Mr. Gooding?" Billy asked.

John paused and replied tentatively, "This is a very small amount of money for you and for your parents. After our out-of-pocket expenses and fees, it would leave you with about twenty thousand dollars. This offer does not begin to compensate you for your illness and shortening your life. I recommend that we proceed with the lawsuit." John did not concern them by disclosing the threat to the firm.

Just then, Jane entered the room with tears in her eyes and said, "I've got some very bad news. I just heard by telephone from friends in Treadwell that the McLean's home was burned down by unknown vandals. Everything is gone. I talked to the sheriff and he said there was no way to determine who did it. Probably this was on Webber's orders, but we could never prove it. There were empty kerosene cans around the house and a burning cross."

John said, "Now we don't have any choice about going forward with the lawsuit for Billy. We'll find an apartment to rent for all of you. It isn't safe for you to go back to Treadwell."

Jane stayed with the McLean family at the motel until early morning, consoling them for their losses. John went back to his apartment and went to bed. Sleep eluded him, because of worry about how nasty the lawsuit would become.

In the middle of the night, he heard glass breaking in the living room. He grabbed his .45 Colt from the nightstand and went downstairs with the pistol at the ready. He found a wooden cross on the carpet smeared with blood. He thought, A visit from the goons who destroyed the McLeans' home.

John knew then that he made the right recommendation about continuing the lawsuit. However, the reaction from Webber and the Klan was very violent, including death threats by telephone. He was apprehensive about where this might lead and fell asleep dreaming about the attack in Saigon City.

CHAPTER 56

CHARLIE AND THE LAWSUIT

June 1972

When Charlie read the pleadings filed by John Gooding, which Reed delivered to him in person in the library at Steadfast, his eyes narrowed in hate and he said, "I'm going to get that bastard Gooding and the McLean family for this. Nobody can file a lawsuit against me and get away with it. The publicity ends my chance to run for governor this year."

Reed said, "Charlie, we might be able to win this lawsuit if you don't do anything rash. However, if persons unknown to you do something without your awareness because of publicity on the TV or in the *Charleston Gazette*, it's not your fault. I suggest you prepare a written statement describing your surprise and shock about the unfounded allegations against you. You can state that you will do everything to protect your good name."

"Okay, but what is my defense against the lawsuit?"

"You can say that you didn't know anything about mercury in the fish or how it got there. That would go a long way with a jury. Secondly, Billy McLean may be a special case, born with a birth defect that caused him to pick up the mercury in his system. Finally, we can say it was an act of God or Nature, unpredictable and, thus, excusable. Your reputation will go a long way in swaying the jury to your way of thinking. Juries in West Virginia are sympathetic to the mining companies since many of the panels depend on coal mining for their living. We can get experts who will say anything for money."

"Well, I did know mercury was bound up in the coal, but I had no reason to believe it would hurt anyone. I have no idea how the mercury got into the fish. Hell, I have eaten the fish from Deep Lake, almost from the time I was born, and nothing has happened to me."

"Charlie, I suggest that you change your story and say that you did not know mercury was in the coal. Did you ever test for it?"

"I learned from a report a year ago, which was not requested, that mercury was in the coal tailings. I told the firm that conducted the study to destroy all copies of the report. They gave me a new one which did not indicate mercury. They confirmed verbally that they did as I requested so no reports of mercury in coal."

"Can you safely say that you didn't know about the mercury?" Reed said.

"Yes, I can say that."

"Gooding is going to claim that you should have known about it. Do you know of other coal firms that test for it?"

"No! Nobody thought it was important to test for trace elements. Lots of other trace elements are present in the coal. How should I know what effect one might have on somebody like Billy McLean? I understand that he was different from birth. Probably he has a genetic defect. These mountain folk intermarry with relatives and have incestuous relationships with their children. I wouldn't be surprised to learn that was Billy's problem."

Reed smiled as he assured Charlie they would teach Gooding and his client a lesson that they would not easily forget. Charlie felt calmer.

After Reed left, Charlie telephoned Sheriff Mackey in Treadwell and informed him of the lawsuit. Charlie said, "I need help locating information for the lawsuit and finding witnesses around Deep Lake in my favor." For years Webber gave Mackey money to ensure he was elected.

Charlie knew that the sheriff could not keep a secret and

drank at the local bar in Treadwell every night. Within twelve hours, everybody in Treadwell would know about the lawsuit including his fellow clan members. It will not be safe for the McLean family to live in that town ever again, he thought with some satisfaction.

Within hours, Charlie heard that the Mclean home had been torched to the ground.

————

CHARLIE TOLD ANN ABOUT THE lawsuit. She said, "It is just like John to take on an unwinnable case like Billy McLean's. So, Charlie, what do you know about the mercury? Are we at risk from eating the fish?"

"The lawsuit is completely frivolous, but we are through eating the fish from Deep Lake to be safe. There is no chance that my company or I have done anything wrong. I was interviewed by the Charleston newspaper about the lawsuit and said we expect to win it."

Ann said, "Maybe Reed can teach John a lesson about the law he should have learned a long time ago."

She kissed him on the lips and he felt the tension leave his body. She did wonder, Where's this going to lead?

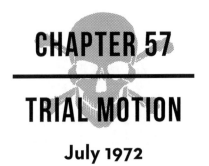

CHAPTER 57

TRIAL MOTION

July 1972

A motion for summary judgment for failure to state a cause of action was filed by Reed. The motion was heard before Judge Gene Hand in state Court in Charleston.

Jake, as senior partner and co-counsel, was present to move John's admission to court. He was admitted in front of Judge Hand who welcomed him to the court bar.

"Without further interruption," Judge Hand said, "I've read the briefs in this matter and the purpose of this hearing is to determine the likelihood of success of this case on the merits. You can proceed with your motion, Mr. Reed."

"Thank you, Your Honor. I brought this motion before the court because the pleadings fail to state a claim upon which relief can be granted. Even assuming that mercury in the coal caused the plaintiff's disease, it could not have been caused by the defendant. The hand of God produced the coal which is mined."

Reed explained the history of coal in West Virginia and its importance to the local economy.

"Can you explain how the mercury came to be in Mr. McLean's body?" Judge Hand asked.

"We have no idea, Your Honor," Reed said.

"Thank you Mr. Reed. Mr. Gooding?"

"Thank you, Your Honor. We are prepared to prove that the fish in Deep River and Deep Lake contain large amounts of mercury in an organic form, which is retained in the body of anybody who eats the fish. Further, we are prepared to show that the waters of Deep River and Deep Lake contain large amounts of washed out coal tailings from Webber's mining. These tailings contain significant amounts of mercury and were put there my Mr. Webber's hand and not God's hand. If the coal wasn't mined, the poisoning of Billy McLean would not have happened.

"We are also prepared to show that the waters of Deep Lake have become more acidic from the coal-burning smoke pouring out of the smoke stacks of the coal powered plant in Charleston, a fact that has been known for many years. Common knowledge in the scientific community is that the acidic waters leach the mercury from the tailings. The water used for washing the tailings from the coal drains into the Deep River and Deep Lake."

"What is your view of the legal standard for liability in this matter?" Judge Hand asked.

John replied, "Established law is that when a food product is contaminated, strict liability is invoked. In our view it does not make any difference that the fish are a wild animal, since it is well-known that people eat the fish from Deep River and Deep Lake. Even so, our view is that there is also the negligence in this case, so gross that there should be strict liability. Finally this case creates concerns for anybody who has eaten fish from Deep Lake. Thank you, your Honor."

"Mr. Reed, any rebuttal?"

Reed stood up at defendant's table, "Yes, Your Honor." Mr. Webber's family has been following standard coal practices for the last one hundred and fifty years, except he has started to strip the coal off the top of the mountains for reasons of economy and safety of our workers. Mr. Webber was unaware of any mercury in his coal."

Judge Hand asked Reed to sit down. "My intention is not to rule on this matter from the bench at this time. From what I have heard, the alleged facts need to be proven in order to provide a basis for strict liability or some form of gross negligence. The law in this matter needs to be fully briefed after we have heard the evidence at trial."

Judge Hand continued, "The motion for summary judgment is denied without prejudice to later presentation again during the trial in light of the plaintiff's proofs. A high burden of proof is required in this case.

"Because of the public interest in the safety issue, I want a speedy trial. I will give you two months for discovery and a month before the trial for further motions. The trial briefs are due in three months. You will provide a witness list and an agreed-upon list of documents to be presented at trial. We will go to trial with the jury in four months from today. I want depositions in my hands within two weeks of their being taken. I can tell you gentlemen that I will not stand for any dilatory tactics in this matter. This hearing is ended."

Judge Hand stood and left the bench. The attorneys and people in the court gallery sat in silence, stunned by the speed at which the case was going to proceed. Usually cases took at least two years to bring to trial.

John heard muttering amongst the attorneys sitting in court, concerned that a speedy trial was also the way their cases were going to go. John thought, They prefer to drag cases out for years.

Reed motioned to John as if he wanted to talk to him. "Boy, this is your lucky day. Charlie has authorized me to offer one hundred and fifty thousand plus medical expenses to settle this case. The only condition is that the record so far be suppressed, to be opened only by order of the court or by an agreement of the parties."

John said, "I'll talk to my client and get back to you."

"You have twenty-four hours to decide. I need to know by noon tomorrow."

Reed turned and left. John would have loved to hear Reed's conversation with Charlie Webber about the result of the motion. He didn't want to accept the offer, but it was a lot of money for the McLeans. John suspected that others besides Webber wanted him to settle. He thought, Fellow members of the CMOA are probably very nervous about this case.

John saw a reporter from the *Charleston Gazette* in the

courtroom listening to the arguments. A small bodied man with steel rim glasses, Wolf was known for in depth reporting on cases involving personal injuries from mining coal. John knew the CMOA would be a powerful influence against any story about the case in the paper.

John was surprised when the Gazette published the article.

Mercury Poisoning

Mercury is one of the elements which everybody knows a little something about since it is used by dentists and oral surgeons often filling cavities. As kids we used to take mercury from the dentist or glass thermometers and rub it onto silver dimes to make them shiny. We allowed our skin to come into contact with the mercury and later learned that the silvery metal could be absorbed through our skin and end up in our body. I have learned that this metal is toxic.

It has been found that fish can contain large amounts of mercury as an organic compound which accumulates in their fat. I wanted to know what damage mercury could cause in the human body.

There is a disease called "Mad Hatter's" caused by mercury metal. In the early 1800's, the makers of felt top hats, who used the mercury metal to brush the felt, contracted this disease.

I learned this week that mercury occurs in coal and can end up in wild fish which are caught and eaten.

It is of public interest to know that a lawsuit has been filed in State Court in Charleston alleging that mercury poisoning from eating fish in Deep Lake, one of our lakes that receives coal tailings from Webber Mining as a result of strip mining.

We will discover whether this is a danger to us, as the case progresses to trial. This reporter understands that an offer of settlement has been made."

Against Jake's advice, the offer of settlement was rejected by Billy's parents, in part because of the burning of their home. They also wanted to go to trial because their friends and neighbors, who ate the fish from Deep Lake, were also poisoned.

John was pleased with this decision. He thought, Webber is going to pay a lot more than the offer.

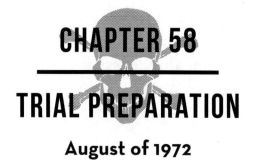

CHAPTER 58

TRIAL PREPARATION

August of 1972

As John began to prepare the McLean case for trial, he worried that a lot more residents around Deep Lake might be poisoned the mercury in the fish. Based upon the recent tests, Deep Lake was becoming increasingly acidic from the coal burning at West Virginia Power and the mercury levels in the fish were going up.

To understand how this was happening, John hired Dr. Andrew Bork, a nationally recognized environmental chemist from the University of West Virginia, to conduct research on the air quality above Deep Lake.

Dr. Bork reported after only a month of study. He said, "Because of weather patterns, the acidic fumes from smokestack emissions from the coal-fired power plant in Charleston are descending into Deep Lake. The distance and prevailing winds are just right to cause the emissions to settle into the lake. Anybody eating the fish is at risk of being poisoned. Even newborn children from mothers eating the fish could be poisoned in the womb."

John asked an out-of-state environmental lab to verify the findings, and the results were the same.

John met with his partners and associates in the library to discuss the test results. Everyone was stunned into silence for a few minutes.

Finally, Jason Mayfield asked, "John, do we have any eminent medical doctors who will testify in court that the effect of mercury in humans from the coal tailings is so bad? After all, the health risk of mercury has been known for well over a century."

John said, "Billy's doctor is willing to testify about Billy's disease, but I am uncertain how much further he will go in asserting mass poisoning of the population around Deep Lake. I think that would require a well- known medical expert in the field. It would require tissue samples from all of those possibly infected."

Jake Masters said, "How is this testing going to help us with Billy's case? After all he is our client. We know with a high degree of certainty that he has been poisoned. Our first ethical duty is to him as our client. It seems to me that other possible poisonings are tangential to his case."

Jason said, "This is a problem for the National Institute of Health or the Environmental Protection Agency."

John said, "It is very unlikely that either agency will consider taking on Webber Mining. I suspect Charlie Webber has been bribing their representatives into silence about any problems with strip mining coal for years. There is no currently proven direct link between coal burning and coal mining with mercury poisoning."

"Don't we have some duty to the public in this matter?" Jane asked. There was only the ticking of a clock in the room for a minute.

Jason replied, "Jane, I would like you to research the law on that question from a legal ethics point of view and get back to us next week."

Jane agreed, and after some further discussion, the meeting adjourned.

John and Jane remained behind to discuss her legal research. It had been a long awhile since John had sex and he became excited by Jane's perfume as she sat next to him. He thought, I don't want to say anything that might offend her. He could feel his body warm and he tried to think only about the McLean case, unsuccessfully.

Jane said, "John would you like to come over for supper tonight? I have some stew cooking, and I can make a salad."

"That would be terrific. I'll bring some wine."

To be fair to Jane, John told her of his experience with Webber and Ann on Deep Lake. Ann's infidelity with Webber was a major cause of my divorce."

Jane said, "That was an awful experience, but I'm glad that you are with the firm now."

With a smile, John said, "I am happy to be here with you today. I like being here with you."

Jane said, "Let's finish this quickly."

John was smiling as he said, "My thought is that we have an ethical duty to do the best for our client. A moral question is not our job. So far, Billy is the only one we know of showing symptoms of mercury poisoning, but it is possible that a number of people have died or are sick. If we stir up other lawsuits now, we would dilute our chance for recovering substantial damages for Billy."

Jane said, "If we settled Billy's case, we could then go after Webber in a class-action suit for the other people who were poisoned and for decreased land values. We might include Lester and his wife, as the plaintiffs in a later lawsuit. Once they understand what Webber has done to the value of their cottage."

John said, "We need to win Billy's lawsuit first." Jane agreed.

It was approaching dinner time and they left for Jane's apartment.

––––––––

THE AROMA OF THE BEEF stew in the crock pot filled her apartment. "I have made enough for six days," she said laughing as she put some French bread in the oven with garlic and butter to bake. Dinner was ready in minutes.

When they sat down for dinner, Jane said grace while they held hands. She said, "It is a tradition in my family". John held onto her hand for a few seconds longer after grace was finished.

As they talked during dinner it was obvious to John that she had a very romantic interest in him. She touched his hand as she talked about their earlier lives.

Jane said, "I've never been married. I have been asked several times. Never found someone I wanted to spend my life with," she said. Her eyes had a twinkle in them.

"I'm glad you didn't accept," John said. He leaned over and kissed her on the lips. She returned the kiss.

They stood and she put her arms around his waist. John said, "My divorce is done, but I realize complications could arise in the office, because you are our associate. You may not want to keep going."

"John, you don't have to think like a lawyer all the time." She kissed him again.

Finally, John told her about the rock thrown through his window and the threats that might turn towards her.

She said, "That doesn't make any difference to me. I'm willing to take the risk." Jane leaned in and kissed him with her body molded to him.

John hardened as he strained against her. She did not pull away.

John said, "I want to stay with you all night. I want to feel your naked body next to me." She nodded her head in agreement. They went into the bedroom, undressed and made love. Hours later they were dozing off to sleep about midnight, they heard a gunshot.

CHAPTER 59

THE WATCHER

August 1972

Max Mull shifted his weight on his feet as he waited for John Gooding to leave the apartment of the woman lawyer. He bit off the end of his cigar and lit it with his lighter. He thought, This business of being a private detective is just plain boring. Occasionally he had clashes with the targets after they had been caught with their peckers in the wrong place, which was exciting.

Mainly Mull investigated spouses who were cheating, primarily representing women who wanted to trap wayward husbands for more money in a divorce. Tonight was different, since Gooding and Seymore were both unmarried lawyers. Not having a specific reason for the surveillance made him uneasy and alert. When he felt that way, the hairs on the back of his neck stood up, like now.

He hoped it was not going to be a long night, since it was beginning to rain. Pulling down his baseball cap, he tilted his head forward so the drizzle dripped away from his face. He thought, At least I remembered to bring plastic rain gear. It was rolled up in his pocket. He could not use the hood for fear it would block his view.

Mull also did not know who his client was or the reason for watching Gooding. A representative of his unknown client had called and outlined the investigation. The money for his fee for two weeks in advance was delivered by courier. Then he had thought it would be easy money, but now he wasn't so sure.

The *Charleston Gazette* published an article about John Gooding filing suit against Charlie Webber for mercury poisoning of a young man named McLean. He wondered whether his present investigation was in any way related. He knew Webber was a pal of Senator Wallenby, as a result of a recent investigation for Evelyn Wallenby, wife of the senator. He had photographed the senator having sex with a woman who was not his wife and testified in the divorce trial, which resulted in a fortune being awarded Mrs. Wallenby.

Mull didn't want to be representing Webber. People disappeared, never to be heard from again when they crossed Webber. He decided to return his fee for this investigation and walk away from. He turned to leave.

Over the sound of the rain, he heard the double click of the hammer of a single action revolver and he felt the muzzle against the back of his head. He heard, "This is for Wallenby." As he started to turn his head, the last sound he heard was the firing pin hitting the primer on the cartridge.

————

JOHN AND JANE WERE STARTLED awake by the gunshot. John climbed out of bed, dressed, and went to investigate. He found a body on the ground across the street. He bent over the body and saw a large hole in the head of the victim. He heard a sound and a man's voice say, "Your firm is next if you don't settle Billy's lawsuit." John was hit on the head, saw stars and blacked out.

————

WHEN JOHN DIDN'T RETURN RIGHT away, Jane ran out into the street dressed in her robe. She found John on the ground alive and the body of another man dead from a headshot. John was unconscious and covered with blood, bleeding from the back of his head. She screamed for a bystander to call the police and an ambulance. He said they were called. As she cradled John's head, his wound bled onto her lap, but he woke up.

Sirens blared and lights flashed as the police arrived. He overheard Jane explaining what she had heard to a policeman, a man who looked like a bulldog with crew cut hair. A police technician started photographing the scene, including Jane and John. The policeman asked John if he needed to go to the hospital.

John said, "No, I'm okay," and related the facts about what had happened, except for the verbal threat.

The policeman said, "I'm a homicide detective. According to a license in the corpse's billfold, the deceased was a private detective named, Max Mull." He showed John the license with a picture.

John said, "I've never seen or met him. The face of the corpse is too disfigured to be recognizable."

Jane confirmed John's story about the gunshot and the detective said they could go back to their apartment and get out of the rain. He wrote down their home and office addresses in his notebook.

While the detective was speaking to John and Jane, the local television crew was filming them and the detective near the corpse. John thought, The crew arrived so fast, as if they knew about what had happened before the killing. In any event, this publicity is going to be very embarrassing to the

An ambulance EMT cleaned and bandaged his head. Then, Jane helped John back to her apartment and then into her bed after a shower. She kissed him and he pulled her down beside him.

Smiling, he said, "You will have to be gentle with me."

She said, "You won't feel any pain."

After they made love again, he thought, She was certainly right. He fell asleep with Jane's naked body beside him.

———

IN THE MORNING, THEY DRESSED and had breakfasted together.

John said, "I want to keep seeing you. However, I think last night was a message for me about how serious Charlie Webber or one of his friends are about my dropping the case against him. I don't want you to become involved and risk something happening to you."

"I'm not afraid, John."

They left in John's car for the office.

When they arrived, the staff was reading the morning newspaper. John was given a copy by his secretary. The headline read:

PRIVATE DETECTIVE KILLED. Last night Max Mull died of a gunshot wound to the back of his head at about 11:00 P.M. Hearing the gunshot, attorney John Gooding of the firm of law firm of Mayfield and Masters, rushed from an apartment where he was visiting with Jane Seymore, a law associate of the firm. The associate heard a second gunshot and ran from the apartment to discover both Mr. Mull and Mr. Gooding on the ground, having been hit on the head by the murderer. Mr. Mull was dead." He skipped the rest.

The morning TV news was even more embarrassing to John and to Jane dressed in her robe. The camera crew had camped on the apartment footsteps all night, waiting for an interview with John.

As they came out of the building in the morning, a reporter asked him questions. His only response was, "No comment." All of this was filmed.

Both Jake and Jason said he should stop seeing Jane until the McLean case was tried, since he was also a target of the attacker, who was probably Webber. They also said Jane could be killed.

John said,"I have no intention of letting Webber or the firm interfere with my personal life," but he did not stay at Jane's apartment again.

CHAPTER 60

OFFERS

August 1972

A few weeks later, John received an offer of two hundred and fifty thousand dollars from Reed for Billy and he immediately informed Jason and Jake as well as Mr. and Mrs. McLean and Billy.

Jake said, "The offer is fair, considering that we have a very difficult case."

John said he was eager to try the case and wanted to reject the offer.

Jason's opinion was that a white jury would likely side with Webber Mining and Charlie Webber. Jason agreed with Jake.

Jason said, "It is likely that a jury will be mostly white men and at least some of them will be Klan members. We believe Charlie Webber is a leader in the Klan. Certainly the Klan will try to intimidate the jury to vote in Webber's favor. I don't see how we can win on the facts so far. We don't even know whether or not the Judge is a Klan member. The family is thinking about the offer and they are in the waiting room."

———————

THE MCLEANS WERE USHERED INTO the library where Jake, Jason, and John were waiting. All of the lawyers greeted them them warmly before they sat down.

Jason reviewed the case again for them, pointing out the firm's fee was one quarter of the amount of the settlement, which

would net them about one hundred and eighty thousand dollars.
"I recommend that you accept the offer."

Mr. McLean said, "I am a lifetime member of the Klan. I don't
think Webber can use the Klan against me. You guys have worked
too hard to settle this case now. I'm thinking that we should go
to trial. Charlie Webber poisoned my son. He also arranged the
destruction of our home. I want to go to trial, even if we lose."

Jake was stunned speechless for a minute by Mr. McLean's
response. Recovering his composure, he said, "Mr. McLean, I
recommend that you settle. Webber is very dangerous, and you
are placing your lives at risk."

Mr. McLean in a country dialect said, "That asshole and his
family have been responsible for the deaths of my cousins,
grandfather, and great-grandfather in the mines. Our lives don't
count for nothing more than the paper the death certificate
is written on, they died in the most terrible way possible,
suffocating to death. At least half our family never had a proper
burial, their bodies left to rot in the mine shafts.

Now he is strip mining to kill people. Webber wouldn't offer
that kind of money to settle without a very sound reason,
probably because of the risk of other lawsuits."

Quickly, John said, "Well that's settled," before Jason or Jake
could speak again. John knew that they had to agree now.

Jake said, "And so, against my better judgment, the decision
is made, we are going to trial."

————

AFTER THE MEETING, JOHN INFORMED Reed of the decision not to
settle.

Reed said, "This is the biggest mistake you have ever made.
This is going to be very costly for your firm and you will lose."
Reed slammed the phone down.

————

JAKE SAID TO JOHN AND Jason that Webber could bankrupt the law
firm because of the legal costs. "Reed will make this case as
expensive as possible."

John said, We will depose Webber first. He is too smart to drop his pants again like in his deposition in my divorce."

He sent the formal notice of Webber's deposition to Reed for two weeks from the day of their conversation.

————

IN PREPARATION FOR WEBBER'S UPCOMING deposition, everybody had to read Webber's deposition concerning John's divorce from Ann. It was not relevant to the present case, but it showed that Webber was very volatile and would be difficult for Reed to control.

Jake then read it aloud to the group. "This deposition is the only hint we have as to how Webber will react in his deposition," Jake said.

Jason said, "John, you are too emotionally involved with Ann and Charlie to be the lead trial lawyer in the case.

Jake said, "John, you will help in the preparation of the case and sit at the counsel table during the trial, but only as an advisor. Also, if another offer of settlement is made, I don't want you to interfere with the decision as to whether or not to settle the case." Jason agreed.

Subdued, John agreed. He said he would do everything he could to help, including making certain he was spending a lot of billable time with his other clients to support the firm.

Jake thanked John. "I am upset that the last offer was not accepted."

Jake said the next item on the agenda was to read their original pleadings to see if they should be amended to broaden the case against Webber Mining and Webber to show a disregard for the health and welfare of the McLean family as a result of gross negligence.

Jake said, "This might help force Webber to settle this case for a larger amount, if the CMOA believes there is a risk that Webber might lose and expose them to a lawsuit."

They agreed to file a motion to amend the pleadings to include negligence as a basis for judgment, which John said would be vigorously opposed.

Jake asked John to prepare the Motion and notice the court for Jake's oral argument on the court calendar ten days from then.

————

ON THE DAY OF THE hearing of the motion, Jake and Reed appeared before Judge Hand. Jake argued first.

"I am appearing for Mr. Gooding who was attacked and injured a week ago in an attack where a man was killed.

"May it please Your Honor, the motion today is to expand the scope of the pleadings to include gross negligence or negligent disregard for the safety of my client on the part of the defendants in sending the coal mining tailings containing mercury into Deep Creek and then into Deep Lake. Until now my client has relied only upon strict liability, where we only had to prove that my client ingested the mercury that caused him harm. We now want to add as an additional legal position that Mr. Webber knew or should have known about the damaging effects of mercury."

"Mr. Masters," the Judge said, "the case before us is not a fishing expedition. Do you have any proof of negligence?"

"No, your Honor. We believe Mr. Webber knew about the mercury in the coal. We will find out more during the depositions."

"Well, Mr. Masters, I don't see why this case should become more complicated. I will deny your motion, until such time there is a basis in fact for it. Are there any other matters to be considered by this court? Mr. Reed's brief correctly suggests you have no basis for the motion, and I am inclined to agree."

In unison both lawyers said, "Thank you, Your Honor."

The Judge said, "The court hopes Mr. Gooding has a speedy recovery and can be part of your team."

Reed gave Jake a smile that said he knew how the motion was going to come out.

Jake just smiled and said, "We'll get the proof we need eventually."

Afterwards, in the Courthouse Bar across the street, John, Jason, and Jake discussed Webber's upcoming deposition. They were certain that Webber knew about the mercury in the coal. They doubted that he knew about the mercury in the smoke from the coal-fired power plants or the acid rain dropping into Deep Lake.

They agreed that a request for production of documents from Webber and his company would be served on Reed. All of them would participate in drafting it. They particularly wanted to have copies of any reports received by Webber showing the analysis of the coal tailings for mercury. The names of the firms performing the analysis would be on them, so they could be deposed.

Jake said," Congressmen, Governor Blanding, and the state representatives who appeared at Webber's party at Deep Lake will be deposed as witnesses for trial. We need the names. They are complicit in what happened to Billy by failing to regulate mercury in the lakes.

Jake said, "John, Ann and you may have to be witnesses at trial as to the politicians who attended the party. You need to find out about their legislative records on strip mining coal. I'll bet they have blocked any reform for years. It is unlikely that we will be able to prove bribes, but we may be able to infer them to the jury."

John said, "Jake, if I am a witness, I may not be able to participate in some of the preparation for trial. Everything I hear or see will be discoverable."

Jake said, "That's right, John, so there may be matters in this litigation to which you will not learn about. It can't be helped."

Jason said, "Ann is a listed as a witness to what Webber told her about the people at the party before they were married. Maybe this will bring a larger settlement offer, so that the trial can be avoided."

CHAPTER 61

THE ANONYMOUS DONOR

August 1972

The next day, John received an unexpected telephone call from a Mr. William White. His secretary said, "Mr. White is from New York City. He said he wanted to contribute to the McLean's lawsuit against Charlie Webber."

Expecting some sort of crackpot who had read the story in the newspaper, he took the call, summoning Jake and Jason.

"Hello, to whom am I speaking?" John said, as he flipped the recording switch hidden from view on the underside of the top of his desk. Taping allowed complete recall of conversations. They would not be introduced as evidence since they were obtained illegally.

"My name is William White and I represent an individual who wants to donate money anonymously to support your lawsuit against Webber. Would that be of interest you?"

John paused before answering. "Yes," he said, "but I need more information. Is the money from criminal activity?"

My client is a very wealthy private citizen who has not even had a traffic ticket. Be assured that I can and will vouch for the character and honesty of my client. Right now, my client does not want to be associated publicly with your lawsuit. My client also is not prepared to face the personal danger associated with going against Charlie Webber and his friends. I believe you understand the risks, Mr. Gooding."

"Yes, what did you have in mind by way of financial support, Mr. White?"

"I am prepared to wire the sum of five hundred thousand dollars to your law firm operating account. Half will go to Billy McLean for his medical and living expenses as they arise. The balance will used by your firm to pay your legal fees. More money is available as the need arises. The only condition is that you not settle the case without discussing it with me. In the long run, your client will receive more money from this arrangement than from Charlie Webber. I know his lawyer made a low offer to settle, and my client wants you to reject the offer."

This was one of those rare times that John was speechless.

Mr. White asked, "Are you still there? I'll call you in the morning. If your bookkeeper can give me the routing codes for your trust account then, I will send the money as soon as I have your acceptance of the terms of the donation."

"Yes, I was thinking that I need to discuss your offer with my client. Your offer is timely. You are correct that Webber made an offer to settle."

"I understand that the offer made by Webber was for $250, 000," Mr. White said.

"You have well-informed sources, Mr. White," John said, and hung up the phone. John was ready to accept the offer. He yelled, "Great!" His secretary came in and saw he was smiling.

John went into Jake's office, who was talking to Jason, and, after explaining the offer, said, "I want to go ahead with the case. What have we got to lose with the guarantee from the donor as long as the money is there? It is probably more than we'll ever get from Webber."

Jake said, "Well, I suppose that is all there is to be said." Jason agreed.

The next morning, with the McLeans approval, John told Mr. White, when he called, that the firm and their client were in agreement with the terms.

After the money was in the firm's account, John called Reed and told him there is no possibility of settlement and that the case was going to trial.

Jake stood up and stretched. "My son is playing Little League baseball. I'm meeting my wife and daughter at the ballpark. I hope we have made the right decision."

CHAPTER 62

REED AND WEBBER

August 1972

"Reed, I want to know what is happening in Gooding's law firm. Who might be bribed to pass on information?" Webber was very upset with Reed.

Reed said, "There is an associate. Ward Temple came to interview me for a job, before Gooding joined the firm. The interview was in confidence, since he did not want Masters or Mayfield to know he was looking. I could approach him with an offer to spy for us, at say $3,000 per month."

"Go ahead and do it."

Reed called Ward Temple at his home and asked that they meet secretly. Ward agreed.

When they met, Reed said, "I would like you to work for Webber while remaining at the Gooding firm to help us get rid of this lawsuit."

Temple said, "When you say 'work, do you mean provide confidential information about what my firm is doing?"

"It would be nothing big. We already know how Gooding is preparing the case. We need to know why he turned down our recently offer of settlement."

Temple thought, I don't know the reason. "This is the disclosure of privileged information of the firm, which is unethical on my part. What do I get out of this?"

"We are willing to pay you three thousand per month, with twelve months guaranteed."

"This could cost me my license to practice law. I would need far more than that. Temple walked away and left in his car without saying anything more to Reed. He did not shake hands with him.

Ward immediately reported the meeting with Reed to John, Jake and Jason in private upon his return to the office. He said, "There is no way I will become involved with Webber. I went so I could report to you."

John said, "I don't want you to communicate with Reed again. You could be killed by Webber. If challenged, Reed would turn it around and suggest that you offered to sell the information to him and he rejected the offer. You could lose your license to practice law.

In the meantime, I want you to keep this from everybody but Jake, Jason or me, including your wife. It will not have any effect on your employment or advancement in the firm. Eventually we may have to tell Judge Hand about Reed's attempted bribe."

"I don't' believe you intended to make me a partner in the firm."

"Ward, we will consider that in a year or two," John said.

"I'll need some time to think about all of this. I'll let you know where I stand tomorrow."

They expected Temple would quit. The firm would give him a favorable recommendation.

The next day, Temple told John that he had called Reed and told him he wanted no part of sending information on the McLean case to him. He also told Reed that he quit his job at the firm.

Temple said, "Reed slammed the phone down."

The parting with Temple was amicable, although John still wondered why he met with Reed in the first place.

The next day John hired an electronics specialist to look for listening devices. They found one in Jake's office. The technician could not say how long it had been there. Any one of the staff or clients could have placed it there.

After that, all conversations were held in the library with the curtains closed. They monitored the room daily for bugs.

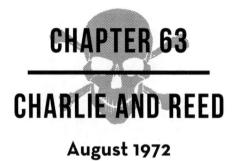

CHAPTER 63

CHARLIE AND REED

August 1972

Charlie waited at Steadfast for Reed to report that the offer was accepted. Reed arrived and reported his failure to recruit Ward Temple. He stuttered on some of the words.

Charlie said, "I have hired Woodward, Barnes and Knowland to take over the case with Nate Hammond as my new lawyer. They indicated they did not need your help going forward, but they do need all of my files."

Reed nodded his head and then his chin dropped to his chest. He said, "I understand."

"Also, I am transferring all my other work to this firm. All of my work is confidential. You must not disclose anything about me to anyone, including anything about my business or the payments to the politicians. You will deliver all of my files today and not retain any copies. Is that clear? My men are waiting for you at your office."

Reed was sweating from fear and he seemed about to faint. He sat down in a chair.

"Charlie, I understand. You know I always had your best interests in mind. Hope this works out for you in the end. I expect that the McLean case is going to get much worse for you before long."

After Reed left, Charlie thought, Reed will have an accident of some sort. He already instructed the men waiting at Reed's office to take care of that.

"Charlie smiled at the thought of Rex Reed's death, burying all he knew about him. He looked forward to working with his new lawyer.

CHAPTER 64

REX REED DIES

August 1972

Reed was scared shitless as he drove towards his office, believing that he had only a short time to live. He called his lawyer, Les Worthey, from a telephone booth, and told him he was coming over. His office was a few blocks from Reed's.

"Webber fired me as his attorney," Reed said. Worthey said he would be waiting. He drove around blocks in circles until he was certain he was not being followed. He then parked and went up to Worthey's office.

Alone in Worthey's conference room, Reed dictated on a cassette tape, all he could about Webber's bribes in fifteen minutes. He named the many politicians who received money from Webber year after year. He sealed the tape in an envelope and sealed it with tape so that it could not be opened without destroying the seal. He directed Worthey to deliver the cassette tape to the county prosecutor in Treadwell in the event of his death.

Arriving at his office, Reed saw Webber's two henchmen waiting for him with a large moving van. He knew them as Duke and Bones. Duke said they had to pick up the files and Reed was to be there to make sure they had them all. Duke ordered him to dismiss his staff without any explanation, which Reed did. It took about two hours to find and load the files into the van.

Reed felt very uneasy as they worked, stopping only to use the restroom. Done, they told Reed to come with them to the van to check the boxes. As Reed stepped into the van, one of them injected him with a small dose of something and he passed out.

When Reed awoke later, he was told he was strapped to a chair. Duke said, "You are going to die, but it will be easier if you disclose any other documents or recordings, not in the files we picked up."

After about fifteen minutes of torture, Reed admitted leaving a tape with lawyer Worthey in a sealed envelope. Bones put a phone to Reed's ear and told him to talk to his lawyer and request him to deliver the tape in the sealed envelope to a drop point. Reed warned Worthey not to open the envelope and he hoped that he hadn't become curious.

Reed and Bones waited while Duke went in to pick up the tapes and return. Duke said, "It's time to "go." and injected Reed with a lethal dose of something which caused his heart to beat irregularly and then stop beating .

In those last moments, Reed thought of his wife and then there was blackness.

CHAPTER 65

CHARLIE'S DEPOSITION

September 1972

Charlie appeared at Nate's offices for his deposition at the same time the court reporter and Jake Masters arrived. There was no exchange of pleasantries.

Charlie was surprised that Gooding was not taking his deposition and mentioned this to Nate. When Jake was asked by Nate, he said John was working on another case.

Charlie saw that Miss Stuart was the same court reporter as in his deposition in Ann's divorce. He became a little concerned about his deposition.

"For the record," Jake said, "This is the deposition of Charlie Webber, the defendant in this case, personally and as President of Webber Mining. The testimony can be used for any purpose at trial. I will waive the signing of the deposition by Mr. Webber."

Nate said "I want Mr. Webber to read his deposition and sign it."

"Mr. Webber, please state your name and address for the record." Jake said.

The deposition proceeded the way Nate predicted, and he answered the questions in the way Nate had coached him. Charlie began to feel relaxed.

"Mr. Webber, are you a member of the Ku Klux Klan?"

Charlie sat up straighter in his chair.

Nate said, "Don't answer, Mr. Webber."

Jake said, "It's a simple question, he should be able to answer yes or no without any difficulty."

"Listen you shit head, you need to back away from that question like a craw daddy in hot water," Webber said.

"Is that a threat Mr. Webber?" Jason asked.

"You can take that any way you want, but you better be careful," Webber said.

Nate said, "Objection! It isn't relevant to this case. I want this line of questioning stricken from the record."

"Well, it is relevant to Billy my client and Mr. and Mrs. McLean. Some people burned a cross in front of their house in Treadwell, and then the house burned down to the ground. They were dressed in white robes. Mr. Webber did you have anything to do with the mob that ended up at my clients' home?"

"No."

"The sheriff for Treadwell said you called him about this lawsuit before the fire. What did you tell the sheriff?"

"I told him that Billy McLean had filed this lawsuit against me. I don't have any knowledge about what he did with the information."

"Thank you Mr. Webber, your phone records that your lawyer provided show that the call was made from your home."

"Now returning to my earlier question, are you a member of the Klan?"

"I refuse to answer on the grounds that it might prejudice my case."

"I'm going to take that answer as a yes, since I don't hear an answer to the contrary."

"On another topic, when did you marry Ann Gooding, John Gooding's former wife?"

"Eight months ago."

Nate said, "I object to further questions about Ann, since she is now Mr. Webber's wife.

Jason said, "Not during the period before the marriage."

They talked to the Judge by telephone about Nate's objection. Jake explained to the judge that Ann might be a witness in the case as to facts bearing on their case related to a party at

Deep Lake before they were married. The Judge ordered Webber to answer the question. That ruling made Charlie visibly nervous.

"Who attended your party that July after you met Ann Gooding in Washington D.C., Mr. Webber?"

"Objection, the question is irrelevant."

"Mr. Hammond, shall we go to the judge again?"

"What possible relevance would the party have to the present case?" Nate said.

"It is our position that Mr. Webber has been blocking legislation regulating strip mining of coal, including dumping of the tailings into Deep Lake, for many years, which could have prevented what happened to Billy McLean. The people at that party are very successful in blocking any coal mining legislation, state or federal, from being passed. Now, Mr. Hammond, would you like to talk to the judge again?"

"I need to talk to my client in private, Mr. Masters. I need a short recess."

"Take as long as you want, Mr. Hammond. All I need is a list of those who attended the party. I might get the information from Mrs. Webber, but that would be unnecessary if I receive the list from Mr. Webber."

―――――

IN A ROOM DOWN THE hall from the library, Charlie was very angry. His face and neck flushed red.

Nate said, "Charlie, I don't see any harm in giving them the list. It will save Ann from being deposed. I can't imagine any of your political guests would say that they were blocking coal mining legislation for anything but the best of reasons. This is just a ploy to get you to settle the case for more money."

Charlie had not told Nate about the bribes to those on the list. He thought, No one can find out about them. I have the only records. And so he reluctantly agreed.

Nate said that they would provide the list of the people at the party. Jake and Nate agreed to adjourn Webber's deposition until another date

Charlie smiled at Jake as they left the office. He thought, Jake Masters is going to die.

CHAPTER 66

JAKE AND CLEM'S BROTHER

September 1972

Jake Masters received a telephone call from Ned Block, the brother of Clem Block. Ned said that he had not heard from or seen Clem in months, much longer than usual. He wanted a meeting outside of Charleston. Clem said, "I think Webber killed Clem."

Jake agreed to meet Ned at a truck stop on US30, ten miles out of town.

Ned said, "I don't want to get involved in your lawsuit. I would lose my job in his mine." More than likely he would kill me and my family.

Ned said, "The purpose of the meeting was to give you a letter and some papers in a sealed envelope, which Clem had left with me shortly before he disappeared."

———

AT THE RESTAURANT, NED SAT waiting alone at a table. Jake introduced himself, shook hands and sat down. Without comment, Ned handed Jake the large envelope, stood up and said, "I'm leaving. "Anything you could do to find out what happened to my brother would be appreciated. I am sure he is dead." They shook hands and Ned left.

On the front of the envelope was written 'To whom it may Concern'. Jake picked up a steak knife and carefully lifted the sealing tab. Inside were a large number of ledger sheets for many years, with abbreviated names, dates, and dollar amounts. The last dates were for the party on Deep Lake, which John and Ann had attended. On the bottom of each page, in the same handwriting as the front of the envelope, was a legend with names corresponding to the abbreviations and signed and dated by Clem Block.

Jake looked around to see if anyone was paying attention to him. He couldn't be sure, so he carefully folded the papers and put them in the envelope, moistened the tab to seal the envelope again. He put the firm address on the outside. Jake had a premonition that somebody was following him on the road.

Jake handed the envelope to his waitress and said,"Please take this to the post office and mail it to my law firm. I am on vacation and my firm needs these papers. Here is a one hundred dollar tip on my client, which more than covers the mailing. He paid his bill and went to his car.

As he drove down the road, he looked to see who might be following him. All he could see was a large semi truck behind him as he drove down the two-lane road. It seemed to be gaining on him, so he went faster as he looked in the rearview mirror. Suddenly, another truck pulled out from a side road so the trailer was in front of him. He swerved to avoid the truck and ran into the ditch and up against a tree at sixty miles per hour. His last thought was that he would miss his wife and children.

———————

THE TRUCKS STOPPED LONG ENOUGH for Webber to light and throw a flare onto spilled gasoline from the gas tank. A huge fire erupted, enveloping the car and Jake.

———————

JAKE'S BODY WAS INCINERATED WHEN the fire trucks and police arrived. The only way his remains could be identified was by the license plate. The firemen said he suspected that the fire had been intentionally set, but there was no evidence of an accelerant.

———————

ALICE COOPER WORKED MANY YEARS at the truck stop as a waitress and had seen a lot, but she had never been offered fifty dollars to mail an envelope. It was addressed to John Gooding, Esq. at Mayfield, Masters and Gooding in Charleston. At a break in the afternoon, she took it to the post office and mailed it. The customer was such a nice man, she thought.

When she read the newspaper the next day there was a photograph of her customer, a lawyer, with a description of the crash and his death. She wondered what was in the envelope, but she was not going to get involved.

————

JAKE'S ASHES FROM THE CAR fire were buried with his wife, son, and daughter standing at the grave side. John cried and knew it was his fault that Jake was dead.

John received the papers in the mail three days after it was mailed. He saw all of the politicians' names and the money paid to them. It was now hidden at his bank in a safety deposit box.

John thought, Webber is going to pay for Jake's death. He held Webber directly responsible for Jake's death, but could not prove it. He hated Webber enough to kill him. Webber threatened Jake on the record during his deposition and done it.

John's firm had no way of replacing Jake. Now it was just Jason and John, who was the lead attorney.

CHAPTER 67

COAL COMPANIES

September 1972

In anticipation of the trial beginning in November, the members of the coal mining association approached Charlie about raising funds from all the owners to settle the lawsuit.

Charlie said, "I don't need any help. With Jake Masters dead, we are going to win the case, my new lawyer says. Gooding's evidence is not good enough to win." He told the men at an informal CMOA meeting. "I am going to trial."

The owners mentioned the problem of the bribes, but Charlie said, "No politician is going to talk about it, since it would end his career and land them in prison.

Webber continued, "The McLean family has no case. If we capitulate on this lawsuit, everyone who thinks that the coal made them sick will sue us. The miners will claim they have been injured and entitled to compensation. The public will start believing their stories and juries will award bigger and bigger damages. With no end of litigation, we will be confined by so many regulations that we will be unable to mine the coal. Trust me. This is the best alternative."

Roy Plant said, "We do trust you Charlie. We expect that everything will turn out for the best. We wouldn't want anything to go wrong."

"Plant continued, "We might dredge Deep Lake and the river to remove the coal tailings and dump them as landfill into a depleted strip mine to restore the land. The gesture would be good for our image."

Webber said, "That is a very bad idea. Dredging would be very costly. It will be like admitting that I did something wrong in dumping the tailings in the first place.

Plant said, "We could have the minerals in the tailings in the lake water monitored monthly. The fish might be tested for mercury levels. I'm told that the acidity of the water in Deep Lake is increasing for some unknown reason. Maybe we can neutralize it."

Webber said, "This is none of your business. I can handle the problem myself."

The meeting broke up without further conversation on the matter.

CHAPTER 68

THE CONSULTANT

September 1972

John hired Dr. Andrew Bork, a professor from the University of West Virginia, as a consultant to discuss the evidence. Using a blackboard in John's office, Bork explained what was happening at Deep Lake in a manner an uneducated jury could understand.

He sketched a diagram showing the Deep Lake and a coal fired power plant in Charleston. The the power plant belched the smoke from the smokestack containing an acid which drifted into Deep Lake. The tailings from Webber mining were at the bottom of the lake. The acid leached mercury from them which was transferred to bacteria. Small fish ate the bacteria on the tailings. Larger fish were eating the small fish which were caught and eaten.

"Acids from the coal smoke are making the water more acidic, causing the mercury to be leached from the tailings. Bacteria in the water feed on sulfur bound to the mercury in the tailings, which goes from the small fish to the large game fish, which are eaten. The mercury stays in the belly fat of the game fish, in the form of methyl mercury, a deadly poison. This form of mercury is what caused Billy's disease. Very small amounts of mercury are also in the smoke from the power plant, but not enough to cause Billy's disease.

The result is a very dangerous situation. Everybody eating the fish will be poisoned."

He explained that methyl mercury was used as a wheat seed coating to kill a fungus before planting. The combination caused the death of thousands who used the wheat to make bread in Iran.

John said, "You can eliminate that story from your testimony. It's too confusing. What could be done to prevent this from happening at Deep Lake?" John said.

Bork said, "The only possibility is to ban eating the fish and dredging the tailings from the lake and river. The power plant could reduce the acids emitted. Traps are available, but expensive, driving up the cost of electricity."

John said, "Should the disclosure of mercury in the fish be kept quiet until your testimony at trial? We need to have the best impact on the jury."

Bork said, "I don't think so John. There is now a known risk of mercury poisoning of everybody eating the fish from Deep Lake. We need to tell people."

John said, "How would we disclose the risk? Tell the story to a reporter for the Charleston Gazette? It's unlikely the newspaper would publish the story. We could report it to the state Environmental Protection Agency, but I doubt that they would do anything because it involves coal mining. There is the federal EPA and we can report it to them through our Congressmen. Maybe one of our representatives is not on Webber's payroll."

And so, John reported the findings to the EPA and to West Virginia Senator Wallenby. He received a polite letter from the EPA saying it would look into the matter. A staff member for the congressmen set him a letter thanking him for looking out for West Virginia. After that there was silence.

The *Gazette* refused to publish the story, saying that people would become alarmed unnecessarily. Probably the newspaper was concerned with their liability for publishing the story in the first place, a sort of trade defamation of coal. Also, the newspaper would risk of loss of advertising again. The TV and radio stations wanted no part of the story. They said they would report on it after the trial.

A letter sent to President Nixon produced a machine signed

photograph and a letter which said he would refer the matter to the EPA. There was no inquiry.

Finally, John decided to focus all of his time on the trial. The witness list included Andrew Bork. Nate Hammond did not even bother to depose Dr. Bork before trial. John thought, Probably Hammond would rather try to destroy his testimony on the witness stand.

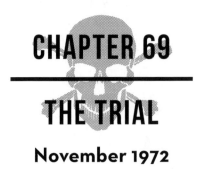

CHAPTER 69

THE TRIAL

November 1972

During the jury selection, Hammond challenged a black juror for cause. In the absence of the jury, he said to the judge, "Webber can not get a fair trial from a black man or woman, since the plaintiff had inferred Webber was a member of the Klan in a deposition.

Judge Hand ruled that in view of recent federal laws on discrimination, he could not exclude these jurors on the basis of race. "The Klan is not on trial here. I don't want them to be mentioned at all in this trial. Am I clear?"

Both lawyers agreed.

The judge said that he could exclude a juror if they said they could not fairly judge Webber. On this basis, five black jurors were excluded, saying they could not find for Webber under any circumstances.

Two black prospective jurors were Professors of literature and science at the branch of West Virginia State University in Charleston. They said that they could judge the case on its merits. They were seated in the jury box over Hammond's objections.

Charlie smiled at them. Finally, six jurors and two alternate jurors were selected and sworn to uphold the law.

ONCE THE JURY WAS IN place, Judge Hand said John could call his first witness.

"I call Billy McLean."

Complete silence gripped the court, as Billy walked up to the witness stand dressed in loose fitting clothes. A Clerk administered the oath. Billy swore he would tell the truth and sat down in the witness chair.

John drew out the usual preliminary answers and then asked Billy why he was dressed like that way.

"I have open sores on my skin and I can't wear anything tight against my body. The white clothes are prewashed cotton, less irritating to my skin."

"Have you had this problem for a long time?"

"I've had rashes all over my body ever since I can remember as a young boy. They itch something fierce." Billy scratched his arm until it began to bleed. The jury saw blood seep through the cotton.

"Do you know what caused the rashes?"

"My doctor told me it was from mercury in my body."

"Objection, hearsay," Hammond said.

"Mr. Gooding?" the judge said.

"Your honor, Billy's doctor, Dr. Richards, is on the witness list, so it is not hearsay." John said.

"I'll allow it subject to Dr. Richards' testimony to corroborate the statement."

"Billy, can you describe how you live from day to day in Treadwell?"

"When I am home, I don't wear any clothes because my skin itches awful. Fishing is the way I pass the time, mainly. I pick plants for my mom to use in potions, which she sells or trades for cash for food. I make friends with those creatures in the forest that Mr. Webber has missed killing, like the deer and raccoons. A teacher, Mrs. Hitchings, taught me to read and write, before she died with a sickness like mine."

"What kind of fish do you catch Billy?"

"Mainly I catch bass and bluegills. Mr. Webber planted some smallmouth bass which fight hard and are good eating."

"How long have you eaten the fish from Deep Lake?"

"For as long as I can remember. Dad doesn't work because of an injury in Mr. Webber's coal mine. We rely on religious groups from up north for food. We eat all of the fish I catch."

"'How old are you, Billy?'"

"I am almost eighteen."

"You have been eating the fish for at least fifteen years, correct?"

"Yes."

"Billy, do you know that there is mercury in the fish in the lake?"

"Objection, your Honor, Hammond said. The plaintiff has no foundation for that question with this witness. The Plaintiff does not have firsthand knowledge of that fact."

"Mr. Gooding?"

John shifted his position to face both the jury and the judge. The jurors were leaning forward with their eyes riveted on John.

"Your Honor, Billy has seen the results on the tests of the fish from Deep Lake."

"Sustained. You have witnesses on your list to testify to that fact. Move on to your next question."

"Thank you, Your Honor. Billy, have you ever met Mr. Webber?"

"Yes, once on the par three golf courses he built near our home."

"What happened when you met?" John said as turned his head towards the jury.

"He said, "You goddamn freak, get off my property. If you know what's good for you, you'll stay away. The next time I catch you here, I will kick your ass good. His hands grabbed me around my neck. Like so." He moved his hands into a chokehold around his neck.

"Objection your Honor, irrelevant," Hammond said.

"Overruled. This testimony is relevant to the regard with which Mr. Webber held Mr. McLean. Mr. Webber will have his chance to testify about the encounter. Please proceed with Mr. McLean's testimony, Mr. Gooding."

"Billy, how did you feel about what he said to you?"

"Well, I was afraid. He took God's name in vain which is a sin."

"And did you stay away from his golf course?"

"Yes. My parents told me to stay away, or they would make me stay home."

"Billy, I want you to show the jury your skin. Please take off your clothes except the swim trunks you have on."

"Objection, your Honor."Hammond said. "This courtroom is no place for such a display."

"Your Honor, the jury has to know the kind of torture Billy has to live with every day."

"Overruled."

Billy took off his clothes. The jury and the gallery watching gasped at seeing the weeping and bleeding rashes over all of his body.

"Billy, I want you to walk over to the jury box so that they can see your skin close up."

Billy walked over to the jury box. The jury moved back in their seats, as if they might catch the disease.

John assured the jury that Billy's disease was not catching. Some of the jurors were visibly shaken, horror on their faces, since Billy's skin was bright red with large mottled, brown, bleeding scabs.

"Thank you, Billy. You can return to the witness stand and dress," John said.

Billy slowly dressed, careful not to rub his sores. The jurors watched every movement.

"Your Honor, I offer these color photographs of the rashes on Billy's skin into evidence. I ask that the jury be allowed to review them in the jury room during their deliberations."

"No objection, Your Honor," Hammond said in a resigned and tired voice, which brought a sharp look from Webber. John did not miss the exchange.

"Billy, the part of your body under your bathing trunks, is that the same as what we can see?"

"Yes, it is and the pictures show that as well."

The jury absorbed that information with their mouths turned down.

"Your Honor, I am finished taking Billy's testimony."

"Mr. Hammond, the court would like to go into recess for the day in fifteen minutes. Would you like to start your cross-examination?"

"Yes, your honor. I have only one question."

"Mr. McLean, do you know for certain what caused your disease?"

"Well, I have come to believe it is mercury poisoning because I have mercury in my body." Billy said.

"Are you a doctor?" Hammond said.

"I am not a doctor, but I have also just been told this morning that I have a late-stage lymphoma, a rare type of cancer. Dr. Richards said there is no hope for a cure and that I will die before too long."

The courtroom was quiet except for the *whosh-whosh* of the ceiling fans. The jury looked with sad eyes at Billy.

After some hesitation, Hammond said, "We are very sorry to learn this, Billy. Do you know for certain if mercury caused the lymphoma?"

"No, I don't, Mr. Hammond"

"Thank you, Billy. Your Honor, I believe we can wait until tomorrow to proceed."

The judge said "Court is adjourned."

John and Jane met with Billy in the office library. They both expressed their sympathy to Billy.

John said, "We didn't know about your lymphoma. I am certain it was caused by the mercury in your body. I will talk to Dr. Richards about the diagnosis."

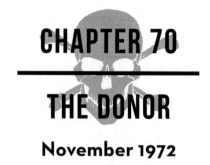

CHAPTER 70

THE DONOR

November 1972

Evelyn Wallenby loved Charlie Webber, and before Ann came on the scene, and was secretly seeing him, cheating on her husband Nick. She hated Ann for taking Charlie away from her. She thought, I tried to have Ann killed by the bomb on the plane.

The former Mrs. Evelyn Wallenby listened to the testimony in the back of the courtroom, wearing a wig, heavy makeup, sunglasses, blue jeans and a T-shirt. Not even her ex-husband would have recognized her. In any event, she didn't have to worry about that. The senator was too smart to be seen at this trial. After today, she would send a lawyer to watch the proceedings to eliminate the risk of detection.

By now Charlie had probably told her ex husband that Gooding was trying to find out about the bribes and other favors, such as the prostitutes. The whores were responsible for the herpes virus she got from Nick.

Evelyn's doctor had told her she would have it the rest of her life and could pass it on to a lover. She hoped Charlie might catch it, but this did not happen since Charlie used condoms.

Detective, Max Mull helped her nail Nick having sex with a prostitute. The pictures proved he was unfaithful. She proved her herpes virus came from the senator by calling the prostitute as a witness. These facts enabled her to take sixty percent of her husband's one hundred million dollar assets as a result of a settlement.

Revenge against Charlie Webber for leaving her was her mission in life. Max Mull was dead. Nick probably talked Charlie into killing him. She financed Billy's lawsuit against Webber through Mr. White.

Evelyn's revenge against Webber would be complete when she testified about the bribes to the politicians. She even knew the numbers of the accounts in the Cayman Islands where millions were deposited by Nick to avoid federal income taxes.

Evelyn knew that the judge in Billy's case might not admit the evidence of the bribes, because of lack of relevance, as her lawyer had explained. If not, she would send the information to the IRS. Her financial support of Billy McLean's lawsuit was worth the cost so that Charlie suffered.

An element of fear controlled her actions. She had no doubt Charlie would kill her, if she testified. However, her grown children were well provided for in her trust. There was nothing more she could do for them. Getting even with Charlie would be worth her life. She thought, There is a better chance of coming out of this alive, if I can send him to jail.

She thought, I do not want this case to settle. As the donor, I made sure that her representative, Mr. White, made it clear to Gooding that I would match anything the other side offered and promptly put the money in Gooding's firm account. With that kind of insurance, John Gooding will not settle. Gooding has his own need to get even with Charlie Webber after what happened between Charlie and Ann at the summer party on Deep Lake.

————

DURING THE SECOND DAY OF the trial, Nate Hammond asked a few softball questions to clarify how Billy felt and to show how sympathetic Charlie Webber was to learn of his disease.

Charlie seemed uninterested in the testimony and doodled on a legal pad.

John noticed the two black jurors watching Webber. He thought, It would be a good idea to focus on these jurors as a barometer of our progress in the case. He asked Jane to make notes on their reactions to the testimony.

John called Professor Andrew Bork, who walked up, standing tall, to the stand. He was sworn in and sat down with an air of confident anticipation on his face. John thought, There will be no surprises here.

"Professor Bork, have you had an opportunity to test the waters and sediment of Deep Lake and Deep River, and if so, what are your findings?"

Professor Bork produced a report which was handed to the Judge. The judge allowed the jury to have a copy of the report, over Hammond's objection.

"My analysis shows very high levels of mercury in the coal tailings in Deep Lake, and also in Deep River, which, if released into the water, would cause mass poisoning of people drinking water. The fish in the lake and river, from samplings taken, contain methyl mercury in levels higher than any tested in any other lakes identified in my report. The exception is for instances where the water itself contains enough mercury from a spill of chemicals sufficient to cause immediate poisoning of those who drink it, dying shortly after ingestion."

The judge and jury were listening very carefully, focusing on Bork.

"The acidity of the water in Deep Lake is higher than has ever been recorded, which in my opinion is responsible for the high levels of mercury in the fish. The bacteria in the lake are absorbing the mercury which are eaten by the smaller fish, which are eaten by the larger and larger fish. The fish contain methyl mercury, a known cancer-causing agent. There are charts in my report."

"Professor Bork, did you perform any other analysis?"

"Yes, I tested the air and found significant levels of sulfur dioxide and trioxide gases. These compounds produce the acid in the waters of Deep River and Deep Lake."

"Did you determine where the sulfur gases came from?"

"Yes, they come from burning coal at the West Virginia Power in Charleston. The prevailing winds are towards Deep Lake. The media's name for it is 'acid rain' in the press and in learned papers. Alone it has a bad effect on the life span of the fish and causes deformities."

"How long has this acid rain been in the air?"

"The acid has been coming in the air for as many years as there has been a power plant in Charleston, at least sixty years. The acid problem has been well-known in recent years. This is the first record of the combination of coal mining tailings and the acid in a lake like Deep Lake. The increasing acidity of the lake was recorded over a period of years by the West Virginia State Department of Agriculture. Until now, no one recognized the significance of the acid combined with mercury from coal tailings."

John thought, I have presented a very strong case. He returned to the plaintiff's table and smiled at Jane.

"Thank you, Professor Bork. Your witness, Mr. Hammond."

"Professor Bork, did you look for mercury anywhere else?"

"Yes, I sampled the soil on the shores of Deep Lake and the air above it."

"And what did you find?"

I found mercury in both the air and the soil."

"And where did that mercury in the soil come from?"

"Some comes from the power plant. We know that mercury is present in airborne ash from the burning of coal," Bork said. Bork appeared to be less certain of his answers.

John thought, I need to prove the mercury in the fish came from the coal tailings.

"Could some of the mercury in the water and the air be a result of the smokestack emissions?"

"Yes, some of the mercury is from the smokestack emissions."

"Then, can you be certain that the mercury from the coal tailings could have caused the plaintiff's disease?"

John objected that this witness was not qualified to answer, since he was not a doctor. The judge sustained the objection.

John thought, That question will linger in the minds of the jurors. I have to prove that the coal tailings are the cause of Bill's disease.

Nate Hammond said he was through with his questions.

On redirect, John asked, "Did you determine the relative levels of mercury in the soil and in the air? If so, what did you find?"

Hammond said, "Is it unlikely that the mercury in the coal burning ash could produce a significant amount of mercury in Deep Lake. I found that the mercury levels in the air were ten to fifteen times lower than in Deep Lake. It is highly unlikely that the ash is the problem."

At that John said he was finished with the witness. Hammond had no more questions. Bork was excused.

John's next witness was Dr. Ronald Richards from the clinic where Billy McLean was being treated. He testified that Billy was suffering from mercury poisoning. The levels of mercury in Bill's body were very high, compared to the norm for the general population. He said Billy suffered from a chronic rash and was in the late stage of a lymphoma, which would cause his death. He said in his opinion the lymphoma was a result of the high levels of mercury in Billy's tissues and bone marrow.

On cross examination, Hammond asked Dr. Richards on what data he based his opinion that the lymphoma was caused by the mercury. Dr. Richards said that mercury was the only probable cause.

"Dr. Richards, in your professional opinion, do lymphomas require the presence of mercury?"

"No, this type of cancer is rare which usually does not progress rapidly to a late stage cancer, as in Bill's case. The only cause I can find is the high levels of mercury."

"So, Dr. Richards, your opinion is based upon speculation about the cause of the lymphoma?"

"Well it's my medical judgment that the mercury is the cause."

"Is it possible that another doctor would have a different judgment?"

"Yes, doctors frequently disagree as to the causes of disease."

"To be clear, Doctor, you have no scientific basis for your judgment that the mercury in the lake and the river caused Mr. McLean's lymphoma, other than your opinion."

"That is true. We are beginning a study to detect if a pocket of lymphomas exists in people who are living at Deep Lake."

"And how long will the study take?"

"At least two years."

"Thank you, Doctor."

John waived redirect examination. Jane said the black jurors were now looking at them and seemed puzzled by Bork's testimony.

John thought, This case should have been stronger at this stage of the trial, before the defendants have their chance to present their evidence.

In his office after the recess for the day, John sat back in his chair and discussed the evidence with Jane.

"Jane, we do not have two years to find evidence that the mercury is causing Billy's cancer. We need to check the records for people who have died in Treadwell within the last ten years. If a doctor is there, maybe we can use him or her as a witness."

Jane said, "I used to live in Treadwell. Dr. Sandborne, who is at least eighty years old, practices there. He still treats patients in his clinic. He uses a lot of herbal preparations from the mountain plants, which most doctors think are useless. If anybody would have detailed death records, he would."

"Let's go there tomorrow. Friday is Motion day and the trial will not continue until Monday," John said.

Jane smiled, "All right. Besides you and I need time alone… and I have something in mind."

John was glad that more than work was involved in the trip. Suddenly his day seemed a lot better.

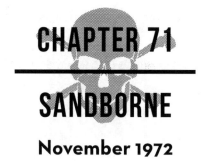

CHAPTER 71

SANDBORNE

November 1972

Jane arranged for them to meet with Dr. Sandborne in his home clinic in Treadwell on Friday. During their telephone conversation, Dr. Sandborne said, "I read about the trial in the *Charleston Gazette* and am interested in learning about the mercury in the fish in Deep Lake."

———

SANDBORNE'S CLINIC WAS IN THE first-floor parlor of an old, rundown Victorian home. Jane introduced John to the doctor. Sandborne had a twinkle in his eyes and a ready smile. His face was leathery from hiking to pick the herbs, w hanging to dry on clotheslines in what must have been the dining room with an old crystal chandelier in the center.

John explained about the trial and Dr. Sandborne listened.

Dr. Sandborne said, "I've always known there was something in Deep Lake that was killing folks here. I've been seeing people with rare cancers and skin rashes for the last twenty years."

John said,"What caused them?"

"I always thought it was something that came from Deep Lake that caused them, probably the fish."

"Why the fish?" John said.

The people in this area, black or white, are so poor that fish from Deep Lake are the only source of protein for them."

"What about other animals?"

"This area has been hunted out by the likes of Charlie Webber so there are no deer. Sometimes there are rabbits, raccoons or possums, but not very many. Not much meat on squirrels."

"What do you do to treat those who are sick?"

"I do the best I can for them. The mountain people call Billy's disease, 'wasting' because they get very thin and covered with rashes before they die. I give them herbs to make them feel better. Sometimes the herbs slow the disease and sometimes it goes away for awhile, but it always returns."

John said, "Do you have records of the people who died from the wasting, Doctor?"

"I do. At least fifty people who have died with the same symptoms. Two others in Treadwell are sick with similar symptoms like Billy McLean."

John could hardly believe what he was hearing. "Would you be willing to testify at the trial on Monday? We need to show that Bill's disease is a result of what people are eating with mercury in it, which is the fish from Deep Lake."

"I would be happy to testify to what I know. I can't say much about the mercury as the cause."

"We will pick you up Sunday morning and take you to Charleston," John said, "We are staying overnight at the motel in Treadwell, if you need us.

Afterwards John said to Jane, "Hammond will object to Dr. Sandborne as a surprise witness, but he was the one who raised the issue of whether mercury was causing Billy's disease."

That night John and Jane made love and slept together in each other's arms. In the morning they ate breakfast at the motel.

They picked up Dr. Sandborne and drove him to Jane's apartment in Charleston. John thought, He will be a great witness.

CHAPTER 72

DR. SANDBORNE'S TESTIMONY

November 1972

John notified Hammond of the new witness by telephone on Monday morning. He said, "Dr. Sandborne is going to testify about illnesses around Treadwell like Billy's.

Hammond said, "I will have a vigorous objection in court since Sandborne is not on the witness list for trial and I haven't had a chance to depose him."

John said, "You raised the question as to whether Billy's lymphoma had been caused by mercury."

Hammond said, "This testimony still will not prove mercury was the cause."

John said, "There were multiple lymphoma cases in Treadwell. Two other people living there have the same rash and sores as Billy.

"These two people are being tested for mercury this week. I am certain they will turn up positive. They have the same history of eating the fish as Billy. At least ten people have died over the years with their bodies covered with rashes and sores."

Hammond paused before replying. "Suppose we accepted for the purpose of settlement that the mercury caused Billy's lymphoma? Would that end the lawsuit if there was a large payment?"

"Would you concede that the mercury from the coal tailings that caused Billy's disease?"

"Let's say for the purpose of argument, for Billy's case only, that it did. Could we then settle on some reasonable basis? After all, Billy is not supporting a family.

Hammond continued, "We would want the settlement to be confidential. If you put Dr. Sandborne on the stand testifying publically in open court, there will be no chance for settlement."

John said he would talk to his client about the offer. He thought, in fact, I have no intention of settling.

To be safe from Webber, John moved Jane and Dr. Sandborne into rooms in a hotel near the court. He thought, Webber is going to be furious and may try to kill Dr. Sandborne.

———

JOHN SAID, "YOUR HONOR, BEFORE the jury is seated, I am prepared to offer the testimony of a new witness, Dr. Sandborne, who can substantiate that numerous other people from Treadwell who have the same disease as Billy. Dr. Sandborne has been treating patients there for over fifty years. I have discussed the matter with Mr. Hammond, and he has said that he will oppose calling Dr. Sandborne as a witness."

Hammond objected to Dr. Sandborne's testimony.

Judge Hand said, "Mr. Hammond, the court remembers that you raised the issue of whether Billy's disease was caused by mercury. It appears that Mr. Gooding has a right to answer that question. Objection overruled. Mr. Gooding, you may proceed to take the doctor's testimony." The jury came in and sat down.

John brought out that Dr Sandborne graduated from Harvard Medical School at the top of his class, and had come to practice in Treadwell because he wanted to help the mountain people. He said his internship was at New York Hospital and his residency was at Children's Hospital there, specializing in the treatment of cancers.

John said, "Your honor I am presenting Dr. Sandborne as an expert."

There was no objection from Hammond who looked dejected.

The judge said, "Dr. Sandborne is accepted as an expert."

John could see that the jury was impressed. Jane gave John a broad smile.

Charlie looked morose as he listened to Dr. Sandborne, as if cash was draining out of his bank account.

John said, "Now Dr. Sandborne, you have treated Billy McLean for years, what is your diagnosis of his condition?"

"In my opinion, he has an incurable, late stage lymphoma. He has terrible skin rashes and lesions which come with the disease. He is dying, in my opinion."

"Could you be more explicit about the disease for the jury?"

"The diseased cells in Billy's body are attacking the skin cells. Billy is dying from the inside out," Dr. Sandborne explained.

"Do you have an opinion as to what caused the disease?"

"Objection," Hammond said.

"Overruled. Answer the question if you can Dr.Sandborne."

"In my opinion, mercury caused the lymphoma. Billy has been sick for most of his life. I learned from Dr. Richards that high levels of mercury are present in his body. I am certain my two other living patients will have the same levels of mercury in their bodies. If we dug up the bodies of those twenty people who died under similar circumstances, they would have mercury in their bodies. Mercury has been known for over one hundred years to produce the kind of skin condition Billy has. Because of the mercury, his own cells are killing him.

"Can you describe how he is going to die, Doctor?"

"The lymphoma will attack his body from the inside until there is not enough living tissue to keep him alive."

Jane held Billy who was crying. The jury was in tears. The judge blew into his handkerchief.

John was silent for almost two minutes.

Finally the Judge asked Hammond if he had any questions and he replied he did not. Billy put his head down on the attorney's table and sobbed. His parents were crying and held each other.

Charlie sat straight-faced.

The Judge said, "We will recess for the day."

Hammond said, "Charlie Webber is our only witness."

———

THE NEXT DAY WEBBER TESTIFIED. Ann Webber was sitting behind him in the gallery. There was a stir when a well dressed woman came in and sat down. A member of the gallery behind Webber said out loud that she was Evelyn Wallenby, the ex wife of the Senator.

Hammond asked about the coal tailings from strip mining on Mt Hope.

Webber said, "I didn't know about the mercury in the tailings or how dangerous they could be. My family has been dumping the tailings from washing coal into lakes for years.

I'm sorry about Billy, but there was no way that I knew that acid rain would cause the mercury to be leached from the tailings and go into fish in Deep Lake. I myself have been eating the fish all my life. My wife, Ann, has been eating the fish recently. I can't be held responsible for something I didn't know about."

On cross-examination, John questioned him slowly, dragging out the way Webber mined the coal in the past and now, washing the coal and dumping the tailings into Deep Lake and the river. Ann had a sour look on her face. He saw that Evelyn Wallenby was smiling for some reason.

By this time, John felt the jury would have hanged Charlie, as if it were a murder case. Finally John was finished and both lawyers made final arguments.

In his closing argument to the jury, John said, "Ignorance is not enough to escape liability. Mr. Webber has been dumping the tailings into the river and lakes for years by his own admission. They could be used as fill to restore mines. Mr. Webber has not done anything about land reclamation after the strip mining.

The Coal Mine Owners Association, of which Webber is a member, has done everything possible to prevent a Federal Land Reclamation Act from becoming law which would require restoration of the land and stop the practice of dumping the tailings into Deep Lake.

John decided to save the evidence of Webber's bribes for another trial, even though the donor's representative insisted that it be introduced. The evidence against Webber was sufficient for Billy's case.

John had in mind filing in Federal Court a civil suit for

racketeering, called RICO, under a new Federal law. The filing would be broadly against all of the mine operators for funding bribes and carrying out murders. The evidence would be Webber's own records of bribes. There were civil and criminal penalties.

THE JURY DELIBERATED FOR THREE days. Finally, the jurors filed into the courtroom. None of them looked at Webber. The judge asked the bailiff to pick up a note from the foreman of the jury. The judge silently read the verdict.

"Mr. Foreman, you can read the verdict."

The foreman said, "We find for the plaintiff and award damages in the amount of two hundred and fifty thousand dollars, medical expenses for Billy's life and two million dollars for his pain and suffering."

Webber was as mad as anybody had ever seen him. He verbally abused the jury inside the Court room, saying, "I'll get you bastards.". He had to be restrained by the bailiff. Judge Hand threatened to throw Webber into jail and he stopped.

CHAPTER 73

THE CHALLENGE

May 1973

The telephone rang in John's office. He did not answer right away, feeling a premonition of something bad. Then he picked up the phone. He was with Jane discussing his next step.

"Yes." He flipped the switch for his office speakers and a recorder.

"So Gooding, we are going to fight a duel on top of Mt. Hope. That's the best way of my getting rid of an asshole lawyer like you. You have interfered with my life for the last time."

"Why would I want to do that? I have you by the balls in Billy's lawsuit. You are millions of dollars poorer. Also, I am going to represent all of the new plaintiffs who were injured by the mercury. You are going to be a lot poorer. Finally, I'm going after your Coal Mine Operators Association and you for the damage your coal mining done by killing any legislation regulating mining."

Webber said, "Watch out Gooding. You know what happened to Jake Masters. My tractor trailers squished him flat. I set his car on fire as the gasoline spilled out of the ruptured gas tank and incinerated him."

John looked at Jane sitting across from him, both stunned by what they heard. She was taking notes.

"I will to kill your girlfriend Jane and Dr. Sandborne as well. They will both die painfully, unless you agree to the duel. I'll also kill your law partner Jason Mayfield."

John said, "You are insanely evil and need to be dead."

Webber said, "Next Sunday at noon at noon."

"I'll be there," John said, without hesitation. "We face off and draw at the count of three using single-action Colt 45 Peacemakers like in the old western movies."

"I'll have your head stuffed and mounted with my other animal trophies," Webber said.

There was a click, and the call ended.

John took out his single-action out his drawer from his desk drawer in a holster which he used fir quick draw shooting. He quickly slid his Colt out of the holster, like he had thousands of times during target practice.

Unlike Webber, John abhorred tracking and killing animals for sport and had never hunted, but he was very quick in drawing on targets. This is a hell of a way to start my career as a hunter, He thought.

Jane said, "How can an experienced trial lawyer like you kill another human being in a duel of all things? It's a crime."

John said, "Webber is the essence of evil. Most likely he has personally killed or injured dozens of people. This is a very real threat. He will kill us unless he is stopped. The law is no help. It is self defense."

"I suspect that Webber killed the Private Detective, Max Mull, across the street from your apartment. Senator Wallenby, Webber's close friend, was caught by Mull engaging in adultery. He testified in Evelyn Wallenby's divorce from the Senator a couple of years ago. She clipped the Senator for more than half of his assets, in the hundreds of millions of dollars."

John said, "I have four days to decide whether or not to fight the duel, but I will not back down for all of our sakes."

Jane said, "Maybe you will see the folly of fighting a duel with Webber. You can find a way out by legal means, rather than fighting the duel and risking going to prison or dying."

John said, "It impossible not to fight." The threat to kill Jason and you is real."

Jane said, "I am afraid for you and us."

John said, "Don't worry Jane, I can kill Webber." He thought, More confident than I feel.

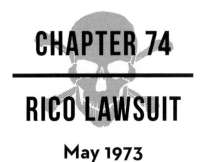

CHAPTER 74

RICO LAWSUIT

May 1973

John decided to file a lawsuit against Webber using the list of the bribes paid to the politicians Jason got from Ned Block before he died. He owed that much to Jason and his family. Webber admitted killing him in the phone conversation. Jason would handle the case if he was killed in the duel.

The bribes by Webber and the Coal Mine Operators Association were enough for filing of one of the first civil actions under the recently enacted Racketeering Influence and Corrupt Organization law of 1971 (RICO).The Complaint was filed against CMOA, Webber and his company in Federal Court for West Virginia. He did not attach Webber's list of payments.

John thought, There are a lot of politicians involved who would want to see Webber dead rather than have this lawsuit go forward. John could hardly wait to see them scramble to distance themselves from Webber and the CMOA.

The Complaint left the legislators who were paid the bribes scrambling to hire lawyers.

There was great speculation in the Charleston Gazette about who might be involved in receiving the bribes. The mood of the public was getting uglier by the day. TV trucks parked outside Webber's mansion trying to get a statement and pictures of Webber or Ann.

Ann telephoned John and pleaded with him to drop the lawsuit telling him that her husband was furious and dangerous and threatening to kill him. He told her, "I will not dismiss the case. Nothing can be done now to avoid the lawsuit. Your husband got himself into this position." John said this with the smugness of somebody who knew he was going to win.

He continued, "You should visit your parents in Lansing with Chas to be safe. I won't disclose your whereabouts to anyone and will try to keep you out of the matter."

She slammed the phone down to end the call.

────────

HAMMOND CALLED GOODING AS WELL and threatened a lawsuit for libel.

John laughed and said, "The filing of a complaint is not the basis for a lawsuit, since this is a protected right. In any event, everything I said there is true, an absolute defense."

"By the way, are you going to represent Webber in this matter?"

"Well, I suspect that our firm represents some of the people who might be on the list of politicians. It would be a conflict of interest to represent Webber."

"It sounds to me like the scurrying of little feet deserting the sinking ship." Hammond called John a son-of-a-bitch and slammed down the phone.

That conversation made John feel really good. He'd bet money that Webber wished he had Rex Reed to represent him now.

The phone rang in John's office again.

Webber said, "You better show up for our duel or Jason and Jane are dead. I don't believe you have a list of my bribing anybody. You are just puffing smoke out of your asshole. One more reason for me to kill you."

CHAPTER 75

CONTRACT

May 1973

Abe approached Angus Campbell with a contract to kill. Angus knew of Abe from his dead father, Ron, who contracted for the attempt on Ann Gooding's life. Angus kept track of what was happening with Webber.

Campbell knew that a Federal lawsuit was recently filed by John Gooding. The pleadings, which he read with interest, said Webber and the CMOA were paying bribes to legislators to halt any regulation of coal mining.

Campbell lived in San Francisco in an old Victorian house. He was muscular, with a blond crew cut, cruel lips and eyes which frightened people. He was a Vietnam vet and using guns to kill people was his business. He was very good at his job, like his murdered father, Ron, who was killed by Webber's goons.

Abe was dressed in a suit. He sat across from Angus in an office he rented for the day. All a matter of money, Campbell was prepared to walk away from this contract.

Abe said "I used your father many times. I'm sorry for your loss. I heard Webber's men ambushed him."

Campbell did not comment. "How soon do you want me to kill Webber?"

"Next Sunday."

Campbell did not ask who was hiring him, but he was certain that anybody who used Abe's services had lots of money and was politically connected at a high level in the government. He knew that Webber was prominent man in West Virginia with lots of money. He thought, I will enjoy killing Webber.

"Abe, what assurances do I have that this conversation is not being monitored? He was pretty certain that Abe was part of a covert service with the most up to date listening devices. "I know you have special resources for listening."

Abe said, "I brought along a device that detects any bugs and also prevents our conversation from being recorded," He placed a small square box on the desk.

"Believe me, we have no interest in this conversation going outside this room," Abe said.

Campbell thought, When ever anybody says that, they mean something different. I suspect I might be expendable as well. Still, if I make enough money, I could retire.

"How much are you willing to pay?" Campbell said, smiling at Abe and sitting back in his chair.

Abe said,"A million dollars."

Campbell got up and said, "Thanks for the offer. You aren't even close to a reasonable figure for such a difficult job, so we'll say goodbye."

Campbell walked to the office door confident that Abe would stop him.

Abe said, "I still believe we can do business. Please sit down."

Campbell thought, Abe needs a lesson in negotiating with me. The people who employed me did not allow for mistakes and usually my life is on the line.

Abe tried not to sweat, but Campbell saw perspiration on his forehead. Campbell thought, Obviously, he has to close this deal today.

"We can start again," Campbell said. "No hard feelings." He returned to his chair and waited for Abe's next offer with an expectant look on his face.

"I am prepared to offer five million dollars, half now and the other half when you meet with Webber."

Campbell leaned forward in his chair as if he was going to

get up, but instead pulled up his chair to the desk and leaned over it.

"I need ten million, all of it up front, in bearer bonds. I'll need to make certain they are genuine before proceeding and delivered to a place of my choosing," Campbell said, "It's going to cost me about twenty percent to fence them." Still, it leaves me with eight million.

Abe said, "I'll have to check with my superiors."

"If you leave this room, the deal is off. I am uncomfortable as it is," Campbell said. He reached under the desk for his 9mm Glock semi-automatic pistol aimed at Abe's gut. Abe wasn't going to leave this room alive if he didn't make a deal.

By this time Abe was sweating profusely. He took out his handkerchief and wiped his brow.

"Hot in here, isn't it?" Abe said. There was no reply.

"We have a deal. Where do you want the bonds delivered?"

Campbell wrote on the back of a fake business card. "To this address in Paris," and he handed Abe his card with the name of a private bank near the Louvre. "Today before you leave. You can make the call from my phone, while I listen."

Abe made the call and merely said, "10M in bearer bonds to…." He gave the address and the name of the bank and then hung up.

Campbell said, "Let's get some breakfast, its 1:00 p.m. in Paris."

As they left the office, Campbell looked around to see if they were being followed. They walked to a busy greasy spoon near the office.

Within an hour, as they finished breakfast, Campbell received a call saying that the bonds had been received and picked up by Campbell's fence. The deal was sealed.

Abe said, "There won't be much of an investigation into Webber's death," as if to reassure Campbell. He smiled as if he had made a good deal.

"We're all set Abe," Campbell said. Nice doing business with you. I will arrange the meeting on Sunday," Angus said.

Campbell walked away down the sidewalk overlooking the San Francisco Bay. The sun was shining in his face. He had been planning to kill Webber for nothing, and now he was being paid a lot of money. Life was good. He decided to splurge on a high class call girl. He even gave ten dollars to one of the numerous beggars on the streets.

The next day, Campbell planned the way he was going to kill Webber. This was not going to be an assassination of an unsuspecting target. He wanted Webber to see it coming. This idea was subject to change, since all he had to do was kill Webber.

Campbell telephoned Webber and said, "I am the son of the man who built the bomb that was planted on Ann's airplane."

Webber said, "I got rid of your father. Too bad I had to lose two men."

"Webber, I can make sure Ann dies along with your son, Chas." Campbell paused and continued, "If you want to end this matter with me and keep your family alive, meet me for a shoot out on top of Mount Hope next Sunday at one in the afternoon. Come alone. It should be a good day for a killing. Bring your favorite hunting rifle to defend yourself. I'm looking forward to seeing you."

Webber said, "I'll bet you're a sniper. You kill without warning, like the coward your father was and you are. I need to be able to see you to kill you. Let's say at five hundred yards."

Campbell said, "That's a deal." He thought, I've no intention of giving Webber any chance to kill me or waiting for one o'clock.

Campbell knew that Webber challenged John Gooding to a duel. He remembered the soldier, John Gooding, in Saigon City, Vietnam. He thought, If Gooding is the same man, he saved my life, deflecting the RPG fired at the Dragon Lady. That Gooding was a very brave man.

CHAPTER 76

THE MOUNTAIN

May 1973

A day early, on Saturday morning, Angus Campbell was in position with his spotting scope waiting for Webber to arrive on the top of Mt. Hope. He was under a camouflage net like he used as a sniper in Vietnam, waiting for days for the enemy target, usually an officer, to cross his path. He killed over two hundred times and kept count.

The day after their meeting, Abe telephoned Campbell and said, "I've heard that the person in question has challenged the lawyer, John Gooding, to an old fashion duel. Webber threatened to kill several people in Gooding's firm, if Gooding didn't show up. I know this sounds nuts, but they will be on top of Mt Hope by Webbers coal mine next Sunday at noon. I want you to interfere. Webber might kill Gooding."

CAMPBELL POSITIONED HIMSELF ALMOST ONE thousand yards from where he expected Webber to land by helicopter on top of Mt Hope. He thought, There will be no shootout with Gooding, since I intended to kill him as soon as the helicopter drops him off on Mt. Hope.

Webber's helicopter landed about eleven thirty in the morning. Webber stepped to the ground with a single action Colt revolver in a holster on his right hip. The helicopter left and circled around several times looking for Campbell and, failing to do so, left to land in the mine. Webber appeared to called helicopter on a Walkie Talkie.

Campbell lined up the shot with his M16 semiautomatic rifle, clicking the safety off. The crosshairs of the telescopic sight were directly on Webber's head. The fragmenting bullets would explode his brain, and the second shot to his chest would explode his heart into mush. Campbell's finger was on the hair trigger when he saw Gooding coming up the hill toward Webber, wearing a holster with a single action Colt revolver at his side.

Campbell recognized Gooding from Vietnam and removed his finger from the trigger. He had wanted to kill Webber before Gooding arrived so that there were no witnesses.

Campbell carefully reached into his backpack, pulled out a ski mask and pulled it over his head. He thought, I'll wait to see what happens.

CHAPTER 77

THE KILL

May 1973

Around seven in the morning that Sunday, Jane picked John up at the office. He tried to sleep on the reception room lounge, but failed.

As they drove, He thought, This is going to be a very bad day for me.

Jane said, "This duel is stupid, you need to let the police handle Webber."

John said, "Webber is insane. I can't risk your life by waiting for the police to arrest him. I could not live with myself if he killed you. Even if I die, I know you will be safe, a price I am willing to pay.

"I know about fighting and killing in combat from my two years in Vietnam, a lot more than Webber. The Vietcong were a much tougher enemy than Webber. I'm proficient with my pistol. I will try to talk him out of the duel, but I have little hope of that happening. That is the best I can do under the circumstances. I can't wait day after day for Webber to kill us."

Jane had tears in her eyes and took a handkerchief from her purse to wipe them away. They rode in silence the rest of the way to the base of Mt. Hope.

When they arrived, Jane said, "I love you," and they kissed.

John said, "I'd like you to wait here, but you can leave if you don't want to be any part of this. I will understand why."

"I will wait for you. You feel you have to do this for us. I think you are as crazy as Webber, but in a wonderful way.

Jane continued, "When you come down afterwards John, wait for me in the center of the road so I can see you from a distance. If this goes wrong, I will see that Webber is charged with the murder of Jake and you." She gave John her moist handkerchief.

John kissed her on the cheek and smiled and said, "You've got guts lady," in a voice like John Wayne's. "I'll be back for certain." He waved to her as he started up the mountain.

It was a clear sunlit day for the hike and John thought, I wonder if I kill Webber what will happen to Ann and Chas. However, now this is about Jake's death and protecting Jane. Finally, he was certain that he would meet Webber in the duel.

After an hour of hiking John wiped his face with Jane's handkerchief. He saw Webber in the distance waiting for him in front of the Webber Mining sign with a holstered revolver. His position was above John's so that Webber had a clear advantage.

John said, "So you decided to take the high ground so that you can shoot downhill."

Webber said, "Move uphill so that we are about forty feet apart. Keep your hands away from your revolver."

John moved slowly, always keeping his eyes on Webber, prepared to shoot if Webber's hand moved towards his revolver. Webber turned constantly in tiny steps to continue to face John.

John said, "I don't need to kill you. I'd rather that criminal law takes its normal course in punishing you. It would be difficult to prove that you killed Jake. I believe you are suffering from a form of insanity which could be a defense in a murder trial. You need to think of Ann and Chas."

Webber said, "There is no way that I would spend my life in an insane asylum. I would rather be dead. Ann can take care of herself and Chas. She is the toughest lady I ever met. I love her."

John said, "Suppose I agreed not to disclose what you said to me in our telephone conversation, treat it as a sort of a heat of the moment exchange?"

Webber said, "What I told you about Masters is true. I need to kill you for what you have done to me."

Finally they were facing each other. Bees circled around John's head, making an angry buzzing noise. John broke out in a sweat but did not flinch.

Webber said, "You're a lot smarter lawyer than I estimated. It didn't pay to underestimate you. I'm not going to make that mistake here. You can go for your revolver when you are ready."

Webber cocked the hammer of his revolver as he pulled it out of the holster. His hands shook slightly as he aimed the revolver at John.

At the same time, John drew his revolver and started to fan the hammer and stopped, because Webber's hands were shaking.

Webber fired one shot at John, grazing the skin of his right arm.

After that, John saw that Webber had two bullet holes in his body, one in his head and the other in his chest as he fell to the ground, almost in slow motion.

John landed flat on the ground and then sat up. He hurt from the wound.

He saw someone approaching. He thought, I'm going to be finished off by whoever fired those shots into Webber.

Webber's assassin, wearing a ski mask walked towards John, pointing his rifle at John.

"Gooding!" he shouted, "Please don't move."

Arriving in front of John, he leaned over and picked up his revolver. He rested his rifle on the ground and knelt beside John, examining John's wound.

He said, "It's only a flesh wound. You'll be able to walk down the mountain the way you came."

Reaching into his back pack, the hooded man took out a bandage and wrapped John's wound. Slowly the bleeding stopped. He said, "I carry these, in case I'm injured in getting rid of people somebody wants dead."

The assassin said, "Webber was my target."If you are ever questioned, you can blame his death on me. It's important to me that I killed Webber."

John said. "It's your kill for the record. I wonder about

Webber's shaking hand holding the pistol. I could have killed him, but stopped." The assassin did not comment, but John saw him shrug his shoulder as if that was pure speculation.

THEY WALKED DOWN THE MOUNTAIN together with the assassin helping him, still with only his eyes and lips visible through the mask. John told him that his girlfriend was waiting for him on the road at the base of Mt. Hope.

The assassin said, "Lucky you. You should take care of Jane." John thought, I wonder how he knows her name.

Half way down the mountain, the assassin removed the cartridges from Gooding's revolver and put them in his pocket.

The assassin said, "You should have used your Colt .45 semiautomatic like you did in the attack on the Lucky Lady in Saigon a few years ago. You saved my life that day. It's funny how things work out in the end."

The assassin jogged off down the mountain away from where John had hiked up. John thought, I have no idea who he could be. There is no way for me to find out now. I don't need to know anyway.

John stood in the center of the road. Jane drove up and helped him into the car. They hugged and kissed.

On the way home, John told Jane about Webber's death at the hands of a masked assassin. She had tears in her eyes and said, "I'm thankful you are still alive. I heard the shots."

John said, "The assassin shot Webber in the head and the heart. He was waiting under a camouflaged netting hundreds of yards away. Neither Webber nor I saw him. The shots came as a quiet 'pop.'

"Webber winged me. I didn't shoot at him. His hands were shaking and I don't know why." John did not say anything about the man's connection to his service in Vietnam.

"Jane, I promise you I will not do anything this stupid again. Webber almost killed me. If the assassin hadn't intervened, I might have died."

Jane said, "You were brave and foolish at the same time. I know you needed to protect Jason and me. Maybe you intended to protect

Ann and her baby as well. I love you for what you did. Somebody must have really hated Webber to have hired an assassin."

John said, "I think there is a connection to the person who financed Billy's lawsuit against Webber." He thought, Evelyn Wallenby is the only person I know who hated Webber and had the money and power to finance Billy's lawsuit. Webber said he killed Max Mull, Evelyn's private detective in her divorce proceedings.

When they arrived at Jane's apartment, they made love in a frantic effort to forget the day and then slept together, their bodies entwined.

In the morning, John said, "I want to marry you." He took out small ring box from his pants pocket, opened it, and offered a ring to her.

Jane said, "I accept, my love."

As John put the engagement band on her finger, he said, "I will love you forever."

They hugged and then made love again slowly moving in a crescendo of touching until they had to come together with John on top. They rolled back on the bed smiling again. John thought, I'm finally free of Webber.

That morning, they planned a date for the wedding. They agreed it would be at the Methodist church in downtown Charleston where Casey McTavish was now the minister.

John thought, It's strange how all of the past came full circle.

CHAPTER 78

THE DEAD COAL BARON

May 1973

Webber's helicopter hovered over his body at about 1:30 in the afternoon. The pilot did not land and scooted away, not wanting to be involved, as soon as it was apparent that Webber was dead. There was no response from the Walkie Talkie beside Webber's body except static.

A State Police helicopter, with State Police Commissioner Winfield aboard, arrived from Charleston. An anonymous call had been received at about two in the afternoon, from a number that could not be traced, with the message that Webber had been shot. The woman's voice said he had been killed as revenge for the many murders he had committed over the years.

Winfield had a military bearing and he was a Colonel in the Vietnam War. Few people argued with him and he had no reaction upon seeing Webber's body. The pilot set the helicopter down on top of the mountain at about the same time the County Coroner, Kenneth Williams, arrived from Treadwell after hiking up the mountain. He also had been called by someone unknown woman.

Winfield saw that Webber's faceless body lay near the "No Trespassing" sign. He observed that Webber had been shot in the head and heart at close range. This indicated to Winfield that he might have been killed by a professional killer. Webber's body lay with his head facing the sun. The blood had congealed on his face and chest and his arms and legs were bent as if his muscles had given up control of his body.

State Police Detective Winfield was examining the body when Williams arrived.

"It would be best to not touch the body, before I have finished examining it," Williams said.

"I just confirmed that he was in fact dead. The rest of the examination is up to you."

"Good luck," Winfield said, as he turned, strode back and climbed into the helicopter. As the blades wind-milled against the sky, the helicopter lifted off.

Williams examined the body. He took an underarm temperature and estimated that the time of death was about two hours ago. There were no tracks or other visible human evidence around the body although there were bird tracks in the blood. His eyeballs were gouged out, probably by the hawk circling above him.

A MEDEVAC helicopter landed. The body was placed in a body bag and the paramedics placed it in a pod on one of the runners of the helicopter, like the wounded or dead soldiers in Vietnam. Dr. Williams climbed into the helicopter and they were flown to Treadwell. Webber's body was then taken to the morgue at St. Luke's Hospital, where the autopsy would be performed by Williams.

CHAPTER 79

ANN AFTER WEBBER'S DEATH

May 1973

Ann learned of Charlie's death from State Police Commissioner Winfield at Steadfast. He said that Charlie was killed by an unknown professional assassin, shot in the head and the heart. He conveyed Governor Blanding's and his condolences.

Ann knew about the duel with John and tried to stop it. She thought, I can't believe John would kill Charlie. He certainly could not have made those shots.

Winfield said, "The Governor ordered me to make certain that Webber's original ledger of pay-offs to him and others are destroyed today.

"Your ex-husband, John Gooding, identified the ledger in a pleading for damages filed in Federal Court. We believe he talked to a U.S. government attorney about it.

"We expect that the FBI will be serving you with a subpoena within a day or two. If they get their hands on the original ledger, a lot of your friends will go to jail."

Ann nodded her head 'yes.' "I will take care of its destruction today.

"Is there somebody I can call to come stay with you?" Winfield said.

"Thank you, Commissioner. I have an acquaintance I can call." Ann showed him to the door and he left.

Ann grieved for Charlie. After crying for a half hour, she

forced herself under control and called Ruth from Dr. Brush's office and said, "My husband has been murdered and I could really use your company." Ann gave her the address and told her she was at the Webber mansion. Probably Ruth thinks I am working here as a maid, she thought.

The doorbell rang, and Ann answered it. Ruth said, "Some house, Barb," as she gave Ann a hug and said she was sorry for her loss.

"It's a long story, Ruth. Steadfast is mine now. My name is really Ann Webber and my husband, Charlie Webber, was murdered."

At this point Ruth was speechless and she sat down on a lounge in the library. She took Ann's hand and held it as tears streaked down Ann's cheek. She did not ask any questions. She knew about Charlie Webber from the stories in the *Charleston Gazette*.

Ruth talked about God's will and finally led Ann in the Lord's Prayer. She prayed for Charlie's soul and for Ann.

Ann thought, I'm tired of her. This isn't helping at all. I haven't been to a Sunday service in years. She thanked Ruth for coming and asked her to go home to her family.

"I need to attend to something today, before Chas wakes up."

They hugged. Ruth said to call her if Ann needed her for any reason.

As soon as Ruth left, Ann went into the library and opened the safe wearing calf skin gloves. The ledger was on the floor of the safe. Ann riffled through the pages to make certain it was the one in which she had seen Charlie making entries. She was certain.

She went to the fireplace and tore out the pages one by one until about one-quarter of them were removed. She then lit a match and started the fire. As the flames picked up, she fed the pages into it for the next half hour. In the end, only the binder cover remained, and she put that in the fireplace as well and watched it burn.

When the pages had turned to char, she took a poker and stirred them into tiny pieces of carbon in the firebox until the fire went out, shoveled the ashes into a brass pail and carried them to the backyard. A fairly stiff breeze was whipping the trees that evening, and she allowed the char to go into the wind. She thought, No chance that any part of the ledger survived. It is done. She went into her home and scrubbed her hands with a brush and soap.

She poured a glass full of bourbon and drank it down without stopping. Warmed by the whiskey, she poured another glass. She was feeling much better and relieved.

Charlie had been mean and anxious since the decision in the McLean case, and he was angry with her for some unknown reason. His hands were shaking like he was an old man.

The safe door was still open, and she went over and picked out an envelope which was labeled 'Charles Webber Living Trust'. She thought, I am the trustee along with Nate Hammond. This was the latest version of Charlie's trust prepared by Hammond.

Some months before, Ann and Nate had had a long heart-to-heart talk about Charlie's estate. Charlie was becoming more erratic. The trust ensured that Ann had a life interest in the principle and income. She could stay in Steadfast for the rest of her life. At her death, Chas would inherit everything that was left. Ann took the trust documents up to their bedroom and put them in a dresser drawer. She thought, I plan to work with Nate who is very interested in me in a non-lawyerly way.

Ann smiled as she thought of how she was going to spend Charlie's money. The trust was set up so nobody could touch her or the money. Most of it was in numbered accounts in offshore banks. Independent of the homes and the mines, she was entrusted with over forty million dollars. The government would receive only a token amount in estate taxes.

She returned to Charlie's office and closed the safe, wearing her leather calfskin gloves and wiped the safe. All she had to say to the FBI, if and when they showed up, was that she did not have the combination to the safe. "Charlie did not trust me that much."

———

WHEN CHAS AWOKE IN THE morning, Ann held him close. She wished Charlie was there.

She thought, Evelyn Wallenby was involved in killing Charlie. Another possibility was Governor Blanding. Charlie turned against Blanding. Finally, the CMOA saw Charlie as a liability. She just didn't know whom to blame, but this didn't matter now.

The *Charleston Gazette* ran a positive obituary. The paper in an article quoted Ann who said, "I will find out who killed my husband. "Even though I am in mourning, I will continue mining coal. I will clean up Deep Lake."

CHAPTER 80

FBI AND ANN

May 1973

Two FBI agents were on her doorstep the next day. Ann appeared at the door looking as if she hadn't slept at all. The truth was that she had a hangover and had slept all night. Her hair was knotted in a bun and was flattened on one side. She wore no makeup.

The agents identified themselves as Potter and Coulter. Ann showed them to the library and they sat down.

Potter said, "We prefer to stand."

"Mrs. Webber, we are sorry for your loss, but we need to ask you some questions about Mr. Webber. We are informed that Mr. Webber kept a ledger with the names of people he gave money to every year," the Potter said.

"I have no idea what you are talking about. Mr. Webber and I have only been married for a little over a year. The only thing I know is that he kept papers in his safe which is over there." She pointed to a large floor safe in the corner. "I have no idea what is in there, since I don't have the combination."

"We would like to have one of our men open the safe."Coulter said.

"You are welcome to do that, but my attorney has to be here. How long will it take?"

"It's an old safe. Probably it will take no more than ten minutes. We are to put a seal on the door to make certain it isn't opened in the meantime. Would tomorrow be alright?" Coulter said.

"Will nine in the morning suit you? I have to take sleeping pills to sleep and take care of my son, Chas," Ann said. They left, again apologizing for the intrusion.

Ann called Nate Hammond and told him he needed to be at Steadfast. Ann then drank some whiskey until she fell asleep on the sofa in the library.

Ann thought, Chas is sleeping in his room. He will be picked up for daycare at eight in the morning.

––––––––

THE NEXT MORNING THE FBI safecracker arrived promptly at nine with all sorts of electronic tools. He took seven hours to open the safe, with Nate Hammond looking on for the entire time.

Soon, Ann began to grumble about the mounting legal fees. The safecracker began to sweat.

When the safe was opened, no ledger was there. They did find about fifty thousand in small bills.

"The agents thanked her for her time and left. The safecracker gave her the combination to the safe and re-locked it.

After they left, Ann put her arms around Nate and hugged him, thanking him for being with her. She said she would like to see more of him after things quieted down. She kissed him goodbye. When he was gone, Ann thought things were picking up for her. Her fear of Charlie and for Chas's safety was now gone.

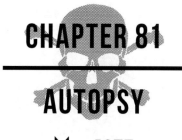

CHAPTER 81

AUTOPSY

May 1973

State law required that County Coroner Kenneth Williams was required by state law to perform an autopsy on Charlie Webber, because he died of gunshot wounds. About seventy-two hours since the shooting, his body was stored in a refrigerator drawer in the morgue attached to the hospital in Treadwell.

County prosecutor Harrington requested the autopsy, since a murder trial was a possibility. He said, "Doc, I doubt that the murderer will ever be arrested. I want the body released this week for funeral services. You just need to remove the bullet fragments. I doubt we can even identify the caliber."

Dr. Williams turned on the recording system with a microphone above his head and began to perform the autopsy dictating as he went. Using a cranial saw he opened and removed the top of the skull to reveal Charlie's brain. He probed and removed fragments of the bullet from the brain and then placed them in a labeled vial on a steel tray beside the autopsy table.

He cut into the chest cavity with a 'Y' shaped incision cutting through the ribs and along the medial line of the abdomen with a motorized circular saw. Webber's chest cavity was revealed. He probed for more bullet fragments around and in the heart and removed them, placing them in a second vial. He said, "The only time I've seen bullet wounds like this was when I was working at St. George's hospital in New York City.

The body in that case was of a man who had been executed gangland style."

Williams saw that that Webber was unusually well endowed, with a penis which was six inches long, as it flaccidly stretched between Webber's legs. He had heard stories about Webber's exploits with women and made a note of the dimension in his record. He said, "Possibly this had something to do with his murder. On the other hand, this style of killing has been well-publicized on television programs. Possibly the killer or killers were amateurs, trying to put off the investigation by duplicating a professional killing, but this is unlikely."

Webber's body was wheeled back into the refrigerated drawer for release to Ann Gooding fir burial.

Williams thought, Webber got what he deserved. Too many times bodies rested on this autopsy table, after having been crushed or gassed by methane in an underground mine. My father died in the Webber's mine thirty years ago. My mother died of grief shortly thereafter.

I remember dad coming home from the mines covered with coal soot, his hands so black from the coal that he could not remove the stain even with soap containing pumice as an abrasive. I grew up in poverty. I hope Webber is in some sort of hell where he had to relive his death over and over again."

Webber's remains were embalmed by a funeral director in Charleston and placed in a casket. There was no viewing. He was interred in his family plot with his father and mother. Only members of the CMOA, Ann and Nate Hammond turned up at the graveside. Hammond stood at Ann's side during the brief service. A minister picked by the funeral director recited the twenty third psalm. There was a mention of the burial in the obituary section of the *Charleston Gazette*. The sensational story gave way to other news.

The RICO case was dismissed by John, since he could not prove the allegations.

CHAPTER 82

ATTORNEY GENERAL

July 1973

John arrived at the Charleston office of Sam Hunt, the United States Attorney for West Virginia, at nine a.m. sharp. Gooding asked for this meeting to convince Hunt to begin a criminal investigation of Webber and CMOA using the FBI. He thought, I want them to file a racketeering case against the Coal Mine Operators Association.

John thought, I'll show the list to a Federal Prosecutor. I was followed to this office and expect to be attacked.

As he sat down behind his desk, Hunt said, "As we discussed briefly on the phone, you want me to bring a lawsuit against the Coal Mine Operators Association, known as CMOA, and its members. You suggested that politicians who have received bribes from Charlie Webber for many years to prevent any regulation of coal mining. Tell me what you know."

For the next hour and a half, John disclosed what he knew, including the deaths of Webber, Rex Reed, Jake Masters, Clem Block, and the union organizers who were missing. He gave Hunt his only photocopy of Webber's list to review. Hunt slowly read the list and put check marks in front of a large number of the names.

After he finished with the list, Hunt said "Ex-president Nixon's re-election committee is on the list as well as the names of a number of prominent state politicians including Governor

Blanding and lots of representatives and senators, as members of Congress. How are we going to authenticate this document and introduce this into evidence? It could be a forgery."

"You authenticate Webber's handwriting, and you follow the money. Clem Block, Webber's driver, copied the list. It was given to me by his brother Ned in a sealed envelope. I don't know where the original is located.

"The members of the CMOA know about the list since I said it existed in a pleading for a civil RICO case against Webber that. It's like I painted a great big target on my back."

Hunt said, "I read your pleading. We searched Webber's safe in Charleston. There is no original ledger book. I will keep this list, since it is the only copy in existence.

"You should hire a body guard. I will discuss this with the United States Attorney General in Washington D.C.

John said, "I'm left to take care of myself?" Hunt did not comment, stood, and shook hands with John as he left the office.

Hunt eventually became Attorney General for the United States. John read that he had a close relationship with Congress and the President. John did not hear from Hunt again.

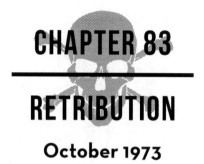

CHAPTER 83

RETRIBUTION

October 1973

John drove his brand new 4-door 1974 Cadillac at five miles over the speed limit on I-90 towards Huntington to meet a new client. The Cadillac was built like a tank and he hoped it would protect him in the event of an attack by the CMOA, blaming him for Charlie's death. The sound of the tires humming on the double lane expressway brought his thoughts back to minding his driving.

Now he was a celebrity lawyer, appearing on TV shows talking brilliantly about the evils and corruption of coal mining and in particular stripping the tops of mountains. The CMOA was very quiet, just going about its businesses as if his preaching about the hazards of coal mining had no effect on them. He thought, *Just a bunch of wimps when they come up against the force of the negative public opinion I've managed to foster.*

Glancing in the rearview mirror, he saw two semi-tractor trailers, side by side on the highway, the one on the outside lane appearing to John to be passing the other. He shifted his eyesight rapidly from one to the other. Increasing his speed to eighty, he hoped he would pull far ahead of them, away from the walls of the pass cut through the top of a mountain on either side of the highway. The semis kept going faster downhill, still gaining on him.

Shaken at the possibility of a collision, he glanced at the

speedometer and saw that he was going almost one hundred down the mountain. He started to sweat, beads appearing on his forehead, in spite of the air conditioning booming out of the dash vents. The semis were close to the rear of his car, rushing towards him.

John's right hand trembled as he reached for his 45 Colt semiautomatic in a shoulder holster, which he used in Vietnam, and laid it on the seat beside him, uncertain about how it would help. It held nine cartridges.

He swerved into the left lane, hoping to avoid crashing into the mountain walls beside the inside lane if he was hit. The semi in the inside lane pulled up alongside him and scraped the right side of the Cadillac, pushing it towards the median.

John pushed a button on the door for the power window to open on the passenger side and tried to point the Colt at the driver. As his car was pushed into the median out of control, the semi's collided.

Too occupied to see what happened next to the semis, he struggled to keep his car under control, but was failing. The brake pedal pushed down as much as possible, he headed over the median toward the southbound lanes. He missed a car with people in it and slammed sideways on the driver's side into the steel mesh that held back rocks from falling onto the highway. Shielding his eyes with his right arm, he felt his left arm scrape against broken glass. At that instant he thought about how Jake Masters must have felt when he died.

––––––––

I SENSE THE SOUND OF a pump noise in a far distance, but I can't open my eyes. I feel like I am floating in a pool of water, keeping me alive. My lungs are expanding and contracting without any effort on my part. He rested for a while, enjoying the feeling.

My eyes blinked open and seeing only shadows of movement, I closed them. I wonder if this is heaven or maybe hell, like a "Thou shall not kill" kind of purgatory. I tried to lift my arms, but could not. Maybe I'm just a ghost, he thought.

Jane's voice said, "Welcome back, John." Her touch and perfume made him start to awaken.

He thought, This time I succeeded.

Jane leaned over and kissed him on the cheek. He tried to move again, but could not, as if he was strapped into place.

Jane said, "Don't try to move. The nurses have strapped you down."

This seemed frightening to John. He moved his fingers and toes to be certain they were there and he felt them.

"You have been in a coma since your car crashed a week ago," Jane said.

A nurse brought in a cup of water with a straw and Jane helped him drink. The nurse gave him a shot in his rump which she said was for pain. "It's best if you don't move. Try to stay awake for now so we can test your cognitive skills. 'Rachel' was stitched in cursive letters on her uniform, and she looked like a Sumo wrestler. She would win any day against John and he was not about to argue now.

A doctor with 'Holmes' sewn on his green scrubs, came into the room. "I'm your surgeon. I thought you might die from loss of blood. A few more ounces and you would have. There was a driver who stopped and used his belt as a tourniquet on your arm to slow the bleeding."

"Your left arm has a long cut from the wrist to the upper arm. I'm amazed that you survived the crash. Jane came to see you every day."

John was silent for a minute. He said, "I dreamed I was in a lighted room with my friend Jake. He said it wasn't time. I'm just glad I'm alive," John said.

Jane pulled up a chair beside him, and the sound of the legs scraping on the floor was like music proving he was still alive.

Jane said, "Hello, love of my life. I thought I had lost you for the first few days."

"There were two semi drivers who forced me off the highway. What happened to them?"

Jane said, "The tractors collided, and then they both crashed into the wall of the mountain beside the road. The drivers died in their cabs from burning fuel. The trailers they were pulling were turned into scrap metal while crashing down the hill. Oddly they were empty.

Jane continued, "The state police found your pistol on the floor inside your car. It was loaded with the safety on. It must have fallen from your holster when you crashed. Witnesses saw the trucks forcing you off the road."

"I don't remember anything about the accident." He thought,

That's a lie. I do remember they were trying to kill me. The members of CMOA want me dead. By now they must know I don't have Webber's list any more. I turned over my photocopy copy to Assistant Attorney General Hunt.

John said, "We will be married as soon as possible. I love you."

Jane said, I will love you forever."

At the next red traffic light, Jane leaned over and kissed John on the lips.

THE END